MONSTERS ARE HIDDEN

GODS AMONG MEN SERIES

ALTA HENSLEY

DEDICATION

For all the people who wanted to invite
the Monster under the bed to join you as you slept.

WARNING

Enter this tale at your own risk. It's dark. It's dirty. It's about the monster that makes the scary bumps in the night.

The problem with secrets is they create powerful monsters.

And even more dangerous enemies.

He's the keeper of all his family's secrets, the watcher of all.

He knows what I've done, what I've risked... the deadly choice I made.

The tangled vines of his mighty family tree are strangling me.

There is no escape.

I am locked away, captive to his twisted obsession and demands.

If I run, my hell will never end.

If I stay, he will devour me.

My only choice is to dare the monster to come out into the light,

before his darkness destroys us both.

Yes... he is the monster in hiding.

And he is the end of my beginning.

CHAPTER
ONE

Ani

I don't know what time it is. I've been sleeping more than I've been awake, and the darkness of the night has deepened. I am curiously removed from the world around me and wake slowly, disorientated, with soft sheets luxurious against my skin. A feeling of stillness hangs in the air, and the room is lit by a soft night light that is always kept on. Somewhere, in the distance, a clock is ticking, and I feel a faint chill.

I've been in this mansion for weeks—maybe even a month. Each day has blended with the next, and I feel as if I'm living in an odd purgatory between the hell I was once in and a potential future of better times ahead now that *he's* gone.

Forever gone.

Gone.

My phone vibrates on the nightstand beside me, which makes me wonder if that is the sound that woke me. It's my sister calling, so I answer quickly. If I don't, she'll start to panic.

"Hey." I reach for the glass of water beside my bed. My voice is scratchy, and I don't want Daphne to worry even more that I may be getting sick or something.

"Did I wake you?"

"I really need to start sleeping on a regular schedule. I'm losing all sense of time."

"You're healing. Your body went through a lot," Daphne says, softly. "Your mind did, too." This isn't the first time she's given me this reassurance. Every time I bring up how I should leave and get out of her hair, I receive this same lecture.

"I know, but I'm feeling better. The bruising is fading. Nothing I can't hide with a little makeup." I leave out the fact that I have the kind of makeup that covers the bruises back at my trailer and have done this multiple times.

"You aren't ready to leave Olympus," Daphne says, clearly reading my mind. "I don't want you in that tin can any longer."

"That tin can is my home."

"It's a piece-of-shit trailer, and it doesn't need to be your home. I can help you—"

"I'm not taking your money," I say.

"Ani..."

"I'm serious. You and Apollo have already done far more than I'm comfortable with."

My sister and I have been having this argument ever since she married into the Godwin family. Just because she has access to money now doesn't mean I do. I don't take charity or handouts. Never have. Never will.

"Tell me about the house you visited today," I say. "I'm assuming you've seen it by now."

"It's so pretty. Everything inside is what I imagined it would be. It's perfect. Apollo said we can buy it. It has three bedrooms, so if you want to move—"

"I'm not moving in with you guys," I say. "No way. Don't even think that's a possibility. It's bad enough I'm staying in the infamous Godwin family estate. I'm sure I'm an uninvited guest."

"I invited you. Apollo invited you. And both of us want you to remain there until we come up with a plan to get you in a better situation."

"*I* need to come up with a plan. Not *we*. This is my problem. My messed-up life."

She sighs heavily on the other end of the phone but doesn't argue any further. Instead, she says, "Thank you for remembering this house and giving the information to Apollo. It was by far the most romantic thing I could have experienced. A true Cinderella story."

"You deserve it," I say, and she does. My older

sister has always done whatever she could for me, and it's time for her to put herself first.

"We're going to stay in Seattle for a couple of days while Apollo does some work for Medusa Enterprises and also does what it takes to buy the house. Do you think you'll be okay on the island without me?"

I suppress the urge to groan as I sit up all the way, peering into the darkness. I've spent way too much time in bed, and my body is shouting for me to get up and stop feeling sorry for myself. *He* did this to me. *He* put me in this dark space. But he's gone now, and it's up to me to bounce back and rebuild. I can't be the victim any longer.

He's gone. He's gone.

It's as if I've been in prison. Doing my time. And, though my accommodations have been nice—extremely nice—I'm finally free. It's time I start acting like it. Yes, I'm in a mansion, but I can't hide in this luxury forever.

My room's furniture is opulent—a four-poster bed, a vanity, and a tall armoire all dominate the room. An ornate rug spreads out across the floor, and expensive tapestries hang on the walls. Despite the interior's elegance, there is something vaguely menacing about it. The shadows seem to lurk in the corners, and the objects that decorate the room appear to be watching me.

I always feel watched.

I have to keep telling myself that he's gone. He's

gone. He's not watching. Stop thinking he's watching.

"I'll be fine," I reassure my sister, who has worried about me since the day I was born. She takes being a big sister to a completely different level.

"Apollo told me that a housekeeper and cook will arrive tomorrow. He wants the house to be staffed again, so you won't be on your own completely."

"I really need to get back to my home," I say. "There's no reason for Apollo to pay to have people here just for me."

"Ani..." Daphne audibly draws a calming breath. "A few more days, okay? Then we can revisit this conversation. That's all I ask."

I can sit here and try to argue, but I know my sister. She'll win. She always does.

"Fine. A few more days, but then I'm serious. I need to get home and deal with my mess of a life."

A silence stretches out on the other end, which tells me Daphne isn't going to just agree to let me go, but I'm not going to battle this out yet. I'm going to need a plan of action to even have a chance of convincing her I'm going to be all right, and I don't have it yet.

"It's getting late. We'll talk tomorrow," she says. "There's food in the kitchen and—"

"I can fend for myself," I say, "but thank you. I appreciate it. Love you."

"Love you."

When I hang up, my stomach growls at the

mention of food. I do indeed need to find something to eat in the kitchen downstairs. As I get out of the bed, an ominous creak echoes down the hall, and I shiver. It's not the first time I've heard a creak, bump, or shuffle of what I swear are feet when no one is supposed to be in the manor.

Godwin ghosts are everywhere, and I have to keep reminding myself that they're harmless, even though I know living Godwins are anything but.

After I throw on a borrowed robe and step out into the hallway, my heart pounds, no matter how much I'm telling myself I'm being ridiculous. But when I hear another bang at the end of the hallway, I know it's not just my imagination. Daphne said the housekeeper and cook don't arrive until the morning. The house should be empty... and quiet.

Olympus Manor is old and drafty, and the darkness seems to stalk me as I move down the hallway. Still feeling as if I'm being watched, I peer into each of the empty rooms as I pass them but see nothing. I'm not sure what exactly I'm expecting—the Boogie Monster, a ghost, or maybe it's just bats in the attic fluttering around that I hear.

I reach the end of the hallway where a staircase leads up to the attic. I hesitate, suddenly feeling very foolish in the darkness. This is how people in horror movies die.

That creak comes again, this time, from the attic. Something inside of me wants to go up, but I feel like I'm trespassing if I do.

But then again, maybe I can put my mind at ease by checking it out. It could help me believe that all thoughts of monsters are simply in my head.

After taking a deep breath, I start up the stairs, my footsteps echoing in the darkness. As I reach the top, the creaking becomes louder and more insistent. I step into the attic, my heart in my throat, but then I quickly stop and turn back around.

This is the part in the horror movie where you scream at the screen at how stupid the actor is being. They go places they don't belong. I will not be that dumb girl. Besides, it's probably just a raccoon or rats or something, and I'm far from an exterminator. I'll just tell Daphne that the Godwins better get someone out here to take a look.

Another creak behind me has me jump, so I leave the attic's doorway and quickly make my way to the kitchen. It's like when I was a kid, scared of the dark at night. I would pull the blanket up over my head and think of rainbows and flowers.

You can't see the monsters if you don't open your eyes.

CHAPTER
TWO

Phoenix

I can't take my eyes off the screen in front of me. It's a live feed from the guest room below, showing her lying there, asleep. She looks so peaceful, so innocent, but I know the truth. I've seen the bruises on her face, the cuts on her arms. Someone did this to her, and I'm going to make them pay.

Ani is prettier than her sister. The same dark hair, but it shines more as it lies on her pale skin. Her eyes are green, so green and intense they remind me of a panther's. I see strength in them even though she sleeps broken and beaten in a bed. I watch her as her long eyelashes flutter open and see the way she stares into open space—thinking. She's planning. She's plotting. Maybe she wants revenge, but she doesn't have to. I will do it for her.

I know the way I feel is wrong, obsessive, possessive, but I can't help it. I need to know who did this to her. I need to make them suffer the way she has. And so I sit here, day and night, watching the video. Watching her heal and recover. She doesn't know I'm here, doesn't know I'm watching. But it's the only way I can protect her.

I have intrusive thoughts.

Dangerous thoughts.

Compulsive thoughts.

And I can't stop them. Even if I wanted to.

My computer screen lights up with an incoming message. I know who it is even before I hit the connect button.

Athena refuses to call me like a normal sister would, but then again, members in my family are far from normal. She claims she wants to see me. She needs to set eyes on me to make sure I'm actually alive. A voice on the other end of a phone isn't enough for her, and though I have many weaknesses in life, my sister is the ultimate one. I can't say no to her, even if I tried.

"Athena," I say as I connect with the message.

She's sitting in her office at Medusa Enterprises, where she spends most of her time. "Did you hear?"

"What?"

Athena leans closer to her computer, peering at me through the screen. "You look pale."

"I always look pale," I say. "What should I have heard?"

"You need vitamin D. You can't stay cooped up in that attic and not see the sun." She jots a note to herself. "I'm sending you vitamins. You need to start taking them."

Athena is the family caretaker. I'm not sure if it's truly compassion that makes her fulfill this role or the fact that she is a control freak. Regardless, my sister is a general in the army, and I've learned to be her obedient soldier unless I want a fully-fledged war—a war she will win.

"When is the last time you've been outside?" she asks.

"Today," I lie.

Her eyes lock with mine, and she gives a deadpan face. "Seriously, when?"

"I've been busy working."

"We have a security department for that. You don't have to sit in front of all those damn screens day in and day out looking at footage of Medusa."

"I do. Look what happened the last time I got lax. Apollo got caught killing someone, and our family nearly imploded. Our security team didn't catch it. I didn't catch it," I say.

"Overseeing the security footage of Medusa is not a one-man job," Athena lectures. "You have a team. Use them. Come into the office and train their asses. Whatever. I don't care. It's your department. But get out of the fucking attic, fly to Seattle, and get some goddamn vitamin D."

Getting frustrated, I ask, "What were you calling about? You asked me if I heard."

She looks up from her computer, reaches over for a file, and hands it to her secretary, who has just entered the room. Then she returns her attention to me. "Apollo and Daphne. He's having a baby with that bitch."

"What?" I say the word on an exhalation. It feels as if my lungs have been punctured, and shock edged with rage is oozing out.

Athena rolls her eyes. "So yeah. Looks like there's a new heir to the Godwin fortune and empire coming to play."

"How the fuck did this happen?"

"Did no one ever have the birds and the bees talk with you, brother?" Athena's getting distracted again, texting something on her phone. It's rare anyone gets Athena's full attention. She is the queen of multitask. "A man puts his penis in the va—"

"Athena..." I'm not finding Athena's dry humor amusing. I rarely do. "Daphne betrayed this family. Doesn't Apollo get that? She's a liar. Nothing is worse than a liar."

Athena shrugs. "Love."

I huff. "Apollo is as capable of falling in love as you and I are. Not possible."

"Then she's good in bed. I don't know. But she's pregnant. That much is for sure."

"Fuck."

"Yeah. Fuck," Athena agrees. "They bought a house or something, too. A new one."

"Yeah, I knew that." I refocus on the monitor where Daphne's sister sleeps.

Ani is the most beautiful woman I've ever seen. It's not just her physical appearance, although that's certainly part of it. She has a kind of inner glow, a light that shines from within. It's like she's made of magic, of pure goodness.

As I watch her on the screen, something stirs inside me, something I haven't felt in a lifetime of loneliness. I've always been a recluse, a hermit. I've never cared about anyone, never let anyone get close. But watching her, seeing the way she moves, the way she smiles, it's like she's reaching out to me, pulling me in.

I shouldn't feel this way. I'm a stalker, a predator. Godwins are bad and can't be good. She should be my prey and nothing more. But as I sit here in the attic, watching her, I can't control my raging emotions. I'm drawn to her, irresistibly. No matter what happens, no matter what the consequences, I'll always be here, watching her, because she's the one thing in this world that makes me feel alive.

I thought I was dead. Just a ghost. Phoenix Godwin, forever haunting Olympus Manor.

But then she came...

"They left Daphne's sister here. Alone," I say.

Athena nods, obviously she already knows that, too.

"What does dear ol' Dad say about this baby?" I ask. "He wanted Daphne dead. Why does that suddenly change?"

"A Godwin is a Godwin," Athena says. "If the baby turns out to be a boy, then even better. You know him. He wants a mighty bloodline. Ares is dead, and you and I sure aren't going to give him grandchildren. So this is his only hope."

Her reminder of how I have failed my father once again doesn't sting like it would have when I was younger. I've become numb to my inadequacies.

"So, does he plan on having her killed after the baby is born?"

Athena's eyes darken. "Every child deserves a mother." A long pause breathes between us as her words sink in. "Godwins deserve the best. No way in hell is our father going to allow another Godwin to go through life without a mother. He won't allow another mother to leave a child, and I can't say I blame him. So Daphne was smart. She saved her life by getting knocked up."

The walls are closing in on me. the air in this attic growing thin, heavy with the stench of lies, deceit, cover-ups, and hatred. This conversation needs to end.

"Ares would be in jail right now if he didn't die in that accident. Because of *her*. Because of what *she* did."

Athena nods. "You don't have to tell me, but it is what it is. Besides, why do you care? You hide up in that attic all the time. You don't have to see her around like I do. So you have nothing to complain about. And Apollo is... different lately. He never seemed to love Daphne before, but now he's a fucking weak-kneed, pussy-whipped ass. It concerns me in regard to where his head is. Apollo and I haven't always seen eye to eye in how Medusa is run. And Ares was always on my side in the boardroom. Now that he's dead... I'm afraid I'm going to get outnumbered in votes."

I don't want to talk about business anymore. I most certainly don't want to talk about Daphne Godwin for another second.

A knock sounds on Athena's office door, and she motions for whoever did it to enter. "I got to go. But vitamins are coming. And it wouldn't kill you to take a walk or something."

"Or something," I say as I end the connection.

I scan all the monitors before me, taking in every detail of every office, every hallway, every elevator of my family empire. But I'm constantly drawn to the woman in the room below me. I could stare at that monitor for days without ever coming up for air.

The hours tick by, and I start to feel like the stalker I am again. A predator. But I can't stop. I can't tear my eyes away from the screen. I need to know she's okay. I need to know she's safe. And so I sit here, in the darkness of the attic, watching her. Waiting for the moment when I can finally have my revenge on whoever hurt her.

Days turned into weeks since she first arrived, and still I sit here, watching her. She's getting better, the bruises fading, the cuts healing. But I can't shake the feeling of anger, of desperation. I need to know who did this to her. I need to make them pay.

Before Ani, I lost track of time, of reality. It was just me and the screens.

But now, the sound of her breathing is the only thing keeping me grounded.

I'm losing my mind more and more with every year of my life. It's like I'm trapped in some sort of twisted reality. I can't leave, can't tear myself away from this attic without extreme work and discomfort. I'm trapped here, watching the outside world.

But she's not on the outside.

She's here.

And, as the days go by, I think about her more and more. I watch her every move, memorizing every detail of her face, her body. It's wrong, but I can't help it. She's a drug, an addiction, and the more I watch, the more I need.

I get bolder, taking risks I never would have before. I leave the attic, sneaking down to the guest room to watch her from a closer advantage point. It's dangerous, and I could get caught at any moment, but I can't stay away. I need to be near her, to feel the heat of her skin, the sound of her breathing close by.

And then, one day, she wakes. She sits up in bed, rubbing her eyes, and for a moment, our eyes meet on the screen. I freeze, feeling like I'd been caught. But she doesn't seem to notice me, doesn't seem to realize I am there. She doesn't see the hidden camera.

Just like now.

She gets out of bed, stretches, and heads to the bathroom.

I release the breath that I have been holding as I watch her every move. But as she's getting ready, I see something that makes my blood boil. Her phone lights up on the end table, and I know it's her sister.

The enemy.

The betrayer.

The woman who should be dead.

I hate when she talks with her. I hate it.

Ani is better than her sister. So, so much better.

And what kind of sister just leaves her here by herself? Apollo and Daphne just left to worry about themselves.

Well... Ani has me. I'm here. I'm always going to be here.

THREE

Ani

Who could stay locked within four walls day in, and day out and not go crazy? Although this room is bigger than my trailer on the Eastside of Heathens Hollow, I feel as if it's getting smaller and smaller as the days go by, which tells me one thing.

It's time to leave. It's time to start my life.

But how? I have no actual skills to get a good-paying job. Not that there are many of them on Heathens Hollow. I could be a fish monger again, and most likely will have to be to put food on my table, but I haven't done that job since marrying Mark. He wouldn't allow me to work. He wanted me to completely depend on him and his next-to-nothing income he brought home every month.

I get out of bed and start pacing the room. My

body hurts from immobility. I need to stretch and work my muscles again. Deciding to do some basic yoga moves to get blood flowing into places of my body that feel frozen in place, I sit down on the hardwood floor and take a few deep breaths to center myself. I slowly stretch my body, bending my arms and legs in different directions and working up to more difficult poses. I twist my back, extending one arm over my head, with the other reaching for the floor.

Without warning, something gives beneath me, and the wood plank I am balancing on comes loose from the floorboard. Startled, I jump back on my heels while frantically trying to pull the loose piece of wood back into place. My heart pounds with the realization that I have caused serious damage to the Godwins' home.

I frantically try to press the loose plank back into place. As I struggle to secure it, something catches my eye. It's a small gap at the corner of the floorboard that reveals items within the hole. My pulse quickens as I realize what this could mean: someone has been hiding things inside this floorboard.

Whatever it is, is tucked away in this hole beneath the floor for a reason. But curiosity is most certainly killing this cat. I want to see what's inside. What is in hiding?

I reach inside and withdraw four leather-bound journals. Though old, they appear rich and elegant.

They are tied with a piece of leather string, not strong enough to take away my temptation to see what's inside, however.

But as much as I want to read each one, the person who wrote what's inside wanted these hidden for a reason, and something deep inside of me wants to honor their wishes. These are someone else's secrets.

I should resist. I should put them back where I found them and continue with my yoga. But I can't. Shit...

After climbing back in the bed, I pull the blankets over me like I did when I was a kid and wanted to read by flashlight.

This will be my secret. Mine and whoever wrote these journals.

I open the leather notebook and see the name Freya Godwin written in perfect script. I don't know all that much about the Godwin family, but from what I do know, Freya was the mother of Apollo, Athena, Ares, and Phoenix, and was married to Troy Godwin. I met everyone briefly at Daphne and Apollo's wedding, but they weren't exactly welcoming or chit-chatty with me. Freya didn't attend the wedding. If I remember correctly, it was because she died. In fact, I think it was suicide. Daphne knew some of the story and had told me that Apollo didn't like to talk about his mother. No one in the family discussed her or brought up her name. I don't remember any pictures or anything being present of Freya in the house anytime I looked around either. It's like they wiped her from the Godwin history.

I consider returning the journal. I'm invading a dead woman's privacy. But then again... I'm so freaking bored and... Yeah, I'm the cat that curiosity very well may kill.

Dear Diary,

I can still feel the excitement I had as Troy and I set off for our special date. Our destination was a beautiful cabin in the mountains, and as we drove, I could feel my heart racing with anticipation.

The morning sun was shining through the trees, and we stopped to take a hike through the forest. The dewy mist still lingered in the air and the greenery was vibrant and luscious. It was so peaceful, just him and me, that I felt as if we were the only two people in the world. We found a tranquil pond, where we sat in silence, my heart singing with joy.

We returned to the cabin, and what I saw took my breath away. Troy had prepared a romantic dinner for two — candles lit on the table, with wildflowers in vases. The fireplace was lit, and it provided a warm and inviting atmosphere. We enjoyed a delicious meal as we talked about our future and shared our secrets.

We stepped out onto the deck that overlooked the stars and lay down on the hammock. The blanket of stars seemed to stretch on forever, and all of my worries melted away as I felt Troy's firm embrace. His heart beat in sync with mine, and it felt like time stood still – nothing else in this world mattered but us.

My heart swells with emotion when I think back to that special day when our love was still new and fresh, when every moment felt like an adventure, every touch like an electric shock going through my veins. This day was a reminder of how strong our love was and how much we had grown together.

Dear Diary,

Today, I found myself reflecting on my relationship with Troy. We used to be so in love, and it was as if the stars had aligned when we first met. He had a strong presence, and I knew from the moment I saw him that we were meant to be together. I felt like nothing in the world mattered when I was with him. I thought back to the way Troy and I had been when we first met, how our love just seemed to fit together like two pieces of a puzzle. When we were together, it felt like nothing else mattered in the world. We could stay out all night or just sit in comfortable silence, and either way, it felt right.

Our bond was so strong that it was almost tangible. I could feel the connection between us everywhere we went. We'd laugh at the same jokes, finish each other's sentences, and knew exactly what the other one was thinking without having to say a word.

It's so sad that as the years went on, our relationship slowly changed. We started going through the same motions, and I could sense a distance growing between us. We stopped talking and laughed less until eventually we stopped laughing altogether. We became strangers in the same house, and I guess I always knew inevitably, things would end between us.

Nothing lasts forever.

I know our love is gone, and it is time to move on.

But I do miss those days when it felt like we were two star-crossed lovers who were meant to be together. I miss the way he looked at me, the way he touched me, and the way we talked about our dreams for our future.

But now things feel so different. I wonder if we'll ever find our way back to those days when our love was new and untainted. Or have we lost each other forever?

I should stop reading. I really should. But... one more entry and then I will. I will put the journal away to join the others in their hidden coffin. Just one more...

Okay, now I'm hooked. It's better than finding and reading an old romance novel. I should stop reading before I get completely hooked, but—just a little more.

Dear Diary,

Today, I told Troy that I had to leave him. His fury was expected, but his declaration that leaving him would mean choosing death, took me by surprise. How could he think our love was so strong that death was the only way out of it? As I sat there silently, tears streaming down my face, I asked myself what had happened to us.

We had started out as two star-crossed lovers, living in a fantasy world of our own creation. We promised each other nothing but happiness and forever togetherness; but now here we were – bound by an ever-tightening grip of desperation and despair. We were no longer two people connected by a shared passion, but rather two people clinging to survival in a world we created out of fear and uncertainty.

I wonder if things would have been different if we'd taken our time to properly cultivate our relationship instead of rushing into things head on. If we'd taken the time to really understand each other and work through our differences before making any commitments or promises, then perhaps things wouldn't be so strained between us now.

In the end, maybe it just wasn't meant to be – some relationships never survive beyond their passionate beginnings and maybe ours is one of them. All I know is that while my heart breaks at the thought of leaving Troy behind, I cannot stay in this place where love is overshadowed by hurt and pain. It's time for me to bid farewell and start anew on my journey of self-discovery and healing.

Dear Diary,

I don't think Troy will kill me. He says he will. He reminds me that Godwins don't divorce. He tells me I can't leave.

I see obsession in his eyes mixed with pain all the time. I know he doesn't want me to see how badly my need to be free of him and free of Olympus Manor hurts him, but I see it.

I thought of running away, but I don't think that would be wise. It would only make him angrier, and I'm not sure what he is capable of. Still, it may be the only way I have left to protect myself from his wrath.

The days drag by like an eternity. I can feel Troy's presence in every inch of this cursed place. He's watching me, waiting for me to make a move so he can respond. I know his response won't be kind.

And then it happened...

A loud commotion came from downstairs interrupting my constant dark thoughts. The staff were all shouting, and chaos was all around. I slowly crept down the stairs, my heart pounding against my chest. I could feel the fear in the air as I made my way to the front door. As I got closer, the smell of something burning filled my nostrils.

My stomach churned as I looked out the window.

Everything outside was engulfed in flames, and in the center stood Troy, his face twisted with rage, as my car was surrounded in a ball of fire.

He did it. He proved that he won't let me go, and I was too terrified to move. I could feel the heat from the fire emanating from the window and smell the scorched metal from my car. I knew that this was a sign of the things to come unless I found a way to escape.

He looked up, and our eyes met. I could see the burning hatred in his gaze before he turned away and disappeared into the night. I knew I should have listened to my instincts and ran away when I had the chance. Now it was too late.

I ran back upstairs and frantically stared packing my belongings. I knew I had to leave and never look back. As I grabbed the last of my things, I heard Troy's menacing voice coming from the foot of the stairs. He was screaming at me, telling me that if I did not come down and submit to him, he would burn this entire house down with us in it.

I took a deep breath to steady my nerves and prepare myself for one last battle. There was no escape from Troy, not anymore. I had to face him, and I had to win.

The children. Where were the children?

Jesus Christ. I knew there was a darkness about this family. Everyone who lives on Heathens Hollow knows the Godwins, though rich as fuck, have demons around them. Rumors and stories about this family are downright chilling. But reading this. Seeing this...

It makes it easy for me to get out of bed and put the journal back in its home. I don't want to read about another fucked-up marriage. I had my own, my own nightmare from which I barely escaped.

I feel for Freya. I can relate to her, but Freya's secrets died with her, and I need to let them remain that way.

The instant I've replaced the journal, I look around the room and rub the chill off my arms while trying to shake off the overwhelming sense that I'm not alone. Another loud thump sounds from upstairs in the attic, but I know no one is here. No one should be here...

A creak that follows sounds as if weight is being placed on the floorboards from above. Or at least I think that is what I hear.

Someone's got to be in this house. I feel it. I hear it. I open the bedroom door and step into the hallway.

I need to see it.

CHAPTER
FOUR

Phoenix

Jesus Christ. She's stretching. Doing yoga. What man could resist the urge to watch?

Soft, dark hair falls in waves down her back and shimmers in the light. I imagine wrapping my fist around it and holding her in place as I...

Fuck. No. I stop the thought before my cock can respond. That way lies destruction. For both of us, even if I want to be the one to give her... feelings. Feelings besides the kind that roil in your gut, churn, and burn until there is nothing left. I want her to hunger for me. Need me. Desire my touch to the point where she can't go a day without my presence. I want to have the power over her just as her seductive vision in the screen has the power over me.

But it's not meant to be. It never will be. The

darkness that lurks beneath my skin, the shadows that call out to me like a siren, will never let me have her. Even if I wanted to, I could never give her what she deserves.

I can't give her anything beyond four suffocating walls.

I can feel her in my bones, calling me like a distant whisper, beckoning me with promises of something far more powerful than mere feelings. I can feel the darkness consuming me, and it won't be long before it has taken over completely. I just hope I can keep it under control until she leaves this place.

I reach for my cock but stop myself. I can't jack off to her lean body while she extends her limbs as if tempting me to do so. But that's when I see it. A flicker of something in her eyes, too quick for me to make out. But in that one moment it's like she can read my mind. Like she knows what I'm thinking and approves.

And then it's gone, like a candle snuffed in the night. But her gaze still lingers on me—or the camera—heavy and full of something I can't quite identify. Something that feels both dangerously exciting and ominously foreboding. Deep in my heart, I know that if I make contact with her, something will happen. Something irreversible and forever changed.

I free my cock from my pants, lick my palm, and begin stroking while I watch her body beckoning me. Calling me.

This is wrong. It's as fucked up as can be. I'm going to cum in my hand as I watch her, and she has no idea. I can't resist the temptation.

Up and down, I tighten my grip. I imagine her pussy wrapped around me as I can only hope that the darkness won't consume me entirely.

I imagine my fingers finding their way inside her, exploring her depths as I feel her slick wetness. I want to push deeper, feeling her muscles contracting around my digits as I find her pleasure spot. I want to hear her gasps as I caress it, her body quivering with each stroke. I want to send wave after wave of pleasure through her body.

I want her to cry out my name. I want to hear her screams of erotic pleasure with my name woven within.

The heat in the room rises as my breathing gets heavier, and I'm close. My heart thunders as I move faster, pushing myself closer and closer to the edge. Her eyes flicker in the shadows, as if she's watching me, and I imagine her wanting me without a word spoken.

I slide one hand down to my balls and massage them, letting out a deep groan as I do. With my other hand I continue to pump furiously, my fingers slipping through the slickness of my pre-cum. I close my eyes and imagine what it would be like to be inside her. I take my time with the vision, savoring it.

And with one final stroke, I come undone. White-hot pleasure radiates from my core as I fill my palm with my hot cum.

Lost in my carnal self-pleasure, I didn't notice when she crawled into bed, pulling the sheets up over her head.

It's as if she's hiding in shame.

Shame.

I should be man enough to go into her room and fuck her like a man would a woman. Not this way. Not like a fucking monster hiding in the attic. I should be more than this. I'm a fucking Godwin.

I reach for the tissues to wipe away my signs of disgrace and knock over a bottle of Jack. Glass and booze splatter everywhere as it crashes to the ground.

"Fuck."

When I check the screen, Ani is out of bed. Has she heard me? How can she not?

"Fuck."

It's a goddamn mess.

I'm a goddamn mess.

CHAPTER
FIVE

Ani

The attic. There is something in the attic. Before I explore the rest of the mansion, I'm going to rule out whatever sounds I hear upstairs as being animal rather than monster or ghost. I've faced far scarier things than this in my life. I'm not a chicken, I'm not weak, and I'm sure as hell not going to play damsel in distress for another second.

I climb the narrow stairway to the attic, my heart pounding. For weeks, I've heard bumps and thuds coming from up here, and I've been too scared to investigate. But tonight, I gather the courage to see what's causing the noise.

As I reach the top, I push open the door and step inside. I expect to see dust and cobwebs, but instead, the attic is impeccably clean. Twinkling lights cast a dim glow, and as I approach, I see wall-to-wall video screens and surveillance equipment. It looks like a high-level CIA operative room. Not an attic.

The interior is completely unexpected. Instead of the cluttered, dusty space that I have expected, it's clean and well organized. Rows of video screens line the walls, each one showing a different view of the mansion. Someone is definitely using this space as a surveillance room.

As I a step closer, I notice the screens show security footage from every room in a massive office building, as well as Olympus Manor. Since these monitors are in the Godwin mansion, I can only assume what I see is Medusa Enterprises. It's like the employees are being watched by someone, or something.

But that's not the strangest thing. There's a bed in the corner, neatly made with crisp white sheets. A leather chair sits in front of the screens, as if someone has been spending a lot of time up here and wants to be comfortable. Little touches make the space feel almost whimsical, like the twinkle lights strung up around the beams, or hanging plants in the furthest corners of the room by the window.

It appears as if someone is living in the attic and has done so for some time. I'm about to turn and leave when there's a scrape behind me. I spin around to see a figure emerging from the shadows. It's a man, tall and lean, with dark hair and piercing blue eyes. He's dressed in all black, and although I can't see all of him clearly, something about him feels dangerous.

"Who are you?" My voice shakes despite my best efforts to keep it steady.

The man steps forward into the light, a small scowl playing at his lips. "Hello, Ani."

My heart stutters. I recognize him. He's Phoenix Godwin. I only met him briefly at my sister's wedding and couldn't tell you a thing about him other than rumors I heard growing up on Heathens Hollow. Rumors that were far from good. Our meeting was so brief, I'm surprised he even knows my name.

But why is he here, living in the attic? I have a feeling that I don't want to stick around to find out. I've invaded his space, and something tells me he's a man who hands out consequences like Santa does gifts.

"I'm going to go now." I try to keep my voice steady. "I'm sorry if I disturbed you, I heard noise and—"

The man's scowl intensifies. "You shouldn't be out of bed yet. You're still recovering."

I'm surprised he knows about my recovery, but then I glance at the monitors and see that one of them is of my guest room. Every inch of my room is visible on that screen.

He can see me sleeping.

He can see me dressing every day.

Oh, Jesus Christ— He can see me *undressing*.

39

"You've been watching me?" I can't process the feelings swirling in my mind. Are they shock or... rage? My privacy has been— What the fuck?

Why would he watch me? And for how long?

What the hell is happening up here in this attic?

I turn and flee, my heart pounding. I don't know what's going on in this house, or why anyone would think it's all right to watch me without my knowledge. I am a guest, but nothing about this is right.

I race downstairs and out of the attic, wishing I could make my feet move faster. I need to get out of here as fast as I can. My bare feet are pounding against the floor as I pelt down the hallway. Phoenix's footsteps slap down behind me, getting closer and closer. I don't know if he's trying to catch me or just following me, but either way, I'm not looking over my shoulder or slowing down to find out.

Once I reach the bottom of the stairway, I burst through the front door, running out into the night. The cold air is a slap to the face, and the cold muscles in my legs threaten to seize as I run across the lawn. I don't know where I'm going, but I don't care. I just need to get as far away from that mansion as possible.

I run until my lungs are burning and my knees feel like they're about to buckle. Finally, I collapse on the ground, panting and shaking. I've spent too much time in bed, and my body is reminding me of this. I'm also barefoot, and I'm grateful I've been running on grass, so I haven't chewed up the bottoms of my feet with gravel.

I don't know what's happening, but I can't just leave the property without shoes. The sane part of my brain is now kicking in, telling me that my phone, and what few belongings I do have, are in the house. I can't even catch a ride back to the trailer, as I have zero money on me. Scared or not, I can't be reckless and think a solution will be out here waiting for me.

Taking a few deep and calming breaths, I stand and head back to the house. Yes, Godwins are known for being dangerous. Phoenix might be crazy, but I seriously doubt he will hurt me.

Correction, he *is* crazy if he's living in an attic watching televisions all day and night.

But if he wanted to hurt me, he would have already. He's had the opportunity since we've been alone in the mansion together. I'm being ridiculous thinking he'll kill me or something. I completely overreacted and now feel really stupid as I have to reenter the house with my tail between my legs, because I truly have no way of leaving right now.

Luckily, he's not waiting in the foyer as I enter. I hope he's returned to the attic and will stay there until I figure out a way to leave. I make my way back to the room I was staying in, my heart still racing. I can't believe what just happened. I am being watched.

I close the bedroom door behind me and lean

against it, trying to catch my breath. I scan the room for the hidden camera, but I don't see any place it could be.

Is he watching me right now?

Of course he's watching me right now.

I cower in the room's corner to stay out of sight as I try to come up with a plan. I have no money, no car, and no way to reach the Eastside of Heathens Hollow. I consider calling my sister, but it's late, and I don't want to bother her with this right now. It could put her in an awkward situation. Phoenix is her brother-in-law. Maybe she knows he is staying here. But no way does she know he's recording me. She wouldn't allow that to happen without me knowing. But for the present, I don't feel like pulling her into my shit—again. Especially not in the middle of the night.

But as I think about it, a nagging thought takes hold. Something about this situation doesn't add up. Why would Phoenix be living in the attic, spying on everyone in the house? At Medusa Enterprises? This is his house, too. Why not sleep in one of the large bedrooms? Why not walk around the house freely? Why has there been zero mention of Phoenix living in Olympus unless no one knows? Is he hiding in the attic?

Sitting on the bed, trying to think, I search the room, looking for any signs of surveillance equipment. And sure enough, I find it. A hidden camera is tucked away in the corner of the room behind some crown molding. It's too high for me to reach and somehow disable.

Disgust washes over me. I've been watched this entire time, and I had no idea. But now that I know, I have to find a way to never spend another night in this room. I can't stay here any longer, not with Phoenix watching my every move.

I gather my things, packing as quickly as I can. I don't know where I'm going or how, but I must leave. Maybe I can hitchhike? Or maybe the walk into town isn't as long as I remember.

But as I make my way out the door and down the stairs, I feel a presence behind me. I turn to see Phoenix standing at the top of the stairs, looking down at me.

"Don't go." His voice is low and urgent. "Stay, at least for the night. It's not safe out there."

The rain is coming down, which is only going to make this walk even more miserable. "It's not safe in here. With *you*," I snap.

I need to keep my emotions in check. No way can he have any idea how much I'm quaking inside at this moment, how my legs are jelly, and I'm forcing them to stand.

But he's terrifying, looming over me from the top of the stairs. Broad shoulders, barrel chest, a chiseled jaw, and piercing eyes. I remember him being tall and big, massive next to my smaller size, but in the positions we're both in, he's a giant.

"You can't leave." Phoenix shakes his head, his

stormy eyes boring into me. "One night. We have breakfast together tomorrow and talk. That's all I ask, and then I will help you leave, if that's what you want."

I solidify my stance. "Have you been watching me the entire time I've been here?"

"Yes."

Well, at least the fucker's being honest.

"But I will turn off the camera tonight," he adds.

I hesitate, torn between my fear and my desire to escape, and reason. I don't know if I can trust this man, but I also don't know if I can make it on my own in the rain.

"Please." His eyes are intense. "I know you're scared, but I promise you'll be safe here. At least for tonight."

I take a deep breath and nod. I don't know if I'm making the right decision, but I don't have any other choice.

"Okay." I ignore the warning bells going off in my ears. "I'll stay for the night."

Phoenix nods, a hint of a smile on his lips. "I'll see you in the dining room at eight for breakfast. Goodnight."

CHAPTER

SIX

Ani

I head down to the dining room in a house that has never felt welcoming. It might as well have a *No Trespassing* sign hanging on the front door for people like me. I am beneath a house like this. I am too poor to enter, and it knows it. But it's not like my life and my current situation gave me much of a choice.

As I descend the staircase and adjust my slim skirt, I suddenly wish I'd gone with one that was longer and dowdier. Maybe I should have just stuck with my go-to jeans and sun-faded tee. I don't think it's smart to appear at all sexy around Phoenix Godwin. And who knows how much of my body he's seen without me knowing.

I stand in front of the dining room door, looking down at my shoes for the briefest of seconds. They're worn, but not dirty. So at least I won't track Eastside filth into the pristine manor. Although my outfit may be too sexy, it is as impeccable as I can get—a black blouse and gray skirt from a secondhand store that costs less than the loose change that can be found hanging around the inside of Olympus. My favorite hair clip—my *only* hair clip—that was a gift from Daphne sits jauntily atop my onyx hair. The ivory clip is the only thing I have on that is of any real monetary value. I never asked Daphne how much it cost when I accepted it as a birthday gift. She knew to not make a fuss over money, or expensive items, or I wouldn't accept it. But the clip shows real thought and care had gone into the gift, and I couldn't turn it away. I saw how much Daphne wanted me to keep it.

Overall, I don't mind being poor that much. I never have much money, so I don't miss it. I am different from my sister. She wants the money. She dreams of the wealth. She'll do whatever it takes— and has—to get close to money. Me? I feel no need. I've known who I am from the moment I attended my first day of school and was called white trash. Yes, I know my position in society, and I don't fight it.

I am a realist, while Daphne is a dreamer.

I knock on the door and wait with a pasted-on smile. I'm not sure if I should just open the door and enter. I'm sure I look like a redneck hillbilly for doing it, but I also don't want to simply assume I'm welcomed in all parts of the house.

The door opens, and someone from the staff

greets me with a polite smile. "Welcome, Ms. Parker," she says, as she leads me into Olympus Manor's grand dining room. The marble floors gleam in the light, and the chandelier overhead sparkles like a constellation of stars.

I don't belong here.

As the woman leads me toward my seat, I can't shake the feeling I'm being observed. Phoenix's eyes seem to be everywhere, always watching, always judging. He's the king of this kingdom, and I'm nothing but a peasant in his presence.

I take a seat at the table and try to steady my breathing. Phoenix's footsteps echo as he descends the stairs, and my heart is pounding. I'm not sure what to expect, and I feel that this is a test. Like he wants to see if I'm worthy of his time and of his help.

I'm second guessing my stubborn pride about calling my sister last night.

He enters the room, and my breath catches. He's even more imposing closer up, with his height and thick body. It's as if a six-foot-six brick wall entered the room. He's dressed in a tailored suit that accentuates his power and wealth. He's the epitome of perfection, and I am small and insignificant in his presence.

"Welcome," he says, as he takes a seat across from me. "I'm glad you took me up on my offer."

I nod, unable to form words. He's so overwhelming, so intense.

I try to gather my thoughts and speak, but my

voice comes out not much louder than a whisper. "Thank you for inviting me," I manage to say.

Why am I being nice to this man? Isn't he the one who just got caught spying on me? And yet, I'm nervous that I'm not saying or doing the right things around him.

Rich people make me sweat.

It results from growing up on an island where the Godwins were treated as actual Gods, and we were mere mortals praying they wouldn't strike us down with one of their mighty lightning bolts. They owned all the land we lived on, which meant they essentially owned *us*. Or at least that is how it often felt.

Phoenix's eyes seem to bore into mine, as if he's trying to read my thoughts. I fidget with my hands with a sense of unease. It's like he's trying to uncover my secrets.

Secrets no one should ever know.

I need to be careful; I must not show any weakness in front of him. I have to keep telling myself that I know him... or I know him through marriage. He's not a God. He's still a man who can bleed just like me. There must be good in him, even if it's blanketed in all the darkness that almost seems to swallow him up.

"Are you hungry?" He motions for the staff who has been standing by the door to bring the food into the dining room.

I nod, not daring to move my eyes away from his.

I'm too mesmerized by him, too entranced. His mere presence is intoxicating. Plus, I've been trained to never turn my back on a wild animal if it's getting ready to attack.

Will Phoenix attack?

How wild and feral is he?

The food arrives, and the smell of delicious herbs and spices fills the room. The tension between us is palpable, and I wonder if he's feeling the same. Am I making him as uncomfortable as he's making me?

"I didn't mean to scare you last night," he says after entirely too much awkward silence passes.

"I didn't realize you were in the attic. Is that where you"—I swallow the food in my mouth—"stay?"

"I like it up there."

I wait. And I wait. Is he going to offer some sort of explanation or apology for having a secret video camera on me?

Apparently not.

"Why were you filming me?"

"There are cameras everywhere in this house other than a few rooms."

"Is there a camera in the room my sister was staying in?"

"No. That's Apollo's room. It's private."

"But *my* room isn't private?"

"It's not *your* room. It's a guest room. It houses strangers. Not Godwins." He tilts his head and studies my face. "If you want me to try to defend my

49

actions, it's not going to happen. I oversee security for Medusa Enterprises and for my family. My job is to watch. I'm not going to apologize for it." He pauses, inhales deeply. "But I do apologize if it frightened you. That was not my intent. My goal has always been to keep everything safe. To remove the fear. Not add to it."

I don't know what to say to that. I am a guest. I didn't ask his permission to stay. Though Apollo said I was fine being here, this is still the Godwin family estate. Who am I to judge what Phoenix does in his house? And his actions seem far from sinister.

"Who did that to you?" Phoenix points to the fading bruise on my cheekbone. He's not the first person to recognize bruising on my body, but the first one to be so bold as to ask.

"My ex." There's no point in lying about it. Phoenix saw me recover in the bed for weeks. He knows I didn't simply fall or have a minor accident.

"Where is he now?"

I look down at my food and shake my head. "It doesn't matter."

"It matters to me." Phoenix puts down his fork and leans forward. "Where is he?"

I glance up at him, surprised to find him caring. "He's gone. For good."

Phoenix sits back and steeples his fingers together at his chin. I can't tell if he's questioning what I'm saying, or if he's just allowing it all to soak in.

I feel the need to add, "He was my husband in name only. We never actually wed legally, so there's nothing I need to do with a lawyer or anything. He... left. So, I don't have to worry about dealing with him ever again. It's over."

It's odd that I'm being so free with my information to a basic stranger, but then again, I've been living under the man's roof for weeks.

The rest of the meal passes in a blur. I can't focus on the food or the lack of conversation. I'm too aware of Phoenix's gaze on me, of the way he's studying me, trying to read my every move. He doesn't smile, but he's not exactly mean. It's as if Medusa has turned his face to stone.

"What's your plan now?" He finally breaks the silence in the room, and I'm grateful.

"My sister doesn't want me going home, but it's time. I'm going to call her today—"

"You don't need to call your sister," he snaps. "I can help you."

"I don't want to put you out." But his offer is tempting.

I don't want to call Daphne and have her rushing back to Heathens Hollow from Seattle. She's excited about the big changes in her life, and I'm also not sure if she will resist me on going back to the Eastside. But after hours of thinking about it last night, I'm going to need some help. I have zero money, and even if I got a job right away, I wouldn't get paid for at least a week. There is no food in the trailer, and I have no way of getting there. Whether I like it or not, I'm going to have to call Daphne and ask for help.

"Your sister just left you here." Phoenix says the words with disgust, and I can see he's not happy with her, judging by his expression. It appears as if he's smelled something bad.

"She and Apollo are busy—"

"She doesn't deserve your defense." The harshness in Phoenix's words has me flinching.

"I get the feeling you don't like my sister. Why?"

"Correct. She doesn't deserve to be a Godwin."

The familiar rage from last night builds inside of me. "Because we grew up poor on the Eastside? What? She's not good enough to marry into your family?"

He sips from his coffee calmly, staring at me with hooded eyes beneath long lashes. "I couldn't care less where she lived. This has nothing to do with what side of Heathens Hollow she lived on."

Still feeling as if I need to defend her, I say, "My sister is a fighter. She's had to be her entire life. She was never one to settle and had big dreams. You may not like her, or feel she fucked her way into your family, but Daphne would throw herself on a sword for those she loves. Can you say the same?"

"I can," he replies simply. "Any Godwin would."

I'm thrown off by how easily he counters my words. "You shouldn't judge what you don't know."

"I know enough."

I wipe my mouth with the cloth napkin on my lap and stand. "I really need to get going. I've overstayed my welcome."

Phoenix mimics my actions. "Allow me to drive you home." His voice is low but demanding.

I open my mouth to argue, but him driving would save me the hassle of trying to get money from Daphne for the cab ride and waiting for it to arrive somehow. Feeling trapped and with no options, I nod. "Thank you."

Phoenix remains in place, forcing me to have to walk by him to go upstairs to get my stuff. I can feel the heat radiating from his body, and I'm overcome with an intense feeling of—

He reaches out to push away a strand of hair from my face. I only come up to his chest, and our height difference is obvious when I have to completely tilt my head back to look up at his towering face. Our eyes lock for a moment too long for my comfort. Feeling as if I'm breaking a powerful spell, I quickly make my way to the guest room for the last time.

SEVEN

Ani

I've never been in the back of an expensive Town Car before, but I suppose I should have expected that when Phoenix Godwin offers to drive you home, what he really means is he'll have someone chauffeur us there as we sit awkwardly on the smooth leather seats in the back of the car, not saying a single word to each other.

I'm not even sure why Phoenix offered to come. It's clear by the way he toys with his cuff links, breathes shallowly, and darts his eyes out at the passing scenery that the man is extremely uncomfortable in my presence. He appears more restless than me, which is really saying something.

"You didn't have to come," I say, although it's a little late now. We are almost there.

"I said I would. I'm a man of my word. When I offer to help, I mean it." He doesn't look at me as he speaks, but instead unbuttons the first two buttons of his shirt to give more room between the fabric and his neck.

"I'm clearly making you uncomfortable." I don't know if I should be apologetic or offended.

"It's not *you* that is making me uncomfortable." He quickly glances at me. "It's not you at all."

We finally turn the corner, and I've never been so grateful to arrive at my home as I am now. This car ride has almost been painful.

The trailer looks like it's been through hell and back. One side is covered in moss and mildew, the other in decayed holes. The outside is the color of dirt, its trim yellowed, and the wood is splintered, the glass looking about ready to shatter. The trailer's walls are made of poorly and irregularly shaped aluminum siding, some of it rusted, as if the whole structure has been left out in one constant storm for years. The aluminum has been dented and pushed back on itself, and the roof is sagging and leaking. The whole trailer reminds me of a melted popsicle discarded on a dirty street.

I'm embarrassed.

But I don't want Phoenix to know just how much I'm ashamed that he's seeing this place I call home.

He's silent as he gets out of the car, taking in every square inch of my home sweet home. He walks around to my side of the car and opens the door for me, offering his hand to assist me out. Gentlemanly manners are forever ingrained in this man.

The door isn't locked, but then it never has been. I have nothing anyone would want to steal. When we go inside, Phoenix is clearly not prepared for what he sees. He doesn't even try to hold back the gasp of shock he makes.

"You can't stay here," Phoenix declares as he looks around inside my dilapidated, white trash trailer in revulsion.

Everything inside is coated in a film of dirt and grime, the floors are stained in dried memories of darkness. Mold—visible from the living room—is growing around the sink, the toilet is cracked and jagged, the TV is crooked on the wall, and thick cobwebs are hanging from the ceiling.

The living room floor is splintered and worn, the carpet stained with food and mold and vomit from all Mark's partying the night before I left. The walls are chipped, the color long since peeled off. The floor is stacked with boxes, mechanic books, men's magazines, and newspapers. The kitchen table is cluttered with dirty dishes and fast-food trash. Cookie crumbs and soda cans litter the countertops, the sink is filled with soured milk, rotting fruit, and scraps of dry food. The couch cushions are stained and ripped open with missing springs, stuffing and filth spread across the floor.

"Absolutely not." He motions to the front door,

where it barely hangs on its hinges. "You don't even have a lock to the door."

"I'll be fine," I say.

"Ani..."

"I just have to clean up. Now that he's gone... I can."

Mark never allowed me to touch his stuff. He didn't like when I tried to clean, even in the slightest. He didn't like anything I did.

"This goes beyond anything that can be cleaned up."

"I know it's not like what you're used to, but it's all I have." I give a weak smile. "And I'll be fine."

He stares at me for a long moment, his face conflicting emotions. "It's not safe." His voice is gentle, but undeniable worry is lodged in his eyes. "You don't have to stay here," he continues, softer now. "I know it's not easy, but I could help you get somewhere else. Somewhere you can actually be safe and secure."

I hesitate, conflicted. Part of me longs to accept his offer, to just let him take care of everything and give me a new, better living situation. But that would mean taking charity, and that's something I've never been willing to accept from anyone.

I draw a deep breath and force a smile, trying to make my voice sound more confident than I feel. "I'm all right here." My words come out more firmly than I intended. "I'm really okay. I know how to rebuild."

Phoenix continues to assess the room as if looking for danger to pop out.

"It's just me now," I add. "I can fix this place up and make it my own. He doesn't have a say. His drunken rages can't destroy what I fix or clean."

Phoenix shakes his head. "I'm not letting you stay here. No fucking way."

I stand my ground, my heart pounding. I don't want to rely on someone else to take care of me. I want to be able to stand on my own two feet and provide for myself. But at the same time, I'm scared of being here all alone—not that I'd admit that.

Fear and determination battle inside of me, the two seeming to pull me in opposite directions. It's like I'm standing on the edge of a cliff, teetering back and forth between safety and danger. Fear of the unknown and of taking a risk makes me want to accept Phoenix's offer. But stubborn pride makes me cling to the idea of self-sufficiency.

I look around the room, studying the worn walls and broken furniture. I've been in worse places and managed to make them livable. A few repairs, and it'll be good as new. I can do this.

"I'll find a way," I say.

"I said no, and that's final," Phoenix pushes. "You're coming home with me where you belong. I should have never even considered allowing you to return here."

"I can't just stay at your house. I've overstayed my welcome as it is."

"You can. You will," he insists.

The walls start to close in on me. Phoenix is only trying to look out for me, but the idea of being under his roof again makes me feel like a burden.

He's right, however. I look around a trailer that doesn't even have running water or electricity. I couldn't wash the dishes in the sink or even flush the toilet. I can't stay here, and even my stubbornness is starting to realize that fact.

"Besides, Olympus Manor isn't just my house. It's the family estate, and your sister is part of that family." A slight grimace at the mention of her, washes over his face. "So think of it as your sister still helping you, rather than me, if it helps." He scowls at the trailer's condition again. "Whatever it takes to get you out of this fucking hell hole." He looks to the open door. "And how do you know he isn't coming back?"

"I know."

His blue eyes narrow on me as he shakes his head. "I'm not going to take that chance. Any man who did to you what he did and forced you to live in conditions like this deserves to be dead. And if he were to walk through that door right now, I'd kill him with my bare hands."

The mention of death and killing turn my stomach, and I feel faint, but I quickly shake it off. I have to. I can't reveal my secret ever. To anyone.

"You are coming home with me where I can keep

you safe from him." He takes in the garbage in the kitchen again. "From all of this."

I draw a deep breath to steady myself, then nod. I'm grateful for Phoenix's offer, but it won't be easy adjusting to being dependent on him. Still, I can't stay here. After one last look around the living room, I gather my courage.

"Okay," I say, "but just until I find another place. Until I get on my feet."

I make my way to head to the bedroom, but Phoenix reaches out to grab my arm. "Where are you going?"

"To pack some clothes."

"We'll buy you new clothes in town. Everything in this place smells of mold and puke."

I try not to be offended by him saying my clothes stink, but the reality is he's most likely right. But I also can't have the man buying me clothes on top of offering me a place to stay.

"Daphne still has some things at the house," I say.

"We're stopping on our way back to get you some items. Final."

"You don't have to do this," I say, offering him one last chance to back down.

"I do."

With that, he places his hand on my lower back and leads me out of the trailer to the waiting car. I don't even look back to say my goodbyes. This part of my life has to be over. Never go back. Never return.

EIGHT

Ani

"Go on inside the store." Phoenix leans his head back against the leather seat as if too exhausted to come with me. He's sweaty at the temples. Why is he so clammy and pale? "I texted Linda a list of everything you'll need. She knows to just charge it to my account."

I look at the boutique store in surprise. "You just want me to go in there and get clothes?"

Lulu's is a boutique that sits on Main Street, and before this day, I wouldn't even consider walking through the doors. It smells rich. It looks rich. It is rich.

I am not.

"I'd go with you but..." He takes a deep breath and closes his eyes. "Linda knows what you need."

Phoenix has clearly hit his limit of helping me. His mind and body seem to be shutting down, and rather than argue with him on not accepting this charity, I enter the store with the intention to make this as quick as possible.

The bell hanging off the top of the door announces my entrance, and my face heats up. I don't belong here. One glance tells me that much. It's raining outside, and I'm afraid I'm going to track in puddles of water, so I stand entirely too long on the mat, swiping the wetness off my feet.

"Hello, hello," a cheery woman calls out from behind the counter on the right of the store. She holds a phone, reading what I can only assume is the text from Phoenix. "Ani, right? Go ahead and look around. Let me know if I can help you with anything. My name is Linda."

I don't want to be in this store any more than Phoenix does, but I can't walk out empty handed. It will make Phoenix feel as if he's wasting his time. So, I'll be quick. In and out.

I don't even know where to start, but if I'm staying at Olympus Manor, I'm going to need something classier than just jeans and a T-shirt. I pick out a black, long-sleeved, off-the-shoulder dress. It looks like one I saw on the cover of a magazine once, and when I hold it up in front of me, I stare at it with joy, unable to believe someone is buying this for me. I've never had a dress like this before. I can't remember the last time I've had anything this nice, and it makes me feel weird. I look around the store, considering what else I need, so I pick up a pair of black skinny jeans and a pair of black boots.

I approach the checkout register and hand Linda the items.

She looks up at me and smiles. "Oh, that's not enough. Phoenix sent me a detailed list of what he wants." She places the dress, jeans, and boots into a bag. "But this is a good start." She takes me by the hand to the changing room. "I just need you to try on a couple things. Once I know how they fit, I can get the rest of the items without having you try on everything. I have a really good eye for sizes.

Linda starts by handing me a blouse, a dress, and a pair of pants. I quickly try on each item and walk out of the changing room for her to assess how they fit. Once done with that, she ushers me to a tufted white chair.

"Here, sit here so we can try on some shoes."

I sit down and pull off my old shoes. Linda has me try on every kind of shoe—ankle boots, peep-toe flats, heels, wedged sandals, wedges, and even go-go boots that make me feel like a teenager again.

A glance at the price tag of the dress I'm wearing tells me it's a little over three hundred dollars. I'm sure the shoes will be triple that, if not more. I can't stop staring at the price tag. This is too much. It's too much for someone to spend on me. I should refuse to take it, but I don't have any other options right now, either. Unless I want to wear moldy clothes or be naked. Plus, Phoenix will hate me for rejecting his offer. I don't have many options right now.

Linda checks her phone. "Okay, so I found a lot on his list, but not everything. I'll have to get the rest of the items elsewhere and have them delivered to Olympus. We don't carry toiletry items here, but I'll still get the best on Heathens Hollow and have them delivered as well."

I run my fingers through my hair and take a deep breath.

"Are you okay?" Linda asks. "You're very quiet."

"I'm fine." I force a smile. "It's just a little overwhelming."

"Overwhelming?" Linda's eyes widen.

My face is getting warm. "I'm not used to this kind of treatment."

"Oh well," Linda says. "This is how Phoenix shops. He texts me a list of what he wants, and I have it sent to Olympus. It's fast and furious, but it works for him."

I nod and smile. I guess it does work for him. For someone who's used to having everything handed to him, I'm sure it does. Yet, it feels weird to me because I've never had anything like this before. I'm not used to someone buying me things, especially something as expensive as these clothes. I don't know what to say. "Thank you" doesn't seem like enough.

Linda turns to me. "Okay, that's it for now. It was

nice meeting you, Ani. I will have all of these items delivered to the manor immediately."

I appreciate that there is no judgment in her eyes. No assumptions made. Linda is simply doing her job and assisting Phoenix with his needs. I must admit this has been the easiest shopping experience ever. I also have no idea what I actually got to wear.

I give my thanks and exit to join Phoenix in the car. Everything has happened in such a blur that I don't even know how long I was inside. The rain is letting up a little, but I still run to the car to try to avoid getting completely soaked.

"Did you get everything you needed?" Phoenix asks as I climb inside.

"I think so. Linda said she'll have it all delivered."

Phoenix nods as he signals for the driver to leave. He seems calmer now. Less sweaty. It seems some time alone is just what he needed.

"Thank you," I say, though I feel I owe him more than just a simple word.

On Heathens Hollow, the Godwins are known for sponsoring charities, donating to causes, and paying their fair share of money to help the community. Although, I've never actually seen a physical Godwin at any of the events or handing the money over in person. It's always felt like something they just do because they are rich. Not because they want to or care deeply about the cause or the charity they are funding. I've never really seen kindness from a Godwin before other than on a surface level.

Until now.

"Can I ask you something?" Phoenix eventually asks. "Why would you allow yourself to settle for that? To settle on a man who gives you that kind of life? You seem like such a strong-willed woman. You don't seem... broken."

"I'm not broken," I respond a little too quickly and defensively, but I inhale deeply and try to give an answer. It's the least I can do for someone who is going out of their way to help me. "I'm not a victim, but I am really fucking stubborn. And I guess I didn't want to give up. I didn't want to admit defeat."

"Why would you want to be with a man like..."

"Mark."

"Why would you be with a man who has you living like that? With a man who beats you?"

Looking out the window at the gray skies, the rain letting up, I say, "Daphne and I grew up with a very neglectful father. Poor would be an understatement to describe our upbringing. I guess you could say I struggled to break the cycle. Daphne was able to do it her way, but that was not the path I chose. When I first met Mark, he offered me something I found very attractive in a man. He was dominant, possessive, and swore he would love me forever and never let me go. I found it sexy and thought that it was everything I wanted and needed. It's still what I want and need. But... I didn't care about money if the man could make me feel protected and nurtured. But I misjudged all the qualities I thought I wanted in him. He didn't have any of them. He was just an ass."

I've never been so open with anyone about this before, not even my sister. Now feeling uncomfortable with how free I'm being with my words, I point to a rainbow that has formed in the horizon as a distraction.

"Look. A rainbow."

Phoenix angles his head so he can see what I'm pointing at. He leans in closer to me so that he can get a better look, and his greater mass seems to take up all my air space. I can only smell him, the faint scent of his aftershave and the spicy fragrance of lotion on his arms.

He's so close I can feel the warmth emanating from his body. I'm drawn to him, uncertain of what that means and why.

He looks down at me with intensity in his blue-gray eyes, and I get lost in them for a moment, as if I'm in a trance.

My heart races in anticipation as he leans in even closer. But then he quickly pulls back and sits back against the seat, his gaze once again focused on the passing scenery of his window.

I'm left to my thoughts, wondering what that was all about, and why the closeness between us felt so... right.

Finally, with enough awkward silence to strangle me, Phoenix seems to snap out of it, looking back at me. I swear I can feel his gaze burning a hole through my skin, but when I look up at him, I see his glare softening.

My heart is still racing, probably too fast. Feeling even more uncomfortable because I don't know what to say, I look out my window, hoping he can't hear the intensity of my heart.

"So why'd you stay?" he asks. "Once you realized he couldn't give you what you needed. What you deserved."

I keep my eyes on the rainbow peeking out from the dark clouds. "Stuck."

"Never again, Ani," Phoenix says with such intensity I'm forced to look back at him. "I don't want you to ever feel that way again."

CHAPTER
NINE

Ani

When we enter Olympus Manor, Phoenix lets out a deep breath, his eyes close for a moment too long, and then he says, "Before you head to your room, I want you to come upstairs to the attic with me. I want to show you something."

I inhale deeply and follow him into his attic, all too aware of how awful the exchange between us was only one night ago. It feels like a lifetime has already passed us by since I snuck up on him.

I was afraid of him. Afraid of the unknown. But now...

I'm not.

The darkness swallows us whole the second we step in the stairway. It's like I'm standing on the edge of a precipice, not knowing what's next. He's taking me to his special place. He's showing me a part of him that he keeps hidden from others. I'm not taking this trip up the stairs flippantly.

My heart is pounding, my palms sweaty. Phoenix's power and influence within these walls is palpable. Deep down, I know that once I take this step, there's no turning back. It's a scary thought, but also strangely liberating.

He's letting me inside his lair.

I take in the shadows of the attic, feeling a strange hunger for something I can't quite explain. I stand still, allowing my eyes to adjust to the room's deep gloom. As they do, I'm surprised by the vastness of the space before me. Now that I'm truly taking the time to absorb everything rather than fleeing so quickly, I see more. This is no ordinary attic; it's an entire world kept hidden away from prying eyes.

The walls are lined with ancient artifacts of the Godwin family, mysterious boxes, and stacks of books that reach all the way to the ceiling. The air is thick with age, knowledge, and Phoenix Godwin.

I turn to find Phoenix standing silently in the corner—watching me as if his presence is some sort of guardian angel protecting this place from intruders. His eyes burn into mine as if he can sense every thought running through my head, and he knows exactly what I'm thinking.

But I don't even know what I'm thinking. Chaos is swirling inside my mind.

He remains still and silent until eventually taking a seat at the station of monitors and control board and motions for me to do the same. He studies me intently as I shift in my chair, unsure of what he expects. I take in all the security footage of Medusa Enterprises and feel like a fly on the wall. I see everything within the building. Every room. Every crack. People are moving about and have no idea that I can see what they are doing.

"This is what I do," he says in a low voice. "I watch."

I nod slowly, still trying to comprehend the gravity of his words. "Every day? Up here by yourself?"

"Yes."

I turn my attention back to the monitors, and as I watch, I quickly develop a newfound respect for Phoenix and his work. He has Post-it notes about someone being suspicious, and there are notebooks full of paragraphs on people he's keeping a close eye on. He's an excellent observer and a master of detail, and I begin to understand why he values secrecy and security so highly. This is his family's company, and he takes it seriously.

"But why not do this in Seattle? At Medusa?" I ask.

"I like it here. I do have a penthouse in Seattle, and sometimes go when I'm truly needed in the office by my sister. But my choice is to remain here, if possible."

"Does anyone know you are up here?"

"Those that matter do."

His hand brushes mine. His large, broad shoulders crowd my space as he leans to flip a switch. Every time he touches me, electricity courses through me.

At first, I'm not sure if Phoenix notices my reaction. But after a few times, it's obvious he does. He always pulls away quickly and apologetically, but the spark between us continues to grow.

"I wanted to bring you up here to show you I'm turning off the camera in your room. I want you to see me do it so you know for a fact that I won't invade your privacy any longer." He turns a switch, and I see the guest room come up on the screen.

"How do I know you won't just turn it back on?" I challenge.

"My word is everything. I detest liars more than anything in this world. If I say something to you, I honor that. I'd never lie." With that, he flips off the camera, and the screen goes black.

Phoenix rises and makes his way to the open window allowing the sea air inside. I follow him so I can take in the view of the waves crashing against the cliff below.

"It's the best view in the entire house," he says.

The Salish Sea is beautiful, twinkling underneath the sunlight peeking out from the storm clouds. Olympus Manor sits on a cliff, but from this angle, it almost feels as if we are floating over the sea. I'm getting a glimpse of what being a God feels like. We are in Olympus staring down at the mortals below.

"It's beautiful outside, and the rain has stopped. We should go for a walk," I suggest.

"I don't like going outside. I rarely leave the attic." His eyes focus on the large willow tree balancing on the edge of the cliff.

I widen my eyes and turn my body to fully face him. Having to tilt my head back far so I can look into his eyes, I say, "But you went outside today."

"For you. I did it for you," is all he says.

Remembering how sweaty and agitated he got, it all makes sense now.

"You never leave?" I'm still not truly processing what he's telling me.

"Not unless I have to."

"Why?"

He shrugs. "Stuck."

He looks down at me, possibly waiting for me to judge him, which I don't. We all have our demons, and if this is his, I've seen worse.

"Thank you," I whisper. Our bodies are so close, but neither of us is taking a step back to make space.

"For what?"

"For pushing past your boundaries for me. I don't take that act lightly."

Phoenix reaches out and takes my hand in his. His touch feels electric, like a wave of heat that washes over me. His gaze is intense, and he doesn't say a word. Instead, he leans closer, lowers his head, and lightly brushes his lips against mine.

He tastes sweet, like honey, and his kiss sends a jolt of pleasure through my body. The kiss lingers for a few moments before he pulls away, leaving me wanting more.

I'm desperate for more of his touch, so I stand on my tiptoes and wrap my arms around his neck and pull him close. Our kiss deepens, and the heat radiates from his body.

His hands wander over my curves, exploring every inch of my skin. He moves his lips down to my neck and lightly nibbles my earlobe. I press myself against him and let out a soft moan of pleasure. His brings his hands further down my body, causing my skin to tingle with anticipation.

My breath is coming in shallow gasps as he stares into my eyes, and he begins to caress my body with slow, gentle strokes. He moves down my neck and over my chest, exploring every inch of me and driving me wild with desire. With each touch, my heart races faster, and I long for more.

His hands wander lower, tracing circles around my navel with his fingers before he reaches my waist. His touch is gentle but firm, stroking my skin and setting my nerve endings aflame. I'm lost in sensation as he slides his hands up and down my body, exploring every curve and driving me to the brink of pleasure.

Finally, we pull away, leaving me breathless and

aching for more. He looks into my eyes and strokes my cheek gently. My heart is pounding, and a warmth spreads through my body. The connection between us is undeniable, but I'm not sure we should continue.

What does it mean if we do?

What does it mean if we don't?

"I should probably settle into my room," I murmur, trying to regain my composure.

My words hang in the air between us, but he doesn't move away. He leans in closer, his breath tickling my face. He brushes his lips against mine in a soft kiss, my skin burning at the contact.

He nods slowly, but his eyes never leave mine. He leans in and brushes another gentle kiss against my lips, sending a thrill through me. It's only fleeting, but it's enough to make my knees weak.

"Let me know if you need anything," he whispers, barely an inch away from my mouth.

Reluctantly, I break away and head to the stairway as I try my best to ignore how this man behind me makes me feel.

CHAPTER
TEN

Ani

I'm back in the room. Alone. And I hate it.

Funny how different I am from Phoenix. He enjoys four walls and being alone. I, on the other hand, am regretting leaving the attic to return to my room. If it weren't for me, I think Phoenix would have had me stay. But then what? What would happen?

Butterflies swarm in my belly, and I feel like a giddy school girl who has just had her first kiss. It's as if I'm expecting angels to sing and the skies to part. I just kissed Phoenix Godwin.

If you would have told the starving, cold, poor girl on the Eastside of Heathens Hollow that I would someday be kissing a Godwin, I would have laughed. I don't get fairytales. I'm not Cinderella.

After taking a deep breath, I try to shake off what happened. It was momentary. Impulsive. He and I had simply confessed some details about each other and were vulnerable and nothing more.

Nothing more.

I need to distract myself and remove the buzzing from my body, so I glance back toward the floorboards and decide a little reading from the journals can't hurt. Anything to get my mind off the man only one floor above me.

I check the camera and for a second wonder if it's a good idea. What if Phoenix is watching me? But then he said he would never lie, and I actually believe him. Ignoring the warning voice of caution, I open the hole back up. I've been thinking about Freya, and I need to keep reading.

Dear Diary,

It all began with a kiss. I see that now. I see how the darkness began...

I can still remember the taste of his lips on mine the first time we kissed. I can still see the way he looked at me when he first saw me across the room, looking like he was about to die for me.

I close my eyes and tilt my head up as he leans down. I can feel his lips on mine and the sweet sensation of his breath on my face. When I open my eyes, he's staring at me, eyes searching for signs that I liked it.

The feeling that had just passed between us was foreign yet familiar. I knew that I had found something special in him, something that I never wanted to let go of.

But as the days went by, my feelings for him started to change. Our conversations became more tense, and his kisses felt forced. I tried to push away any thoughts of doubt, but it was becoming harder and harder to ignore.

Suddenly, one night I found myself walking along the edge of the cliff, my heart pounding and my feet heavy. I looked around, trying to remember how I had ended up here. And then I saw him in the shadows, his eyes glowing in the moonlight.

He reached out and grabbed my arm, pulling me closer. His grip was strong and unyielding, as if he had been waiting for this moment for a long time.

I tried to scream, but he clamped his hand over my mouth. He leaned in close and claimed me as his.

I now can look back and see how Troy Godwin made me his. I see now how I never had a choice. He made it for me.

So why did I think I had a choice now to leave the marriage?

I don't. I know this. I don't.

He had taken my freedom away, taken my decisions away, and I felt like a puppet on a string. He was always lurking in the shadows, watching and waiting for me to make a mistake.

My days and nights were filled with fear and anxiety, and I knew that if I ever did try to escape his clutches, he would be there waiting. I was trapped in an endless cycle of darkness and despair, never knowing when or if I would ever find freedom.

Dear Diary

I'm worried about my son. Phoenix is so different from his siblings, Apollo, Ares, and Athena. While they are brimming with life and enthusiasm, Phoenix is a pale shadow of who he should be. His eyes are sad; an abyss of unraveled secrets and hidden fears that I can only guess at. He does not laugh or joke like the other children. He doesn't seem to have any friends. He is alone in his own world, a solitary figure of sadness. I have tried to talk to him to pierce the veil of sadness that surrounds him, but he turns away from me, like he is carrying a weight too heavy for me to understand.

As a mother, it breaks my heart to see him like this. I fear that I am failing him, and that I am not doing enough to help him. I want to be able to help and understand his struggles, but I am afraid I don't have the ability to do so. I know for a fact his father doesn't.

I try to show him love and acceptance, but it's hard when he is so different from the other children. When I look into his eyes, I feel like there is something more to his sadness, something that is too heavy for him to carry alone. I feel helpless, and sometimes I worry that he may be hiding a family secret from me.

I want Phoenix to know that no matter what he is going through, I am here for him, and I will do whatever it takes to help him. He needs love and guidance, not judgement or criticism. All I want is for my son to be happy and find the strength to confront whatever it is that has been holding him back.

I talk to Apollo, Ares and Athena about their brother, but all they can offer me are shoulder shrugs and lip biting; they don't really understand what Phoenix is going through either. It's like we're all in the dark about this mystery of his, just wandering around blindly hoping that one day it will reveal itself and give us an answer.

My worries for Phoenix are only compounded by my concerns over my other children. Athena, my daughter, is a fiery and passionate soul. She has a strength in her that can be both empowering and dangerous. Her confidence and independence can be inspiring to watch, but it can also lead to recklessness and anger. I try to talk to her about her feelings, but she often shuts me out or gets defensive.

Athena's temper sometimes gets the better of her, leading to raging arguments or fights with the other children. I am scared for her safety. I don't want her getting into physical altercations with anyone, let alone her siblings or friends. I understand that she needs an outlet for her emotions, but I worry that if she doesn't learn how to control them soon, it could have serious consequences.

I have tried many different methods of helping Athena with her anger—teaching her breathing exercises, talking to her calmly when she's upset, encouraging positive self-talk—but nothing seems to help in the moment when she is overcome by emotion. I just want my daughter to know that no matter what happens, I love and accept her unconditionally.

As a mother of four children, it is hard not being able to protect them all at once from everything that might harm them: whether it be physical danger or emotional trauma; external threats or internal struggles like those Phoenix and Athena are facing.

I look at my son Apollo with a heavy heart. He's the son that can do no wrong in his father's eyes. He is handsome, charming and always eager to please everyone—not just his father, but anyone he comes in contact with.

The problem is that I am worried he is too eager to please, and that he's not being true to himself. I have tried talking to him about this, but he either doesn't understand what I'm saying or ignores my warnings altogether. All I want for my son is for him to be happy and fulfilled in life. If that means following his father's expectations then so be it, but if it means striking out on his own path, then I'll be there cheering him on.

I worry that Apollo is so focused on earning his father's approval that he'll lose sight of his own passions and desires. It breaks my heart to think that he might be sacrificing something important for the sake of appearing successful in the eyes of others.

Ares is my hardest child, and perhaps the most difficult to understand. On the one hand he is brave and fearless—always ready to take on a challenge or stand up for what he believes in. He takes pride in being the protector of our family, and his siblings often turn to him in moments of distress. However, I worry that Ares's desire to protect can lead him to act without considering all the consequences of his actions.

I have tried talking to him about this, but he struggles with understanding abstract concepts like consequence and responsibility. He wants so desperately to please us, especially his father, that he sometimes forgets to think for himself. I worry that if I don't help guide him soon, it could have disastrous results.

At times like these I wish ever-so-slightly that Ares was more like his brother Apollo—calm and collected— so that I could trust him a little more at times of crisis or uncertainty. Nevertheless, my love for Ares remains as strong as ever.

It is almost impossible to be a parent. I didn't want to be distant from them but also didn't want to smother them with my concerns. I just wanted to give them space and love and support. All I could do was take them by the hand and escort them through life and hope that they would find their way in the world. But then there is another part of me. A part of me that wants to run and never look back. Hide from it all. Remove myself completely.

I close the journal with a tsunami of guilt. Phoenix would be livid if he knew I was reading these journals. I found the vault of Godwin secrets, and though I can't resist reading them... I know deep down I shouldn't. It's wrong. It's invasive. And yet...

Poor Freya. Reading the words of a tortured wife, and a troubled mother...

My connection with Phoenix feels different after reading these words. He has secrets. And I most certainly do. Maybe that's what's pulling us together. Maybe we don't have chemistry or lust causing that kiss. Maybe our darkness is acting like magnets. It's bringing us together.

But my secret, my darkness, is so much worse than his could ever be. A man died because of me.

Mark, my ex-husband, is dead because of me.

I may not have pulled the trigger, but the minute I brought Daphne and Apollo to the trailer to rescue me... I signed his death warrant.

Trying to gather some self-control, I toss the journal back into the hole, close it, and vow that I won't read anymore. These are not my tales to read. I just need to go to bed and get some sleep. Who knows what tomorrow is going to bring. I have a life to rebuild, and something tells me this is going to be much harder than I think.

CHAPTER
ELEVEN

Ani

The fear I am feeling is like a punch to the gut.

Hands around my neck squeezing.

Chains around my body with no escape possible.

A gag between my dry lips so I can't scream.

This is it. I knew this day would come. Deep down in my moral soul, I knew punishment would be the ultimate ending to this story.

I stare out the window at the cars pulling up. Men in suits and men in uniforms are storming the manor. The full moon hanging over the crashing sea illuminates the army of justice. I fucked up.

I allowed this to happen. I didn't stop it when I could have.

It doesn't take long for them to barge their way into my room.

"Ani Parker. We have a warrant to search Olympus Manor."

I nod with wide eyes. I try to offer a smile, although the effort could very likely crack my face. But if I am nice and cooperative, maybe they will let me go free. Or maybe Apollo hid my misdeeds sufficiently. Maybe he's smarter than them. A chance exists that whatever desk jockey they assign this case to won't be able to overpower the mighty Godwins. Maybe I'll be safe due to association, simply because my sister is married to one of them.

"We would like you to come with us," a man in a suit says. They all blur together, and I wouldn't be able to describe any of them tomorrow in a lineup if I have to.

"Am I under arrest?" My voice doesn't sound like mine. It quivers and is too high-pitched. A stranger is doing the asking.

"That will be up to you, Ms. Parker. We hope you're willing to be cooperative."

I nod again, although I know what they want from me.

Rat.

Narc.

Backstabber.

Betrayer.

They want me to go against the Godwins.

Silly people. Don't they know that no one goes against a Godwin?

I wake up with a jolt, sweat beading on my brow.

A dream. It is just another dream. The same one over and over again. Will I ever sleep without this nightmare haunting me?

I look up at the camera in the corner of the room. He's not watching me. Thank god, or I'd have to try to explain.

But a part of me wishes he is watching me, too. If he knew I was having a nightmare, would he come and take me in his arms and comfort me, to protect me from the boogie monster beneath my bed?

Footsteps pad outside my door...

The fear of my nightmare returning or realizing I haven't fully woken from it yet grips me once more as the door creaks open.

It's Phoenix.

He approaches me with a concerned look in his eyes. The weight of his gaze on me is a physical force, pushing me down into submission. He stands over me, towering above my bed, a god among men. I am nothing but a mere mortal in his presence.

"I heard you screaming."

"I had a nightmare."

"You seem to have nightmares a lot."

I give a weak smile as tears burn the back of my eyes. "As long as my days awake are no longer a nightmare, I'll consider myself lucky."

I must stop obsessing over what happened. Over what I can't change. My guess is Phoenix thinks I'm simply dreaming of Mark hurting me. He has no idea what the guilt of what actually happened is doing to me, a guilt I have to take with me to the grave.

Out of respect for Apollo, I won't tell a soul. Apollo helped me, and he deserves my secrecy forever. But the only way that is going to happen is for me to accept and release this guilt. I must.

"I'm not going to let anyone hurt you again." Phoenix's voice softens. "I can protect you. Even if I can't make your nightmares go away."

He reaches out his hand, and I take it, grasping it tightly. I know what I'm getting myself into, but I don't care. I'll do anything to be free from this fear, this constant sense of impending doom.

"Come upstairs with me. It could help you sleep by not being alone," he says.

"I don't want to be a bu—"

"It's not a request." His eyes narrow in on me. "I'm not going to stay up all night and listen to you have one nightmare after another."

My breath catches, and for a moment I'm frozen. I want to run away, but his dominance silences the flight.

I draw a deep breath, savoring the feeling of warmth and security. I don't know why I feel so safe with him, but I do. I let out a long sigh of relief.

Just then, a chill runs up my spine, and I know he can sense it. He takes a step forward and looks at me with a concerned expression. "What's wrong?"

The words freeze in my throat as I try to think of what to say. I don't want to tell him about my fears, about how I'm scared of being hurt again. It's too personal, too raw.

But he's already seen through my defense. His voice is gentle and understanding as he presses further. "I'm not the one you need to be afraid of."

The sincerity in his voice is comforting, and I begin to relax again.

As he leads me out of the room, I am aware I could be making a deal with the devil. He's a Godwin. I know what that means. Everyone on the island knows what that means.

Gods or Devils—basically the same thing.

But in this moment, it's a deal I am willing to make. Because with Phoenix by my side, I am safe. And that's all that matters. No one can enter the attic without Phoenix knowing. Something tells me even nightmares aren't allowed.

Phoenix leads me up the narrow staircase toward the manor's attic. My sense of unease increases as we climb higher and higher. But I trust him. Everything in my gut tells me I do. As we reach the top of the stairs, he pushes open a door, and I'm greeted with a dimly lit room. What catches my attention is the bed is now in the center of the attic. The large four-poster bed with crisp white sheets and fluffy pillows looks like a sanctuary. He's fixed up the space since the last time I came up here.

"No more nightmares, dove," Phoenix says, as he guides me toward the bed. "It's safe here. No one can hurt you."

A sense of relief washes over me as I sit down on the bed. The sheets are soft and cool against my skin, and I release a sigh of contentment.

"Lie down," Phoenix says, as he tucks me into the bed. "Close your eyes and rest. I'll stay awake until you fall asleep."

I do as he says, my body easing into the mattress. I should be worried about what's to come, about what he expects from me in return for this help. No one can be this nice out of the kindness of their heart. My life has taught me that much. But in this moment, I don't care. I feel safe, and that's all that matters.

But as my mind starts to wander, I remember all the times I've been hurt in the past. All the times I've been taken advantage of or manipulated. A pang of fear pierces my chest, and I worry that Phoenix is no different, that he, too, is trying to take advantage of me in some way.

My breathing starts to pick up pace, and my heart races as I try to process these thoughts. I want to trust him, to feel safe, but I can't ignore the doubts that are creeping in. Fear slowly overtakes me as I grapple with this inner conflict.

I lie there in silence, my mind spinning as I struggle to make sense of my conflicting emotions. I want to believe that Phoenix means well, that he truly wants to protect me, but I'm so scared of trusting the wrong person again. Of being hurt over and over.

I draw a deep breath and try to steady myself. I can't live my life in fear, and if I'm ever going to move on from my past, I need to find a way to open up again. I need to force myself to take a leap of faith and trust Phoenix, believing that he won't hurt me.

My heart feels like it's being torn in two. I want to stay and enjoy this brief moment of peace, but at the same time, my mind is screaming at me to get away while I still can. I'm so confused, so scared.

As I drift off to sleep, I can feel Phoenix's presence in the room. He's here, watching over me, keeping me safe from the nightmares that haunt me. And for now, that's enough.

I wake a few times throughout the night and notice Phoenix asleep in the nearby leather chair. He's facing the bed, still watching over me. Staying near, but not assuming he may come lie in the bed with me.

He's a gentleman. Not a monster.

And he's watching.

And I like it.

TWELVE

Phoenix

"We need to get out of the house. It's been a beautiful day, and we've spent it cooped up," Ani says, holding back the sheer curtains of the attic window.

"It's still beautiful *inside*," I argue. And it is because of her. She's stunning, the sun behind her framing her in a golden-yellow glow. She's a masterpiece in the flesh.

"The sun is going to set soon. We missed the day."

"The sun sets every day. Nothing special when it does."

"Phoenix... Sometimes you need to take in the small and simple pleasures. Mother Nature gives us that. You can't stay locked up in this house forever. I worry about you, just as I know you worry about me," Ani says softly, turning to regard me. Her eyes are so kind and understanding, and I feel my resolve crumbling, but I'm still hesitant to venture outside. "Vitamin D. We need to actually feel the light once in a while."

"I'll get you some chewables," I say. "Orange juice and stuff."

She glances over her shoulder at me and sighs. "Phoenix..."

"I can't keep you safe if we're not here. You say Mark is gone for good, but there is no way of really knowing that. I haven't had time to speak with Apollo and put some additional security in place. I want to know exactly where Mark ended up so we can keep a close eye on him."

The smile and softness on her face disappear immediately. Shadows and sadness take over. "He's gone. Trust me. He's gone."

"But until I know that for sure, we stay here."

Ani takes a step closer to me, closing the gap between us. She places her delicate hands on my shoulders and looks me in the eye. "Phoenix, you were my protector last night, my knight in shining armor. You made me feel safer and more cared for yesterday than I have in my entire life. So, let me repay the favor. Let's get you outside and knock down these prison walls you've made for yourself."

She pauses to see if I'll respond, but I simply

watch her, tempted to go against everything inside of me that screams *stay*.

"Besides," she adds. "If you say no, then I'll just have to go for a walk on the beach by myself, and maybe someone will steal me away forever. Maybe the Kraken will rise from the sea and take me to the depths of the ocean."

Though she's teasing, I feel a pull of possessiveness at the thought of how easily she could be taken away from me, just like that.

She crosses her arms and gives me an exasperated look. "I know you don't like going outside, and I understand. I'm not judging you in the slightest, but if we just stay here in the attic, we'll miss out on so much life has to offer."

I say nothing, but I'm watching the persistence in her eyes and finding it endearing.

"What if we go to Seattle? You said you have a penthouse there, right?" she suggests. "We'd still be alone. We still would be inside... safe. But we'd have a change of scenery from the attic. Maybe I could start looking for a job there and—"

"No," I answer gruffly, feeling constriction on my insides. I'm not ready to see her moving on with her life. Not yet. It's too soon.

Ani is undeterred, her voice gentle and patient. "What about the beach? We could take a leisurely walk, and we wouldn't have to worry about crowds. There's no one around. It's your land. It's private."

I take a deep breath, and my heart beats faster as

I consider the possibility. I'm content being in the attic day and night, but she clearly is clawing at the walls and needs fresh air.

"Okay," I answer. "We can go to the beach. On Godwin private land only."

Her face brightens with surprise as she grins and rushes to give me a hug, her body so tiny compared to mine. "You won't regret it." Her voice is full of warmth and reassurance.

I nod, already regretting my decision but also knowing there is no backing down now.

She takes my hand and leads me out of the attic, down the stairs and out the front door. We walk together, our steps in sync, until we reach the beach.

The salty air greets us, and I inhale deeply. Ani stands beside me, looking out at the vast ocean expanse.

"This is amazing," she says in awe. "It's like a painting."

We walk along the beach, feeling the sand beneath our feet. It is strange but invigorating to be out in the world again after so many years of staying inside the attic. One second, I like it, the next I don't.

Ani looks up at me from time to time with a sparkle in her eye; she's clearly enjoying herself. It's nice to see that something so simple can bring her such joy. I stay close, watching her as she takes in the sights and sounds all around us. For the first time in months, a sense of peace washes over me, and I'm glad we ventured out. The rush of the waves lulls me into calmness, and I relax as Ani and I walk side by side along the shore.

We find a spot to sit and watch the sun set.

Ani wraps her arm around me, and I let myself feel the warmth of her embrace.

"Thank you," she says, as the sun sets beneath the horizon.

"I can't always expect you to want to stay inside," I answer.

"Not just about the walk," she says. "For everything. For giving me a place to stay. For making me feel safe for the first time in my life. For not judging me for my past and who I was. Allowing me the time to figure out who I am now."

I nod, and Ani squeezes me tighter.

For a long time, we sit on a large piece of driftwood in silence, watching the stars come out in the night sky. The full moon is going to light our path back or I'd be nervous about her getting hurt climbing the hill back to the manor. Although I do see some storm clouds coming in, so I consider telling her we need to cut this short, but I also don't want to spoil the mood—her mood.

Ani leans her head against my shoulder. I turn to meet her gaze, and it is full of understanding and contentment. It's almost as if she likes me. Likes the real me. We remain as we are for what feels like an eternity, just being in each other's presence and savoring the moments.

Ani speaks up softly. "I'm so glad we took this

walk. It was exactly what I needed. And I think that even though you may sit here and act grumpy, you enjoyed yourself, too. But I like your grumpy." She looks up at me with a small smile on her face that tells me she means every word.

Warmth spreads through my chest as I squeeze her hand in response. "I like your light. It helps with my dark."

Ani squeezes my hand lightly before standing up and stretching her arms above her head. "I think I'm ready to go home now." Her voice is quiet but determined.

I nod, and we make our way down the beach to where we started. I'm happy to be heading back to a place it'll be safe.

Ani looks at me, as if she's reading my mind. "You know... it's possible to be safe outside, too."

I grunt in response.

Ani just smiles back, her expression full of understanding. I take her hand, and together we make our way back to the attic. But she stops midway and points in the distance. "Look, a lighthouse. I don't remember seeing that before."

I glance over. "It's on Godwin land. You wouldn't have seen it or visited it before."

Her eyes widen. "Then let's go see it now." She tugs my hand. "Come on."

"I thought the plan was to head back."

"Plans can change. Especially when adventure awaits."

CHAPTER
THIRTEEN

Phoenix

Rain erupts from the sky with zero warning, but Ani refuses to head home. Going against every fiber in my body that wants to return to the attic where it is secure and dry, I keep going. For her. I'm doing this for her.

I take her hand in mine and lead her up the lighthouse stairs, our footsteps echoing in the silence. The storm outside rages on, but inside, it's as if we're in our own little world. As we reach the top, we step out onto the platform and look out at the sea below. The waves are crashing against the rocks, the wind is howling, but we're safe in our little cocoon.

I pull her close, wrapping my arms around her and holding her tightly. I don't want her to slip and fall. Nothing can happen to her.

She leans into me, and we stand there, watching the storm rage on. It's as if the storm outside reflects the storm inside me. I like Ani... more than I should.

We take a moment to appreciate the amazing vista. Miles and miles of rolling waves sparkle silver beneath the full moon below us. The sky glows with the stars and brightness of the moon, with storm clouds drifting by like otherworldly entities. The air is cool, yet salty, as if an alchemist had crafted it himself.

Somewhere in the distance, a lone seagull cries out, its piercing call breaking the spell and reminding me who I'm standing next to.

I pull away enough to look into her eyes, and I know that whatever happens next, I want to be with her. Leaning down, I press my lips to hers, and in that moment, the storm outside fades away and it's just the two of us, lost in our own little world.

I wrap my arms around her tighter and lift her off the ground, pressing her body to mine as our lips lock together. It isn't a tender kiss; it's an assertion of my claim on her.

She's mine.

I use one hand to bring her face even closer. "You've unlocked something wild inside me, and I can't get enough of you. You've only given me a taste, and now I want more."

The tension between us is electric, and I'm filled with a desperate urge I can't explain. The passage of time fades away as we stare deeply into each other's eyes. I'm swept away by the power of this moment, wishing it will never end. Finally, our lips part, and the spell is broken.

We pause, acknowledging the gravity of our interaction.

My words sound foreign to me when I whisper, "What is this?"

She looks away and inhales deeply. "I don't know, but I don't want it to end just yet."

The realization that she also feels it, hits me like a bolt of lightning. I have been aware of our powerful chemistry, but until this moment, I haven't comprehended how much we have connected.

I must kiss her again. It deepens as I press her closer. Her body is warm where it presses against mine, and the heat of desire that courses through my veins. In this moment, I realize that I've been fighting an urge to take what I want from her all along. For the first time in my life, I'm keeping a possession that matters to me. Ani is mine, and I'll no longer try to deny it.

Without asking for permission, I part her lips with my tongue and explore her mouth with an urgency that feels almost primal. Our tongues move together like two lovers in perfect harmony, and it feels as if nothing else exists but us in this moment of passion. Nothing else matters. We are completely lost in each other's embrace until eventually our lips part, and we slump exhaustedly against one another.

For a long time afterward we just stand there,

caught up in the afterglow of our passionate embrace until finally Ani pulls away and looks into my eyes.

"I want to keep you, Phoenix Godwin," she says softly, laying her head on my chest as she wraps her arms around me tightly once more.

I nod solemnly in agreement, understanding all too well the repercussions of these words. Yes, Ani is mine now, and she actually wants to keep me as hers.

"Why are you shaking?" Ani asks me.

My hands tremble as I caress her face. "I'm trying to hold back." I feel as if I'm swimming against a tidal wave of darkness.

"Hold back? From what?"

"I'm trying to be gentle. You deserve soft and light, but I don't know how to be anything but rough and hard."

"Don't hold back," she whispers. "Be you. Unleash the monster you claim to be. I'm wanting him. I'm wanting you."

My body aches to do as she asks, and I let go, giving myself up to the darkness with a feral growl. Lifting Ani up in my arms, I take her inside the lighthouse.

She looks up at me, eyes wide and trusting, "I don't break, Phoenix. I can't be broken. Many have tried."

My body quivers in anticipation, and I press my lips against hers. The heat of her body envelops me, awakening something primal inside me. I let go, allowing my untamed nature to take over. Our movements become more passionate and relentless.

I take a deep breath as the darkness within me takes over. My muscles tense. As I look deeply into Ani's eyes, a transformative energy shifts within me. It's like electricity running through my veins. It's like I'm standing on the edge of a precipice, ready to jump into the unknown.

"You can always be broken." I'm not sure if I mean the words to sound like the warning they are.

Ani's eyes blaze with a hunger that I recognize. "Yes." Her voice is a whisper in the night. "Break me. Give me everything you have."

Giving in to the urge, I tighten my grip of Ani with the need ravage her body. I kiss her hungrily as I explore every inch of her curves. She shivers underneath me, her body arching to meet my every touch. Her passion grows as the heat radiates off her. Our movements become faster and more intense, our desire rising ever higher.

Fighting the urge to go any further, I place her on her feet and cross the room, creating distance between us. The splash of cold-water action leaves me breathless.

"I'm too big. You're too small. I'll *truly* break you," I say as I run my fingers through my hair, looking out the window at the sea below.

Ani steps close to me. I feel her warmth against my back as she wraps her arms around my torso.

"You won't hurt me. I can take it. I want to take it. To take you."

I turn to face her, my heart pounding. Ani's eyes are burning with an intensity I've never seen before. I can feel the fire of her soul, and all the passion that she holds within her. I know my answer before I even say it.

"We need to stop. We can't do this right now." I glance outside at the growing storm. "We need to head back to the house. It's really raging outside."

Ani sighs, her body deflating in disappointment. But she nods in understanding, and I'm grateful for her respect. She steps back, giving me space to breathe.

We stand there for a long time, just looking at each other. The energy between us is obvious, no matter how much I try to fight it.

But right now, I need to keep her safe. Back in my attic. Safe.

CHAPTER
FOURTEEN

Ani

Another long day and night passes, and I can clearly see that Phoenix is doing his best to avoid me. He claims work is keeping him busy, but I know better. We got too close, too fast, and I've scared him the fuck away. I can't say I blame the man. It's scared me, too.

Before I can wallow any more in my thoughts, my phone rings, and I know it's Daphne before I even answer. She's the only one who has this number. Frankly, she's the only person I know. The realization of just how alone I am is truly sinking in.

"Hi, sis." I try to keep the sadness out of my voice.

"It's official," she announces. "We are moving into the house! It's ours. My dream house is ours."

"I'm so happy for you. You deserve this."

She pauses. Since I've not been able to hide the underlying sadness in my tone, she has picked up on it. "What's wrong? How are you feeling?"

"Nothing. I'm good." I swallow to try to mask my voice some more. "And I'm extremely happy for you."

"How are you feeling?"

"I'm fully recovered. In fact, I've spent the day looking for some work."

"On Heathens Hollow?"

"I considered Seattle, but I have no real experience, and I think I have a better chance getting something on the island," I say.

"Let me help you," she offers. "I'm sure Apollo can get you something at Medusa. Even if it's not the best job, it will get your foot in the door, and you can work your way up."

"Daphne... I'm not going to accept—"

"Just think about it," she says. "You can talk to Apollo tonight. He's heading to Olympus to check on things. I'd come, but I'm meeting with the interior designer for the house first thing in the morning, and I want to get some concepts together. I hope you don't mind."

"Of course not. I don't want you worrying about me." Will she ever listen to my request? "I'm fine. Truly."

"I feel like such a bad sister," she says. "I've been so preoccupied with my life—s"

"Stop. I kept telling you that you were smothering me. And you were. I have to learn to stand on my own two feet. I know you mean well, but you need to give me space."

There's a pause on her end. I know my sister well enough that she's wanting to tell me something but summoning the courage to do so.

"Spill it," I say. "What did you really call to tell me?"

"I wasn't sure the right time to tell you, considering everything you're going through, but..." There's another pause. "I'm pregnant."

"Oh my god," I squeal as elation erupts inside me. "Oh my god!"

I wish she was standing right in front of me so I can hug her.

"It's still early, but Apollo and I decided to tell our family only. Get further along before we really tell people."

"I'm so happy for you. I really am." I know why she has been hesitant about telling me. The fact that Mark made me lose that baby nearly destroyed me. But I truly have healed in both body and mind. "I'm not sad, Daph. I don't want you walking on eggshells around me. Everything happens for a reason. I wasn't meant to have that baby, and I've come to terms with that. My time will come. But for now, it's your time. And I can't wait to be an auntie."

"I can't wait. Truly. And Apollo is over the moon. He's such a doting father already. He talks to my belly. I'm really happy. *Really* happy."

"A shopping trip is in our future," I offer. "But

first get that house set up. Save the nursery for me, though. I want to help."

"Deal. And please consider my offer about the job, and we can talk more about it in a couple of days. You aren't in any rush to make any big decisions right now. Take this time to figure out what you want. You get a chance at starting over. What do you want your new future to look like?"

We say our goodbyes, and I'm left pondering my sister's question. What do I want my future to look like?

Growing up, I never had any big dreams or ambitions. I simply wanted to be a wife, maybe a mother, and live a comfortable life. I didn't shoot big, and I'm still not sure I want to. I simply want to feel safe, secure, and know I have the ability to support myself. But even that right now feels as if I'm shooting for the stars.

Needing a distraction and to focus my mind on anything but me and my fucked-up situation, I return to my trusty hole in the floor and pull out a journal so I can read some more of Freya's story. I pick up a different journal in the hope that maybe something good is in another diary entry since the other one was dark as fuck.

After settling on my bed, I dive in.

Dear Diary,

I watched my son whip himself beneath the tree of forgiveness today. The willow tree on the edge of the cliff has become a staple in our family. I hate it.

It's not the first time I've peered down from my bedroom window at one of my children punishing themselves for one of their crimes. Troy didn't believe in punishing the children. He believed it was on them to conduct their own penance. So like a highly devout Catholic priest, Phoenix rained the leather down upon his bare back. The sound of the leather striking his skin echoed through the night air, and I could feel the pain in my own chest. Watching him take on this burden as his penance was heartbreaking. He shed tears with each lash and no matter how much I wanted to, I couldn't stop him.

I wanted desperately to run down, to stop him from this self-inflicted torture. But something kept me from doing so, some force stopped me from interfering. I heard a voice whisper into my ear that this was how it was meant to be.

It was the way of the Godwin family.

But even as I watched, I could feel a darkness gathering around the tree. Its tendrils snaking towards my son and wrapping around him as if to embrace him in a cold embrace. I felt an eerie chill run down my spine as I watched Phoenix take his last lash of the whip, standing tall before the tree as if nothing was amiss.

The sensation of dread only grew as I watched the night sky darken, casting a menacing shadow across the entire yard. It was as if the gods were watching, waiting for something to unfold. Something that I could only guess would be far more sinister than any punishment Phoenix could ever dream up for himself.

I watched in horror as Phoenix spread rice from the nearby bucket along the ground. His back was still red from the earlier beating, but he didn't seem to be deterred by that. Instead, he calmly pulled up his pants to his lower thigh and kneeled down on the ground.

His movements were deliberate and smooth, almost as if this was a ritual he had done many times before.

My son was so brave in the face of pain and remorse. He acknowledged his mistakes and sought atonement for them through self-sacrifice. I found myself inexplicably proud of him for this even though I wanted nothing more than to run out there and stop him from hurting himself further.

Maybe I'm just as demented as his father.

He began to mutter words I could not understand. He lifted his arms towards the heavens above, his eyes closed in concentration, his body shaking and wracked with sobs. I could feel the emotions emanating from him, feel his sorrow and remorse as if they were my own. His anguished plea cut through the night air, a plea for forgiveness that would not be granted.

And then, with a heavy heart, I turned away from the window and went to bed, hoping that whatever future awaited my son, it would be one he could bear.

Jesus. Fucking. Christ.

What kind of mother would allow this? What kind of father would expect this? What could a boy do that would make him feel he needed to seek penance? Although I grew up in an abusive household, something about this seems so much worse. I feel for Phoenix, but it also helps me understand him more. Maybe that's why our connection is so strong. The pain of our past is pulling us together.

Not wanting to read any more about Phoenix and the abuse he went through, I skip a few pages of the journal, with the intention of reading something else. Anything other than the awful tree of forgiveness that remains on the property even now.

Why hasn't anyone chopped it down?

Dear Diary,

I watched my husband attack his brother today. I wasn't surprised as I've always seen the hatred Troy has for Leander. But today... if it wasn't for Ares stepping in between the two of them, I fear they would have fought to the death.

The tension in the room was palpable and everyone in the family was on edge, expecting a fight to break out at any moment. We all breathed a collective sigh of relief when Ares stepped in and stopped the violence.

But I feel as if this is just the beginning of something terrible. I feel a darkness looming over us, like a storm cloud waiting to unleash its full power. I'm afraid what will come next.

"Medusa Enterprises is mine," Troy said. "Mine."

"And Poseidon is mine," Leander boomed back. "You stay in Seattle, and I'll stay in Heathens Hollow."

"Poseidon is only a division of Medusa Enterprises," Troy said as he took a menacing step toward Leander.

"I don't give a fuck. You manage your part of the business, and I'll manage mine," Leander countered.

I could feel the hatred between them, and it was so thick that I almost couldn't breathe. The thought of these two coming to blows was terrifying. Troy had always been hot-tempered, but Leander was no slouch either. I knew that if they did actually fight, one of them could easily get seriously hurt.

And then Apollo stepped in. He said something calming, something that made both brothers pause and take a deep breath. He spoke in a gentle yet firm tone, reminding them that they were Godwins and that they needed to be more reasonable. There was plenty of the family legacy to go around. Apollo reminded them that their father, Cronus, wouldn't want them to divide the family empire. That they should fight their enemies united.

I was thankful that Apollo and Ares were there, but I was still filled with so much dread. I have a feeling that this won't be the last time I'll see Troy and Leander face off.

Damn. This family is fucked up.

Growing up on Heathens Hollow, where Poseidon is the main industry for the workers here, we have always known that Leander Godwin is the king. He isn't a man to mess with, and everyone knows that Poseidon isn't exactly on the up and up, though no one, not even the sheriff will question him.

I glance up at the clock. I've been reading for longer than I intended, but it's so captivating. It's truly a book I can't put down. I don't know if it's just that I'm entertained or if I'm actually trying to find out more about Phoenix. Maybe deep down, I'm trying to find something that can help me connect to the man more, rather than having him push me away.

Dear Diary,

My son hasn't left his room in days. I know it's normal for pre-teen boys to be moody, sullen, even distant. But Phoenix is different. He hasn't left the house in I don't know how long, and he seems content to simply be locked away within the walls of Olympus Manor.

I don't know what it is about this house, but it feels as if I'm suffocating. I want nothing more than to leave... even though I can't. And Phoenix wants nothing more than to stay. He seems to get comfort from the darkness of our home.

I don't understand what's happening. I try to talk to Phoenix, to get him to open up and tell me what's wrong. But he just closes himself off. I can see the sadness in his eyes, but I can't seem to reach him. He's too far away.

My heart aches for him, yet I know I can't fix it. I have to stand by helplessly as my son struggles through this pain that he won't or can't put into words. No matter how hard I try, my words always fall on deaf ears. It's as if he's surrounded by invisible walls that I can never seem to break down.

Sometimes I hate this place. The walls seem to be closing in on me more and more each day. I can feel the darkness of its secrets seeping out from the shadows. I want nothing more than to leave, to escape this feeling of being caged. But at the same time, I'm not ready to leave my children.

My son's always watching. Studying. Maybe Phoenix knows something that I don't. Maybe he knows why we can't seem to escape this place. All I know is that his sadness seems to be rooted in this house, and I don't know how to help him.

I've tried to be strong for him, but it's hard. I feel like I'm failing as a parent, like I'm not able to provide him with the comfort he needs. I just wish I knew what was going on inside his head. I'm just trying to do my best, and yet it's not enough.

I fear for the future. I fear for what will happen to my son when we finally leave this place. Will he be able to find the happiness he deserves? Or will the darkness of this house follow us wherever we go?

As soon as I've closed the journal, I place it back in the hole. Wiping a tear that falls from my eye, I fight the urge to run upstairs to the attic to give the man a hug and tell him I'll be the sunshine to his midnight, but I'm not sure that's even possible.

CHAPTER
FIFTEEN

Phoenix

"Come on, brother. I thought you left this place," Apollo says as he enters the attic, inspecting every inch with his judging eyes. "I thought you were hiding out in that apartment of yours in Seattle."

"I still have the Seattle home," I say, "but I like it here better."

Apollo heads over to the window and stares down at the land below. He doesn't need to tell me he's staring at the tree of forgiveness for me to know where his eyes are locked.

"I don't see how you could. I don't know why anyone in this family would want to keep coming back to this house." He turns and looks at me. "How long have you been here?"

What he's really asking is if I have been here in

the attic the entire time he was with Daphne while they created their demon child.

"There weren't any cameras in your room, or the study, if that's what you are wondering," I say. "The last thing I wanted to see was you with *her*."

"Careful," he warns, subtly telling me that attacking his wife is not a good idea.

I have no desire to fight with my brother. "I'm glad you're here. You are saving me a phone call." I lean against the edge of the console with my arms crossed. "I need you to help me hunt down Ani's ex. I want him killed. Actually, I want to do it myself."

Apollo turns his head slowly, his eyes narrowing. "You've never been the killer in the family, brother."

"Ares is dead, so it's not like I can ask him to do it."

He nods slowly. "Still. Killing someone isn't in your nature."

"It is if it means keeping Ani safe. Guaranteeing it. My job in this family is security. So I need to do whatever it takes to make that happen."

"Ani isn't family."

"Close enough," I counter.

Apollo remains quiet for several moments, studying my face. No doubt he is reading just how serious I am. "The ex is dead. No need to worry about that any longer."

"What do you mean dead?" I ask.

"Dead. Let's leave it there."

"No. We aren't going to leave it there. How do

you know he's dead?" Ani made no mention of him no longer being alive, and surely she would know if that were true.

"It's a long story," Apollo begins with a sigh, "but Daphne asked a favor of me. For her sister. She wanted the ex to be killed, and after what I saw he did to Ani, I made it happen."

"You killed him?" Apollo's not normally the killer in the family either, but then again, his twin brother who was the killer died, so I suppose he felt the role fell to him.

"Yes. And the less you know, or anyone knows, the better."

This was the way Ares used to work. He told no one of the details when he made a hit. Clearly, Apollo has taken notes from our brother.

"Does Ani know you killed him?"

Apollo nods. "Yes, but not all the details."

My disbelief is quickly morphing to rage. Why wouldn't she tell me? Why would she lie? She told me he was gone. Not dead. Just gone.

"And Daphne knows you killed him?"

Apollo nods. "And before you start bashing my wife and telling me she'll turn me in to the police—"

"Again," I snap. "Turn you into the police *again*, brother." My hands shake, so I put them in my pocket to try to control my emotions. I don't want my brother to see me lose my shit. "That woman nearly destroyed our family. And you just handed her the tools to do it again. Her sister, too. Those two women now have the ability to hurt the Godwin family *again*."

"It's not going to happen."

"They are both a security risk!" The heat in my face, the shaking of my hands, and the way my breathing feels it's seizing is betraying just how furious I am. "I oversee security. Don't you think I should have been made aware of this? Where the fuck is the body?"

"Taken care of," Apollo says calmly. "There's nothing for you to worry about."

"Except the two women in this situation who are not Godwins."

"Daphne is my wife. She is a Godwin. And I was doing her sister a favor. Ani will never turn against me. Plus, it would mean putting her and her sister in jail, too, if she did." He takes a step toward me and places a hand on my shoulder. "There's nothing to worry about. I know how to clean up my messes."

"And what does Father say about this? Athena?" I ask.

"They don't know, and we'll keep it that way." Apollo's eyes darken in warning.

"Because you know they'd want both those women killed to keep this from spreading like a goddamn disease."

"I told you it's taken care of. It's over. Done."

I don't like being blindsided. Of being kept in the dark, completely unaware. And that is exactly what has happened.

And Ani... I trusted her.

I thought she was genuine. Honest. Someone I could open up to.

Lava erupts in my gut, and I have never been more relieved when Apollo says, "I need to get back to Seattle tonight."

That would explain why the helicopter is still on the pad rather than flying back to Seattle.

"But I wanted to tell you in person that I'm going to be a father," he adds.

"Congratulations," I say between clenched teeth. "Athena told me."

"I figured she did. But still. It's news I wanted to tell you face to face." He pauses. "I'm happy, Phoenix. It's a rare emotion in our family, I know. But I am genuinely happy."

He remains in place. I don't know if he's waiting for me to bust out the cigars or something, but I have nothing to offer him. I'm not happy. I'm fucking furious.

Daphne trapped him. She trapped us all.

The minute Apollo leaves, and the blades of the chopper are swirling, I march to Ani's room. I can't see straight. The ringing in my ears is deafening. There is a traitor in my sanctuary, and I must get rid the cancer now.

She jumps as I open the door. "Phoenix? Is everything okay?" She doesn't move, which is a good thing. It's smart to remain very still when face to face with a beast.

"I'm going to ask you something, and I want the truth." I'm giving her an option to try to fix this situation, if that's even possible.

"Okay..."

"Where is your ex?"

She licks her lips, swallows. "I told you. Gone. Why are you bringing him up again? I don't want to think about him for another second."

"Where is *gone*?" I press.

She shrugs and avoids eye contact with me. "I don't know. Baja maybe. He has a brother there. My guess is he's riding dirt bikes and drinking cheap Mexican beer."

And there it is. Ani Parker is a liar.

Controlling emotions has never been one of my strong suits. However, up until this very second, rage and fury were not emotions I had often experienced. Usually, there was something darker inside of me that sort of numbed those feelings, allowing me to take a step back and observe the world around me with a disaffected calm. But not now.

The sight of her sitting on the bed, her small frame filling the space with a betraying energy, is enough to ignite a fire in my heart I have never known before. Ani and her sister could now be the source of all my family's pain if they open their mouths, the ones responsible for shattering the Godwin name into a million pieces.

Daphne and Ani have all the power.

My hands tremble as I clench them into fists. I

want so desperately to lash out, to give in to my anger, but I've never been violent toward a woman. I don't want to start now.

Slowly, I step forward and speak. "You are a liar," I seethe, my voice deceptively steady despite the emotions raging inside of me. "I just spoke with Apollo." I lean towards her, my face towering over hers. "You are a liar. I detest liars."

Ani doesn't say anything right away, but she scrutinizes me with a calculating calm. After a few tense moments, she speaks. "This wasn't just my secret to tell. It involved your brother, my sister."

"I trusted you." Saying the words feels as if I am vomiting.

"I'm sorry, Phoenix. Truly. I didn't mean to lie to you."

"But you did."

Ani looks away, her expression a mix of guilt and sorrow. Her silence speaks louder than any words she could say. She's clearly struggling to come up with a valid excuse for lying to me multiple times. And even if she's truly sorry, it's too late. The damage is done.

"Get out of the house now," I boom, my voice vibrating in my chest. "Now. You have ten minutes to gather your stuff." I spin and storm out of the room.

She calls out behind me, "Phoenix, wait. Please. I'm sorry."

I pause in the hallway, feeling a pang of guilt by

simply throwing her out of the house in the night with the rain coming down in sheets.

"Phoenix," she says again as she runs to the doorway. "Let me make this right. I'm sorry. I truly am. You're right. I did lie."

I snap my head around and glare at her. "It's more than just that. My family can't allow danger to enter our bubble, and you delivered it on a motherfucking silver platter. You put my brother at risk. Because of you, he risked everything."

"I didn't ask Apollo to kill him!"

"But your sister did. And for that, you must pay the consequence. You both will."

"What do you mean by that?"

"Your sister has caused issues for this family for the last time. If no one else will do something about it, I sure as hell will."

"Please, stop and listen to me. Everything happened so fast that day. Mark had—" Her voice cracks and she looks up at me with big wide eyes. "I'm sorry."

"Words aren't enough," I counter. "Consequences and actions are how the Godwins respond. Your sister has already been alive longer than she should have."

She takes a step toward me. "Fine! This was my mess. Allow me to face the consequences. Not my sister! I'll do whatever you want." She pauses, looks toward the bedroom window through the doorway, then takes a deep breath. "I'll pay my penance if it means you trust me again. If it means you don't go after my sister. After me. Let me prove to you that my sister and I will never do harm to your family. Let me prove to you that I never meant for you to feel this way. Never."

Ani has the ability to hold a noose around my neck. She's strangling me with her pleas. She's fucking pulling the air right out of me.

"Out of this house. Now," I demand.

I march downstairs and pop my head in the kitchen where the staff are working, acting as if they haven't heard a single word of the commotion. They are used to keeping Godwin secrets. Years of being in this den of sin is enough to school them that they keep their heads down and their ears closed.

Behind me, I can hear Ani scurrying down the stairs to leave. I issue some orders for them, and they act on my commands immediately. I then turn to head to the foyer where Ani is, putting on her shoes that she had left by the door. She has a backpack slung over her shoulder, and I know—without even checking—that she didn't dare pack a single thing I bought her. She's leaving the house with nothing.

She's kneeling on the ground, which makes my height over her even more ominous.

Ani scurries to her feet. "I really am sorry I lied to you. I would never want to hurt you. Not after how kind you were to me. Especially after what we just... had."

Her fucking words are stabbing my heart. But

even through the pain, my rage is still there. I had tried to contain the monster inside of me for her. I had tried to behave. To be the man who could take romantic walks on the beach. And look what that got me. Lies. Nothing but lies.

Chaos of thoughts swirl in my head. So many thoughts. So many fucking thoughts.

Is there a way to fix all this? Can we turn back time to where she and I are alone on the top of the lighthouse?

I want it back. I want it back so fucking much.

But I let down my guard with Ani. I became soft with her. Weak. Never. Fucking. Again.

She's a liar. A liar.

And her sister, and that fucking Godwin baby...

But I want it back. Ani back. I want my sunlight back. I do.

Is there a way to fix the wrong?

No. She's a liar! Or...

Maybe...

She reaches for the door and something inside me makes me shout, "Stop!"

She freezes, turns to face me.

"If you are serious about suffering the consequences for your crimes," I take a step toward her. "Then get back on your knees now."

Without hesitation... she does.

CHAPTER
SIXTEEN

Ani

I adjust my weight to relieve the pressure on my knees. The small movement is not a good idea, however. Phoenix, who now has a handful of my hair in his grasp, jerks me up to a standing position. The sting on my scalp has me crying out, but I don't resist in any way.

"First rule," he says between clenched teeth. "You do nothing without my permission. Nothing at all. I don't care if you're uncomfortable, in pain, or just in the mood to do something of your own free will. You won't do anything without my direct order, or you will suffer the consequences. Liars, deceivers, and Parker girls get punished, and you will soon see just how severely."

He pauses and waits for some type of response from me. I can't talk. I'm so terrified I can only stare and nod. What type of consequences?

"Let me explain in more detail why you're still here," he begins. "I have graciously decided to grant you mercy. Of sorts. I believe in paying for your crimes, and that a girl like you can repent rather than just being shot between the eyes as any other Godwin would want me to do."

"I didn't mean to lie to you," I begin as Phoenix still grips my hair by the roots. "It was a secret. One I didn't feel you needed to know. It's my darkness. I don't have to share that."

"Well you are about to see my darkness. And what happens when I'm betrayed."

"Why are you being so mean?" I somehow get the courage to ask.

"Mean? Mean?" He pulls harder on my hair. "I *was* nice. I was so fucking nice. And look what that got me. A liar. It got me a fucking liar."

"Are you going to kill me? Is that it? I told you I wouldn't tell a soul. Not one."

"A death sentence is not off the table, but you have a chance to remove it by being a good girl rather than a bad girl," Phoenix says. "I'm not a man to say no to. Regardless of what your heart is screaming right now, your intelligent mind has already accepted the fact that you will have to pay a price. But life doesn't have to be difficult here. It can be quite comfortable if you *earn* the comfort."

"How do I earn the comfort?" I feel the first spark of hope since Phoenix learned of the murder.

Still holding my hair, Phoenix leads me to the stairs. "You have two choices every single day. To be a good girl or to be a bad girl. So, the choice really is up to you. Just as the choice of whether you would lie and deceive me was up to you. You clearly chose wrong, but hopefully when I'm done with you, you'll never make that mistake again. And you are going to have to make the ultimate sacrifice."

"What's that?"

"Your body," he states. "Your sister trapped my brother by becoming pregnant with his child. She's bringing another Godwin into the world. He can't act against her now. None of us truly can. So, as payback"—he locks gazes with me—"you are now going to be trapped with *my* baby."

"What?" There is no way I heard that correctly.

"Tit for tat," he says. "Your sister trapped my brother, and I'm going to counter the move by doing the same to her flesh and blood."

"I don't want to have your baby. Please. There has to be another way." I try to turn my head to look at Phoenix in desperation but am rewarded with a sharp yank on my hair as he leads me up the stairs. "I'll do anything else you want. I'll go to the police and take the fall. I'll claim that I did it and leave Apollo's name out of the story completely. Anything. You don't really want me to have your baby, do you? Or I'll leave and disappear if you want. I swear that

I'll never betray your family. Please just tell me what I can do. Let me pay for what happened in some other way." I stumble up the stairs to try to keep up with his stride.

Out of the corner of my eye, I can see Phoenix smirk. "Oh, you will pay. You will definitely pay."

When we reach the landing, I try not to focus on the way my ears ring and my vision fades in and out as we go down the long, expansive hallway. My head spins as I try to process what he's telling me. He was wanting to have sex with me for a different reason than just lust and attraction, and I'm to have his baby. This all seems so normal to him.

Simple.

A sentence issued for my crime.

"You will soon be the mother of my child. But before that day comes, you'll need guidance, structure, and a firm hand to teach you right from wrong. I don't want you to be the untrustworthy liar that you are." Phoenix opens the guest bedroom door and shoves me across the threshold as he follows close behind. "Every single day, I will ask you the same question. Have you been a good girl or a bad girl? I hope you answer correctly."

Looking around the room, it surprises me to see that it's completely empty. There is no longer a single piece of furniture, a painting, curtains, or even a rug on the aged hardwood floor. The large, canopied bed mastering the room with lush bedding and pillows is gone. The floor-to-ceiling window draped with heavy velvet curtains is bare. Antique furniture that adorned the room and even the large oriental rug that covered most of the marred wooden floor now missing. The room was lovely, elegant, and welcoming, but no more. What I had is quite the opposite of what the reality currently is.

Bare. Completely bare.

I turn and look at the man who stands by the door watching me examine the room. "Where is the furniture?"

"I had the staff remove it all," he says.

"Am I to stay in this room?" I'm almost too scared to ask this in fear of what I will hear.

He nods.

"But there is no furniture," I say softly. Am I to be expected to sleep on the floor? What about my clothing and personal items?

"By doing every single thing I say without protest, you can start earning some items of comfort," Phoenix explains. "If you argue or put up a fight, I'll still do what I intended to do, but you will earn a consequence instead. Good girl versus bad girl."

"What do you intend to do to me?" My voice cracks, and I think I might have to run to the bathroom and throw up.

"Have my baby. Behave," Phoenix answers.

"And do I just stay in this room until the baby comes?"

Phoenix takes a step toward me. "Until you earn

the comfort of exiting the room." He reaches into a leather holder on his belt and pulls out a knife I haven't seen before.

Did he bring it from the attic with the intent to use it on me?

The blade's silver glimmers beneath the light cast by a small chandelier. "But it's time we begin." He takes another menacing step toward me as my heart stops. "Remove all your clothing."

His command is accented by the heavy step of Phoenix circling to my left, as if I need a reminder of what will come if I say no.

I reach for the top button of my blouse and slowly unbutton it. "Am I to be a whore to you whenever you want?" I stare him directly in the eyes. "So, I have to fuck you at your beck and call? Is that what I'm understanding?"

Phoenix closes the distance between us and places the knife at the side of my neck, right below my earlobe. "Fucking you would give you pleasure. And the last thing I plan on doing to you right now is giving you pleasure." He runs the knife along my collarbone and down until it reaches my fingertips holding the button of my blouse. He then forces the blade between the button and the fabric and starts plucking the buttons right off, disrobing me his way.

I remain perfectly still. The knife's so close to my flesh that I worry the slightest move will have it slicing my skin instead of the blouse.

"I'll put my seed in you many times. Over and over until the swell on your belly is evident," Phoenix says as he uses the knife to cut through the thin band connecting my bra between my breasts.

He pauses and looks me directly in the eyes as the cool air kisses my now exposed nipples. Phoenix takes hold of the fabric and rips the bra off me.

Phoenix steps back. "Now, remove the rest of your clothes and stand naked before me. I will give you the first opportunity to earn an item of comfort." When I don't move right away, he raises one eyebrow. "You'll be naked standing before me one way or the other. I'm giving you the opportunity to at least earn some comfort for the act. Your choice. Good girl or bad girl?" Phoenix crosses his arms against his chest, awaiting my answer.

Glancing at the knife in his hand, and then at the way his jaw clenches while he waits, I decide it best to do exactly as he wishes. At least for now. I have to regroup. Think everything through. I need time to process, but I need to be alive to do so. If all I have to do is stand naked before him, then so be it. Trying to not overthink or allow my pride to get in the way of my survival, I disrobe as fast as I can.

"Leave your panties on," Phoenix instructs. "For now. I like the way they look on you. Delicate and sexy."

I pause as his deep voice breaks my spell of compliance.

"Please don't make me do this." My voice quivers as much as my body does. Fresh tears erupt and run down my cheeks as I watch Phoenix, who maintains the cold expression he has had since the beginning.

He once again closes the distance between us and puts the knife under my chin so I have to look up into his blue eyes. He inhales deeply. "I love the way your tears smell against your cheeks." He presses the tip of the knife into my skin, forcing a gasp to break free from my closed lips. He then darts his tongue past his lips and licks a trail up my cheek, collecting my tears for his tasting. "These will not be the last of your tears," he nearly growls as he then lowers the knife to the edge of my panties.

"Please," I say softly. Another sob breaks free. "I'll do as you ask. I'm scared. Please don't hurt me."

The knife dips below the waistband of my panties and rests against my mound. The coolness of the steel against my intimate skin makes me gasp again as Phoenix brings his lips to my ear. "Stay still, Ani. It would be a shame to scar this pussy of yours."

"Please..."

"You saw the nice part of me, and the one thing I've learned in my life, is that nice gets you nowhere. It fucking blindsides you. Godwins aren't nice, and I have to remember that. *You* will remember that."

He taps the metal of the knife against my clit, causing a surprising surge of sinful arousal. Horror at my captive situation, combined with my desire, weakens my knees. Beads of sweat form on my upper lip as I focus on not collapsing to the floor, thereby jamming the blade right through me.

"By the time I'm done with you, you'll be the perfect partner and the perfect mother to our child. You belong to me now. I will be your master, your sir..." He pauses for a moment to examine my body from head to toe. He gives me a wicked look, clearly pleased with his thoughts of what that will mean. "I will be the man who controls every single breath you take and move you make. You were a bad, bad girl, Ani. But I can learn to be a forgiving man, and I know you will give me a beautiful baby. Another Godwin to take over the Medusa empire."

He's serious. This man is fucking serious.

"Do you understand what I'm saying, Ani?" Phoenix asks. "What my expectations are?"

I nod, trying to stay as still as I can while the knife resting on my pussy reminds me how precarious my situation is.

"Answer me the proper way," Phoenix says firmly.

Not sure what he means exactly, I try to guess and reply, "Yes, *sir*."

"Good girl."

I swallow hard and with wide eyes try one last time to beg for mercy. "Please don't do this. I swear I won't say a single word to the police. I'll go to jail. I'll do whatever you want me to do. I won't try to run away from you again. I promise you that I have learned my lesson. We don't need to do this."

"But we do," Phoenix says.

"Please," I plead as fresh tears fall. "I beg you."

"You aren't begging yet. Trust me. But you will. When I'm done with you, you'll be begging for more. You'll beg for my cock to be inside of you. You will plead with those tears in your eyes for my tongue to go lower and deeper. You will beg like a dirty girl. You will beg." He presses the knife a little harder against my mound. "Now say it. Say yes, sir."

"Yes, sir," I whisper.

Who is this man? This isn't the Phoenix Godwin I kissed not that long ago. I see my very own Jekyll and Hyde.

"Say it louder." The knife goes even lower, rubbing my clit with the burn of seduction on its descent.

"Yes, sir!" I say louder as I tense. The sensation sets my body ablaze in arousal, but it's so fucking wrong.

"Say it again and look me in the eyes like a good girl."

I open my blurry, tear-filled eyes wide and stare at him. "Yes, sir."

"Very good," Phoenix says. "You just earned yourself a comfort item."

Phoenix removes the knife and replaces it with the palm of his hand. Without warning, he inserts a finger into my pussy and begins pumping it in and out of me. "Look me in the eyes while I finger-fuck you," he orders. "Get used to seeing my face when I make you come."

I gasp as I struggle to not close my legs in an attempt to protect my virtue. Tears of indignity run down my face as I also fight the urge to grind against his hand to drive him deeper inside me.

Another finger is added to my degradation. Two fingers, but only my one tiny hole now being raided.

He spreads me wide as he claims what is now his. I want to scream, to demand for him to stop, but the only sound that escapes my lips is a deep, guttural moan.

Just as the most embarrassing orgasm nears, he pulls out his fingers as quickly as he started and chuckles.

"Too soon for pleasure," Phoenix says.

He replaces his hand with the blade and begins rubbing the knife up and down in a slow and sensual manner. He inhales again, brings his lips to my ear, and whispers, "I smell you, dove. I can smell those naughty juices of yours. I have a feeling we are going to have great fun paying your dues."

I begin to cry harder— this time more out of shame and humiliation than fear. My body hungers for more, and I hate myself for it.

I am his. His.

No. Wrong.

He is *making* me his.

There is nothing I can do. Nothing I can say. My cries grow louder and echo off the walls of the empty room. It's a symphony of misery. A chorus of terror. And as I look at Phoenix, I realize he'll be the man orchestrating it all.

Phoenix then leaves briefly and returns with a thin gray wool blanket. He tosses it to the floor and smiles. "Your first item of comfort." He goes without another word.

CHAPTER
SEVENTEEN

Ani

I stand alone with Phoenix. He has a thin scar that runs down his left cheek. It's subtle but just visible enough to make me wonder what caused it. I'd never seen it before, but then again, I was lost in the daze of butterflies and first kisses.

"I've upped security surveillance of the house. So, if you even think there is a chance of escape, I will get that thought out of your head right now. You can run, but I'll hunt you down, and you won't like the consequences for that act. I'll allow every single man who is involved in the hunt to have his chance to punish you. So, the choice is yours." Phoenix smiles, but it is not warm and inviting. No. A smile of evil. Phoenix removes the knife from my panties.

He raises the blade to my eye level. Glancing at it,

I can see it's coated with my signs of fucked-up lust and twisted sexual need.

It glistens with sin.

Phoenix is right. I am a dirty girl. Yes, filthy. So fucking wrong. I should be screaming. Demanding freedom. I should be fighting to escape, but instead I'm nearly coming on a weapon used to kill.

There is a sparkle in Phoenix's eye and a smirk on his face as he returns the blade to its holder on his belt. "I advise you to be a good little girl. Do you understand?"

I nod and say softly, "Yes, sir. I'm not going to try to leave. I want to prove to you that I can be trusted." I don't want me or my sister to be on the outs with the Godwins—whatever that means. I don't want to suffer either and be miserable the entire time I'm here. I don't. I can do this. I can earn my comforts. I already have one. I have a long way to go to furnish this room, but I know the only way to survive this ordeal is by focusing on one comfort at a time. I can do this. I have no choice but to do this. I also want my Phoenix back. I want the man I first met in the attic, and I know he's there beneath the anger and the fury. "What are you going to do to me now?"

It suddenly dawns on me that I am still standing with my arms at my sides. Like I'm a private in the army standing before a general.

Yes, sir.

No, sir.

Whatever you say, sir.

Only this time, the private is wearing nothing but a pair of white lace panties. I don't have to look down to know my nipples are hard, nor do I have to press my legs together to feel the leftover wetness from the kiss of the knife.

Phoenix takes hold of my hair again and circles it around his hand. He then guides me out of the room as if my hair is a leash, and I'm his mangy mutt. We head down the hallway, where cameras are placed strategically. Is Phoenix recording so he can watch later? How many cameras are there? I can practically feel eyes burning holes into my exposed flesh.

When we reach the bathroom door, Phoenix turns to me with seriousness washed over his face. "A new camera has been placed in here. This is going to be filmed the minute we walk into the bathroom. I'm going to be rewatching. I don't want to miss a thing. I want a close-up recording so I can truly examine how grateful you are for your life and my mercy. Are you going to be able to behave and act as I would expect someone who wants to earn items of comfort would behave? I'm serious when I tell you that what you do from this point on is crucial. So, will you be able to do exactly as I say?"

Do I have a choice?

I swallow hard and take a deep breath. In a very tiny voice, I answer, "I think so... sir." The word still feels foreign but doesn't necessarily feel more fucked up or wrong than my current situation.

My body trembles with the overwhelming nerves

exploding within, but I don't want Phoenix to see that anyone has the ability to break me. Inner strength is all I have left. This is my new reality, but I need to stay strong. I've tried begging, and begging didn't work. So I have to regroup. Approach this situation differently. I need strength and determination to survive this.

I can survive this.

It's temporary.

It's just until Phoenix feels safe enough to know that my sister and I mean no harm.

And there will be a time when he lets down his guard again and allows me in. Then I can somehow wake from this nightmare. But for now, I have no choice but do as commanded. I need time... time to figure out how to fix this situation. I will remain strong no matter what occurs on the other side of the door.

Phoenix's face lights up, and he strokes the back of my head. The act doesn't feel loving, but rather condescending. Humiliation is clearly a tactic of his. What's worse is I'm not sure I totally hate it. I should hate it, but tingles in my core disagree.

"That's my good girl. You just do as I say, and don't fight me in the slightest. Swallow that pride raging inside of you. Your pride is only the first of what you'll lose while here." He opens the door and guides me inside.

I enter a pristine bathroom, fiddling with my fingers as I try not to view my reflection in the mirror. I don't want to see my new reality staring back at me. I'm standing in nothing but my panties with a man who is nothing but a monster. I have already been more vulnerable and intimate with Phoenix than most men in my past, but now... I don't even know what to call this. I look up to see a camera in the corner of the room with a red light on and know there is no turning back. Phoenix will be watching the replay of this later.

"All right. Let's get you out of those panties." Phoenix's command is firm.

Only pausing to appreciate my breasts for a moment, Phoenix takes hold of my panties, squatting as he pulls them down all the way to my ankles and lifts my feet one at a time to step out of them.

Glancing up and staring at my exposed, completely naked body, he scowls and stands up. "Bad, bad girl."

I flinch at his words and his stern expression. I have no idea what I have done wrong. I've done exactly as he's asked.

"Only very bad girls have hair on their pussies," he lectures.

I glance down at my little brown curls and then back at him in disbelief.

"This is not acceptable."

He takes a step forward, lifts my arm, and runs his fingertips along my armpit, nods, and then runs his hand down the front of my leg and nods again.

"Lucky for you and your ass, you at least take care of the rest of your body hair. But," he says as he goes and sits on the edge of the tub, "you'll still be punished for a hairy pussy." He pats his lap, which I assume means he wants me to lie over it since he used the word *punished*.

"I... I'm sorry." The man sitting before me is not the same man I thought I knew before. It's like I'm presented with a dominant man on steroids. Once a man, now a monster.

I have no idea what to say or do. The humiliation of this entire conversation is almost too much to endure. And the fact that it's all caught on camera makes it even worse.

"Mistakes happen, but that does not mean that there won't be consequences." He pats his lap once more. "Now come here. I haven't got all day."

Oh, Jesus.

This is it. I am about to be spanked for the first time in my entire life. Spanked over a man's knee. Is this really happening? Am I really standing naked in front of a man and a camera? All because of me keeping a secret of murder from a powerful and now clearly ruthless member of a fucked-up family. My choices are either death or... shame and humiliation?

My legs tremble, and when I take my first step, I wonder if my knees will buckle from beneath me. As if I am moving in slow motion, I somehow reach Phoenix and place my body over his lap, feeling the firmness of his thighs beneath my belly.

"Now, before we start," he says as he runs his palm along my naked behind. "Some punishments will also earn you extra comforts if you submit properly."

I nod as I stare at the tiled floor beneath me.

"Each comfort will depend on severity and how well you take the discipline."

I nod again.

"To begin with, we will only do a single comfort punishment," he says. "So, expect this show of discipline to be far easier than any of the future ones. Now, I'm giving you this spanking today to remind you that good girls keep their cunts nice and smooth." His hand comes crashing against my flesh, and I flinch more out of surprise than pain. He swats me again and again, before saying, "After every swat, I want you to say 'good girls keep their cunts smooth.'"

The next swat stings far more than I expect.

"Good girls keep their cunts smooth." The words sound as if they are spoken by someone else other than me.

The second swat hurts even more than the first.

I gasp when the sting begins to set in. "Good girls keep their cunts smooth."

The third swat brings on panic. How will I be able to endure this?

I squint. "Good girls keep their cunts smooth."

The fourth swat makes me squeal.

"Ow!" Fuck, it's starting to hurt. Far more than I thought it would.

Phoenix spanks me several more times. "What are you supposed to say?" he warns.

"Good girls keep their cunts smooth!" I cry out as my ass heats up with every second that passes. Each swat hurts more and more, and I'm not sure how many of the searing blows I can take.

He brings his large palm squarely down on my punished cheek, and I gasp at how the pain radiates through my core.

"Good girls," I squeak, "keep their cunts smooth!"

He spanks me again, but this time hitting the tender flesh that meets the tops of my thighs.

"Please!" I beg. "It hurts!"

I'm begging again, even though I'm trying to be strong. I don't exactly have a choice. My self-preservation overtakes any sense of pride or conviction I had.

My plea is rewarded with a volley of spanks that are far worse than the ones given seconds before. He continues with a ferocious spanking as I kick, wiggle, cling to his calf, and cry out in pain. The sound of his palm connecting with my punished flesh echoes off the walls of the tiled room, the only sound louder is my cries for mercy. Over and over, Phoenix holds my helpless body to his lap and spanks my butt, even taking some time to once again spank my upper thighs and the area where my bottom meets my legs.

It's excruciating, and that he can do all this with just his hand and little effort on his part terrifies me as to what else he is capable of.

Finally, as I lie gasping for air, Phoenix pauses, rubs my skin, which feels as if it has been stung by a million hornets, and asks, "Shall we try this again, dove?"

Swat!

I don't hesitate in the slightest. "Good girls keep their cunts smooth."

"Now that is truly my good girl," he praises, which actually does fill me with a sense of warmth and pride.

Swat!

"Good girls keep their cunts smooth."

"We will do ten more, and then your spanking will be over. You have earned a comfort item, dove."

EIGHTEEN

Ani

I forgot the video had been recording. Not once during my first spanking of my life did I even stop to consider that the camera pointed at my upturned ass the entire time. Funny how the only thing going through my mind was how I will never let even a hint of hair grow on my 'cunt' ever again.

Phoenix keeps me in position over his lap while I slowly regain my breath and sniffle back the tears. I didn't sob, but the pain brought tears to my eyes, and I'm not sure if I should try to hide them. Do I try to be brave and endure my spanking with little emotion? Or does Phoenix want to see the pain? The fear? I must ask when the time seems right. Will tears earn me extra comforts? Or will showing strength earn respect, hence more comfort items? However, right now, I can't speak, even if I want to.

Phoenix rubs his fingertips in small circles over my heated flesh. "Good, dove. This is the first of many punishments to learn your lesson." Without warning, he moves his fingertips down the crack of my ass until they reached my pussy. Dipping them past my folds, he moves them around and collects my juices. "Someone likes having her ass spanked, I see."

I shamelessly wiggle against his hand, desperate for him to move his fingertips beyond my folds and to enter inside of me, or at the very least to play with my clit. Something, anything... He is right.

I did enjoy it.

Maybe not the actual pain of it. I don't think I like the feeling of being spanked, but my body is on fire, just as my ass is. How can a spanking that I am literally begging for him to stop do this to me? The only explanation is that the feeling of desire is far better than the feeling of fear.

"Do you want me to make you feel all better? To kiss away all the pain?" His fingers only run along my folds, teasing me with how close they are to giving me what I want so badly.

"Yes, sir." My voice cracks as I all but plead my answer.

He pulls his hand away quickly and gives me one final swat before helping me to a standing position.

"Bad girls with hairy cunts do not get to feel all better."

He turns on the faucet and adjusts the temperature, placing his hand under the water until he's satisfied. He then takes the removable showerhead off the base and pulls the lever to make the water burst from the showerhead. He keeps it face down and motions for me to get into the bathtub.

Mortified, I step into the tub. How I wish I had been better prepared and shaved down there. Although I have never done so before. All the men I have ever been with before just got what they got. I don't care or have even given it a thought. But with Phoenix, who will be rewatching my humiliation, it fills me with so much shame that I'm not *presented* better. Phoenix has made me feel like a dirty girl. Yes, a filthy dirty bad girl as he so often likes to call me. I am his dirty captive, and yet, the thought of that makes my tummy flip in anticipation of what that will mean, and how he will try to cleanse me of my soiled ways.

"I'm sorry, sir," I whisper as Phoenix directs the stream of water between my legs.

"Sit down and spread your legs wide. Lean back and stay very, very still."

I do as he asks while he reaches for a razor and a bottle of body cleanser. And though maybe I should be embarrassed that my sex is on full display for the camera, the main humiliation I feel is that I have

153

disappointed Phoenix, and for some odd reason, I hate that. I am hairy, and I want to be rid of it as quickly as possible.

Is this submission? Or is this just plain insanity?

But I've never been one to judge people for their sexual kinks, so why am I judging my body's response now?

I've always found dominance sexy, and I longed to be truly submissive to the right man. Being faced with the chance now is not only exciting, but highly confusing. Is this all a sexual kink game, or is my future truly on the line? Do I hate this? Or do I like this? Do I want to run away, or do I want to stay forever?

Phoenix squirts a generous amount of liquid soap between my legs and then with the utmost care, he swipes the razor in one long motion, leaving a trail of bare skin behind. I watch him as he expertly angles the razor, and as he uses his fingers to open and hold back my folds so he can get every last hidden hair. In fascination, I watch as my pussy becomes free of the hair, and I can see what the most intimate, secret part of my body truly looks like. It's odd to see a body part of mine that I haven't really examined before. Or at least seen as an adult. I really don't know what my pussy looks like completely bare until Phoenix grabs the showerhead and once again directs it at my spread legs.

I gasp and release a tiny moan when the pressure from the water makes contact on my highly sensitive clit that is so needy for attention. It takes everything I have not to put my hand down there and pleasure myself, but I figure such an act would land me back over Phoenix's lap for a repeat session on how good girls are supposed to act.

My gasp and moan, however, makes Phoenix smile. "My dirty dove likes her shower time." He keeps the water where it is, watching as the flowing streams build my pleasure.

"Yes, sir," I moan as my orgasm nears.

"But," he says as he shuts the shower off, "bath time is not fully over yet. Although I will give you another comfort item for remaining so still."

He reaches for my hand and helps me out of the bathtub. I groan in disappointment, and my head feels a little light from getting up so quickly. My bare pussy screams in protest with the need for completion, but there is nothing I can do.

I'm at my monster's mercy.

"Let's get you dried off," he says. "I want to see every bit of the enema clearly."

"Enema?" I ask as Phoenix wraps a pink fluffy towel around my body.

"Yes, Ani. Bath time is for getting all parts of your body clean. My guess is that you have never had one." Phoenix ducks under the sink and pulls out what looks like a large, deflated rubber whoopee cushion with some plastic tubing. And what kind of house just happens to have one under their bathroom sink?

Oh... Olympus Manor, of course.

"No, I haven't." Of course I haven't. Who does this? Why would I do this?

Phoenix looks over his shoulder with a stern expression. "No, what?" A warning laces his words.

"No... no, sir. I have never had an enema before." I don't want one. Unlike the idea of a spanking, this does not give me butterflies in my tummy. This doesn't look like it will be worth any comfort item at all.

Hell, I'll give them all back to avoid this.

"Which is exactly why you're going to receive one," he says. "You need to be nice and clean for any anal discipline later on."

Anal discipline?

"But I..." I look up at Phoenix, my panic growing as I stand there trying to process what's going to happen. I really have no idea what an enema feels like, what it will do, or if I will truly even hate it.

"Now, now, dove." Phoenix places the enema tools on the floor.

He stands up and smiles, offering a look of kindness, which does help... a little. Very lightly, he places his palm on my tightly closed fist that clasps my towel securely around me.

"Let go of the towel," he commands softly, which I don't hesitate in doing.

He spreads the towel on the tiled floor and looks at my freshly shaven pussy for long and hungry moments.

He then squats and pats the fluffy pink fabric. "Kneel down on the towel and get on all fours."

I glance at the camera and remind myself that this will forever be on tape. For a split second, I think about running. All I have to do is grab my clothes and be out the door and into freedom. I can leave. I can flee this house and never look back. Phoenix will allow me to go. Maybe not my sister. But something inside me tells me that Phoenix won't harm me. But his anger toward my sister is something I have to fix. I have to stay to fix it all.

Make wise choices, the words of wisdom ring in my ears.

Yes, running isn't wise.

Phoenix doesn't want me resisting, and if I do, the punishment... will be severe.

Not wanting Phoenix to have to repeat himself, I get on all fours, my ass facing the camera. Phoenix pats my behind, reminding me of the spanking I just received. I wonder if it's red or bruised. I'm sure Phoenix, who will be watching this video later, will enjoy the signs that I had just been spanked. He probably wishes I was bleeding while lash after lash scarred my creamy flesh. Maybe he plans to be far stricter next time.

"You are such a good girl," Phoenix praises. "I'm going to take all the bad away from your body. Every single toxin left inside. You just have to endure for a short time, and I will give you a comfort item for good behavior."

He pulls the enema bag and nozzle his way as he positions himself behind me. I hear the snap of a bottle, some shuffling around, and the feel of a wet nozzle touching my anus.

"Okay, I'm going to put this tube in this tiny little hole of yours. It will sting as it stretches you, but I want you to be a good girl and not give me any tears. Take it up the ass without a fight, and just know it won't be the last thing spreading your hole wide while you reside at the manor."

As the tube enters me, I gasp at the foreign sensation. It doesn't hurt, but it feels odd having something inserted in a place so... private. As it slides all the way inside, Phoenix spreads my legs wider and then presses down on my back, forcing the front half of me to lie flat on the floor. My breasts press firmly against the terrycloth, while my butt, high on display, causes my face to burn in humiliation. The room's air is cool on my stretched anus and along my bare pussy. There isn't a part of my privates not on full display for the camera.

"I'm going to start filling your ass with the water. I'm feeling merciful so I'll go nice and slow, but you're going to have to take deep breaths and just allow the pressure to build."

I feel it the instant the water starts entering me. There is a moment of panic as I worry I will have to go to the bathroom right then. It almost feels as if I have to go, but not quite. But then the pressure he speaks of sets in. My belly begins to expand, and cramping attacks my lower region.

"I need to go to the bathroom now!" I'll be mortified if I have a bowel movement by accident—especially on camera—but that's what my body is threatening to do if I don't run to the toilet that sits off in the corner in this small compartment of a room.

"No. You have to take it all before you're allowed up." Phoenix holds the nozzle firmly in my hole and places his palm over the small of my back to remind me to stay in position.

"I can't," I moan. "Please. You don't understand." I don't want to tell them that I have to go bad, but I can't hold it any longer.

"Ani," Phoenix warns. "Listen to me."

The cramping intensifies, and I feel as if I will explode at any second. Sweat begins to coat my skin. "Please! I..." I clench my anus as tightly as I can to hold it back. The action only reminds me that something foreign is inside of me. "I can't," I whine.

"Do you want me to distract you?" he asks.

I nod and whimper in response.

Phoenix reaches around and gently massages my extended belly, which does seem to relieve some of the pressure. When my whimpers stop, he sits back and runs his fingers down the seam of my ass, circling the nozzle, massaging the stretched flesh of my invaded anus. His fingers then leave the taboo spot and dip down to my sex. When he touches me, I realize I am dripping wet.

"Ahhh, my dirty dove is all nice and wet. Dirty, dirty girl."

He runs his fingertip around my clit and then dips down to the folds of my pussy, collecting my juices, and then back to my clit for more delicious ministrations.

The one thing I have to admit as I moan in both agony and pleasure is Phoenix has successfully managed to help me relax enough to take all the water. I'm not comfortable, but at least I'm not in a panic that I will have an accident while the camera captures every embarrassing moment.

"Now that's a good girl," Phoenix praises as he stops playing with my clit and pats my butt cheek. "You took all the water. Do you have to go to the bathroom?"

"Yes..." I moan. A sharp slap to my ass has me quickly saying, "Yes, sir."

Will he make me use the toilet on camera as well? I don't want to, but at this stage, I don't care what it will take to relieve the immense pressure. The control required to hold it all in makes my legs quiver.

"All right, dove. I'm going to pull out this tube. When I do, you are going to have to work extra hard to hold it all in. It's going to feel like you have no choice but to release. But if you do, a severe consequence will follow. So, you need to be a good girl, and get up and run to the toilet."

I nod and moan loudly as waves of cramps attack, one after another.

"You can close the door for privacy since you have been such a good girl. I will be waiting in your bedroom. Meet me in there when you are finished. You have a long way to go, but you just earned yourself some more comfort items."

He pats my behind softly before he slowly eases the nozzle from my puckered hole. He was correct when he said it felt like I will go right here and now. I cry out in fear of having an accident in front of his watchful eyes. Clenching tightly, which only makes the pulling of the tube out more uncomfortable, I somehow manage to run to the small room that only holds a toilet and close the door behind me.

Is this all worth the number of comforts actually earned?

How much more of this can I endure?

How long will this take? Is this my new life? If I have his baby, will the discipline cease? Is this temporary or forever?

Penance is owed, and I clearly will be paying in the most wicked ways imaginable. My sinful sentence has begun. I am now a possession of the Phoenix Godwin. Does this mean I'm now part of the Godwin family? And what does that truly mean if the answer is yes?

CHAPTER
NINETEEN

Ani

When I enter my room, Phoenix is standing by the window with his back toward me. He seems lost in thought, and I wonder if he has even heard me enter. I take a few more steps inside, unsure what I should do next.

"You did good in there," he says, still not turning around. "You showed you can be submissive. That pleases me."

I had no idea Phoenix wants a submissive woman. We didn't get that far into the 'getting to know you' stage before we had each other's tongues down our throats.

I hold my hands in front of my bare mound and have never felt so exposed before in my life. The camera in my room is still there, and no doubt is turned back on. But it's not nearly as invasive as having one in the bathroom.

Phoenix turns around and stares at me, examining my nudity as if he's making sure I am 'dressed' properly for this twisted party of which I am a forced guest. The room's cool air combined with Phoenix's cold stare has my nipples hardening and shivers running up my spine.

"So, answer me this." His eyes finally make their way to mine. "Why did you submit so easily? Most women in your position would put up much more of a fight. They'd scream. They'd demand. They'd beg and plead for mercy far more than you have. Some would even rather die than endure what you just did."

"Would you have preferred that?" I shift my weight from one foot to the other. I feel faint from the ordeal and want to sit down, but I remember the words that I was to do nothing without his command to do it. "To break me?"

"No. I find your already-shattered pieces all the more interesting."

Phoenix approaches me, takes hold of my hair. Is that the only way I will ever walk again—guided by a fist holding my hair at the scalp?

He lowers me to the only item in the room—the gray wool blanket—and releases my hair. He takes a few steps back and crosses his arms against his chest. "Do you truly understand why I am so angry?"

"Secrets were kept from you," I begin. "You pride

yourself on knowing everything so you can protect your family. The secrets I held from you could destroy."

I look up at him and see an eyebrow rise. He's reading me, or at least trying to.

I lick my dry lips. "It's not as simple as you not trusting me. You don't trust the fact that you didn't see through me. You couldn't see this secret from the minute you first met me. You don't trust yourself with me now." I draw a deep breath. "And now I'm here. You're angry at my sister. You're angry at your brother for keeping the secret, too. You're just angry."

Phoenix nods. "Yes, now you're here and will be for a while. So, let's get a couple of rules out of the way. You'll remain in this room unless you are escorted out by me. There's a bathroom across the hall you will have to ask permission to use, and all food will be delivered here unless I choose to bring you to the dining room. You will remain naked from this point on. Get used to having your body belong to me. I will come here when I feel like it. It could be several times a day, or not at all.

I say nothing but only look into his eyes.

"You will not question what I ask. You will not resist me in any way." He looks toward the window. "You can try to escape but won't get far. Cameras are everywhere, and I will catch you. You have the opportunity to earn a comfortable and well-kept life if you understand and follow these rules. Do you understand?"

I nod.

"Do you have any questions?"

For the first time since angering Phoenix, he seems to soften somewhat. His eyes are less severe, and his jaw is no longer firm. I believe he truly is giving me the opportunity to ask whatever I want without penalty.

Drumming up some courage, I ask, "When do you plan on impregnating me?"

"Depends," he answers.

I pause. How far can I go with the questions? I don't want to push too far in fear of the possible consequences.

My hesitation must be obvious because Phoenix adds, "Ask your questions now if you have them."

"What else will you do to me? To earn these comfort items."

"Whatever I want."

"After I'm pregnant, will you continue to fuck me?"

Phoenix closes the distance between us and kneels down on the floor next to me. He takes hold of my nipple and pinches. It hurts but not unbearably so. I gasp at the uninvited touch but don't try to pull away.

"Would you like that, dove? For me to fuck you over and over forever?"

"No," I say in not much more than a whisper.

"You lie, Ani. I can smell your desire. I can hear the way you breathe. You seemed to enjoy what happened in the bathroom. It was far from a punishment. It was as if everything was so natural for you. It fit you. It fit you like a fucking glove."

He pinches my nipple harder as I shake my head to try to deny the fact that, yes, my body had responded in a shocking way.

No. He is wrong.

Fuck. Is he wrong?

His smile grows as his shadowed eyes narrow. "Which I'm going to enjoy. I'm going to have a good time finding an actual punishment for you. I may have to get creative."

I press my thighs together to try to hide that his words and his biting hold on my nipple make me wet.

"Why do you want this?" My words come out on a gasp, so I wonder if they are even clear enough to be heard.

"Want what?"

"Why would you want to have a baby with me? Or to have a baby with someone you don't even love?"

"You serve a purpose. I need an heir and nothing more," he says in a deep, solemn voice. "I'm not going to allow my brother to be the only one to have one with... *her*. We aren't going to open ourselves up to more lies and betrayal. Our entire life is one deception after another, but I'm going to make sure I don't just stand by and allow it to happen. I can't play the twisted chess game if I don't have any pieces."

"A baby is a chess piece."

He shrugs.

His answer surprises me, and my eyes widen. "So why would you want me? I'm one of those people who have lied to you."

"Because I know you already have. It won't come as a surprise if you try again." His face is expressionless. I can't tell what he is feeling in the way he quickly responds.

His hand leaves my nipple, which oddly my body seems to miss. But my longing for his touch doesn't linger because he lowers his hand between my legs and presses past the silky folds.

I can't hold back the whimper and close my eyes in shame.

"Why are you wet, dove? Is it my words, the thought of what's still to come, or simply the pain from my hand?"

He runs his fingertip along the wetness, and no matter how hard I try, I can't control my breathing or the little noises of forbidden desire that escape my dry lips. Just as quickly as Phoenix has touched my pussy, he removes his hand and takes hold of my hair at the scalp again.

He yanks hard.

"You're hurting me."

"Not yet, dirty girl. Not yet." He tugs harder, forcing my head back, exposing my neck as a vampire would do before feasting on his prey's blood.

I whimper, not really out of pain but anticipation. My body sizzles with need, and my very core screams for more. Every word, every touch, every single thing about Phoenix sets my body aflame. He's right. I should be screaming. I should be fighting. I should be resisting this nightmare the best I can. Instead, I welcome it. No... I fucking crave it. Phoenix is right. I am broken. I am shattered. I am scattered into a million pieces and need this man to fix me. I need the fix. I need this sickness.

"Stand up," he commands. "Stand right in front of me between my legs."

I do as he asks, though how I stand on such weakened legs, I have no idea. My head feels light and my breathing even tighter.

"Part your pussy for me. I want to see my dirty dove."

Never imagining myself engaged in such an act as this, I do as he asks. As if I am hypnotized by the silkiness of his directions—because that is the only thing that can explain the complete madness that is raging through me—I bring my shaky fingers to my smooth pussy lips and spread them wide for his viewing.

Phoenix reaches up and pushes his thumb into my mouth. "Suck my thumb, dove. Suck on it good so I can rub it around that tiny clit of yours until you scream for me to fuck you."

I run my tongue against the rough, callused skin and never move my fingers from my pussy. I am still spreading myself wide as I suck on his thumb just as he wants me to do. My eyes connect with his for a moment, and I wonder if it is hunger I see hidden in their depths.

"Beg for my cock. I told you that you would eventually beg for it. So, beg." He pulls his thumb out of my mouth and presses it against my clit.

I cry out in pleasure but hold my position. I don't want to let go of my spread lips in fear he will stop the most wicked of his touches so far.

"Beg," he commands again.

"Please, sir. My little hole wants to be spread open by your cock." The words are so natural they flow from my lips without the slightest hesitation or thought.

His ministrations freeze, and he chuckles. "Oh, my dirty, dirty girl. Having you call me sir was a spontaneous request, but I like it. I think we'll keep it that way. And I think I finally have found your first real punishment. That building orgasm inside of you will remain right where it is." He spanks my pussy hard, forcing me to release the spread of my skin. "For now."

Phoenix stands up and pushes me down on all fours. "Stay bent over."

I try to regain my breath and steady my raging emotions. Tears well up in my eyes, and I can't think straight. I can't process. All I can do is stare at my spread fingers against the wooden floor as I hear the sound of a belt being removed from the loops of Phoenix's pants.

"Every single night and every single morning you will receive a lashing from my belt. The severity will all depend on how good of a girl you have been leading up to it."

Before I can process his words, the stinging crash of leather against skin has me howling out. The pain radiates all the way to my needy pussy, only intensifying my out-of-control hunger.

"Please," I plead as he whips me once again.

"Yes, dove. Keep begging."

"Please..."

"Are you begging for me to stop belting you, or to fuck you?"

He brings the belt down against my sensitive ass again, but rather than crying, I moan.

The belt falls upon me again, and I moan some more.

"Little pain slut. You like when I spank your ass as you pray I'll eventually fuck you."

Tears of shame and humiliation fall as my orgasm builds inside of me. My body becomes more alive with every searing swat. Yes. I want to be fucked. I want to be fucked hard. But not before he finishes the discipline—the most twisted and sexual punishment one could imagine. My mind screams no. My ass screams for mercy. But my core, my inner being, my soul begs for more.

Just as the most intense explosion is about to release, Phoenix ceases the spanking.

I cry out even louder than I ever did during the spanking.

"Yes, my dove. I'm going to enjoy this very much."

His footsteps head to the door, and I turn my head to see him holding the door handle. My heart falls to my stomach as I still remain in position for more.

"No," I whisper so low I am sure Phoenix can't hear me. I don't want him to leave. No.

"I'll be back. I'll come in later with the comforts you have earned today."

CHAPTER
TWENTY

Phoenix

I can't watch the video of Ani any longer or my cock will explode.

"Holy fucking Christ," I say to myself.

She's a hot piece of ass. I can't look away from this woman I shouldn't like. I shouldn't.

Liking her has made me weak. Liking her has made me act like a Godwin never does. Liking her has made me soft.

A sense of primal possession surges through me. Part of me wants to be outside her door. Keeping her safe. Making sure no one can enter the room. Ever.

Yes, she's a captive, but she is *my* captive. Any man who dares to go near her will be a dead man. Don't even talk to her. No contact at all.

There's no one here... but if there was.

Insanity is taking hold again. She brings out the madness. I feel it. I hear the beating of the crazy drum.

No one will ever even lay eyes on this woman again. Only me. Only me!

My attention is pulled back to the screen where Ani's shaved pussy is visible. Holly Hell.

Smirking, I shake my head. I am a kinky son of a bitch.

Trying to refocus, I glance down at the list of comfort items, making sure I don't forget anything. Ani will be earning her items one at a time. For now, I furnished the room next door to hers so I have all the pieces on hand. I'll hold back no expenses. It will be better than the guest room furniture she recovered with. Only the best linens, a four-poster bed more elegant than the last, rugs, drapes, art. Have it all. Hopefully, my dove earns it all.

When I glance back at the monitor, my cock grows hard. She's so bare. Her sexy pink pussy is smooth and mouthwateringly delicious.

Focus, asshole. Focus.

I'll want security beefed up during her stay here. Her location is on a need-to-know basis. Only my most trusted inner circle and no one else. No one.

There's Daphne and Apollo to consider, but I'll address that as it comes.

I will execute every detail with the utmost

attention. I run a tight ship, and everyone who works for me knows just how detail-oriented and what a perfectionist I am. My demands are high, but my rewards are plenty.

I peek at the screen again only to see Ani's naked body is on full display. She's not even trying to cover herself.

My hardening cock is dying for attention. Dying a slow death.

How long will I have to wait to fuck her?

How long *can* I wait? That is the actual question.

Pulling my eyes away, I focus on the plan. Welcoming a new Godwin to the family. I need to make my family impenetrable. To those who want to invade my bubble...

I'm going to have a baby. I've never had any desire to have one before. I didn't want a family. Frankly, I wanted to stop the poison root of the Godwin family tree from an early age. But then there is right and wrong. It's wrong that the next heir is going to be from Daphne. That can't be. I can't let that happen. And Athena mentioned before that she has no plans to have children, which means it's up to me to not give Daphne and Apollo all the power of the future. Daphne could be the puppeteer, and it's my job to cut the strings.

Am I doing this for my father? Fuck no. But am I doing this for me? I suppose I am.

Not being able to watch Ani from afar any longer,

I leave the security console to begin phase one of my plan.

Teach this lady a lesson.

Time to pay, Ani Parker. Time to pay.

CHAPTER
TWENTY-ONE

Ani

Sweat coats my body as I wake in a panic. I have no idea what time it is, how many hours have passed, what day, and for a few terrifying moments, I have no idea where I am. Hell? I might as well be in eternal damnation. Same difference.

I sit up and notice that I am still naked and curled up on the single wool blanket that scratches my punished skin. Not that any of it matters. I slept, and I consider that a good thing. The door to my room remains closed, and I wonder if Phoenix has come in to check on me. Will he, soon? The ceiling light is on, so at least I am not in complete darkness, and I scan the room for the extra comfort items that Phoenix had told me would come.

To my right is a single glass and a pitcher of

water. A mirror has been hung on the otherwise empty wall. A few hardback books are stacked nicely by the water, and I see a hairbrush. Comfort items...

So he has been here. Now what? Will he come back soon, or will I have to call out for him? The idea of calling him to assist me to the bathroom makes me cringe, but my protesting bladder doesn't give me much of a choice. After a glance around the room, I quickly realize there isn't even a bucket to use if I wanted to. I could certainly urinate in the corner somewhere if I absolutely must, but I have to remain in the close confines of the room for however long it takes to get pregnant and then the nine months of carrying the child, and I would much prefer not to have to smell my own waste if I don't have to. I need Phoenix, whether I like it or not.

I rise from the blanket and stretch the kinks out of my body before I go to the door. Knocking firmly, I call out, "Excuse me? I would like to use the bathroom, please." I turn and look up at one of the cameras in the hope that I am being monitored. "May I please use the restroom?"

As much as I don't want to, I decide there really is no reason to be rude. I am at his mercy. Giving attitude or demanding he come immediately will not work in my favor, and right now, my bladder screams for me to behave.

There is silence and not a single sound or approaching footstep in the hallway.

Knocking again, I say, "Hello? I could use some assistance."

Silence.

Feeling the tightness in my bladder increase, I cross my legs in an attempt to not wet myself while waiting.

Just as I am about to knock again and throw some curse words his way, the door to my room opens. Taking a few steps back to allow Phoenix enough room to enter, I quickly realize he's not exactly happy to be here. I've woken him from his slumber. He's the big, hibernating bear who has emerged early from his cave.

God, the man truly is huge. And I'm smaller in size, most likely thanks to childhood malnutrition stunting my growth. Before his anger, I found our size difference comforting. His mass made me feel safe. But now, he's intimidating.

Phoenix takes two large steps into the room and stands before me. Dark hair, stormy eyes, and dominance. Phoenix doesn't have to say a single word to make me understand that he is not a man to be messed with right now. Power, mystery, and alpha power pulsates from his body at the same rhythm as my heartbeat. His firm jaw that clenches while he examines me from head to toe draws my attention away from his hypnotizing glare.

"It's late. Why aren't you sleeping?" he asks.

"I... uh... may I please use the restroom?"

He remains silent, stony, and cold.

Swallowing back the large lump in the back of my throat, I say, "I need to use the bathroom badly."

He nods and leaves the room. Once past the threshold, he looks over his shoulder to where I still stand frozen. "Follow me." His deep voice is firm, direct, and so silky smooth.

I will my body to follow the man, even though warning bells are going off that he is not to be trusted, no matter what. His energy is off. I'm not getting the calm Phoenix. I'm getting the cold, distant Phoenix. He's a flame that seems to be growing, and I sense it. There could always be something up his sleeve, and I remember what he did to me the last time I entered the bathroom. But again, my bladder doesn't give me much of a choice.

Phoenix leads me to the restroom, opens the door, and steps inside. I follow him in then turn, expecting him to exit and wait outside the door.

When he remains in place, I ask, "Can you leave?"

"No."

The idea of relieving myself in front of this man infuriates me. "I don't need you to watch over me." I glance at the small room that has the toilet and think about just going inside and shutting the door, but something also tells me to not attempt doing anything without his direction.

"Please. I'll be quick."

"Go," he snaps, which only makes me angry. I am a fucking human being who deserves an ounce of decency and privacy to relieve myself. Grant me fucking bathroom privileges, for Christ's sake!

"Are you enjoying this? It's sick," I declare. "I'm not going to go piss in front of you."

His expression hasn't changed since the moment he came for me, but his eyes darken at my refusal.

"Go now." This time his voice stabs into my soul. I am not going to win this battle, but I still am not going to go pee in front of him.

"All I ask is that you leave the room. I would like a little privacy. Take away a comfort item if you have to in exchange for allowing me this brief time alone. Please."

"Either go now, or I'll take you back to your room. You can sit in your own filth for all I care. I don't care where you go."

He is lucky I don't have a knife in my hand. I'd kill him right here and now.

"Fine," I say. "If you don't care where I go," I add as I squat right in front of him. "I'll piss right here, thank you very much." I empty my bladder in the middle of the room, staring directly into his eyes as I allow every ounce of liquid to release from my body. It isn't like I have much of my dignity left to lose anyway.

Phoenix remains emotionless. He doesn't say a single word or do a thing. His lack of anger is far worse than any wrath he could inflict. My knees wobble as I remain in my squat, and I just hope I won't fall. He scares me. There is no doubt about that, and yet here I am. The fool pissing on the floor mere inches from my captor's shoes.

He doesn't move. He doesn't speak. If I don't know better, I would say he isn't even breathing. My actions have no effect on him, and I instantly regret it. My childish act empowers him. I am now the woman squatting in front of a man with piss dripping out of me. Humiliation for me, honor for him. Without doing a single thing, Phoenix wins this battle. Damn him.

As I rise and try to control my anger, Phoenix raises one eyebrow and asks nonchalantly, "Are you done?"

"I am a fucking human being. Not a fucking slave. Remember that." Clenching my teeth, I straighten my shoulders and try to muster as much pride as I can. I glide past him, leading myself back to my room. His footsteps follow behind me and can almost feel his smugness burning against the back of my head.

When I approach the door, Phoenix takes hold of my upper arm. It doesn't hurt, but his grasp is tight. He leads me into the room and forces me to sit on the wool blanket by pushing me down. He kneels down and reaches into his pants pocket, pulling out a pair of handcuffs.

"I don't want you to put those on me," I say as panic begins to set in. I'm not sure what his plan is, but I can see how pissed off I made him now. Seeing the handcuffs throws me back into my twisted reality.

I am a captive. Not a guest. No rights, no options, nothing.

He doesn't reply but instead grabs my wrists in front of my body, clasps the metal rings securely around them, and locks them with a small key. The cuffs are tight enough that when I move even slightly, they pinch. I can feel my flesh connect with the cool restraint, but considering how tight they are, how long will it be until I lose all feeling?

It doesn't take me long to recognize a metal butt plug when he pulls it from his pocket. Placing it at my lips, Phoenix says, "You'll discover soon enough that I have little patience for bratty tactics. I don't find bratting sexy at all, and I will put an end to it quickly. Open your mouth."

A butt plug? Is this my punishment for pissing in front of him? He has warned me to behave... repeatedly.

Not giving me the chance to comply, Phoenix pushes the metal past my lips and moves it in and out of my mouth, rubbing it along my tongue with each pass. "I'd advise you to get it nice and wet, because that's the only lube you're getting."

He doesn't allow it to be in my mouth long enough for me to do as he orders, instead he pushes me onto my stomach. The movement is awkward thanks to the handcuffs, so lying there is far from comfortable as my body is contorted. He only makes it worse when he spreads my legs wide and pushes the butt plug inside me without any warning. The biting pop has me crying out in surprise more than pain.

I try to wiggle and push the invading implant out of me, to no avail. "Please. It stings. It's too big. It's stretching me."

"Yes, that's the point." He stands up, not caring in the slightest that I am growing more distressed by the second.

"Please, I'm sorry. I'm sorrier than you can know." I take a deep breath as I turn around and kneel before him. "The cuffs are too tight." I extend my wrists to him so he can see for himself and hopefully have mercy.

"Enough with the pleading," he says. Without another word, he opens the door and exits, leaving me alone in my prison.

Hysteria sets in. There is no way I will be able to endure what this man has in store for me. I am a strong woman, but no one is this strong. I look up at the camera in the corner hoping he's watching.

"I'm scared! Terrified. Please. There has to be a way that you'll let me go. Please."

I can't do this. I can't do this!

Every time I move, the handcuffs seem to tighten. The rough edges are rubbing my skin raw as I push and pull in the hope that I can somehow move them up or down my arm like a loose bracelet.

Kneeling as I am, the butt plug seems to be

stretching me so wide, I worry I will tear. The weight of the metal sits heavy inside of me. How long will I have to wear it? Will Phoenix ever take it out? I can't with my wrists in the handcuffs. There is nothing I can do.

I get up and walk to the full-length mirror to find out if I can see the plug in my ass. When I see my reflection in the mirror, the pink skin of my ass from the earlier discipline makes my horrid plight even more of a reality. Staring back at me is nothing but a woman who is at the mercy of a Godwin—the most ruthless and feared men in the world.

I run over to the door and pound my cuffed fists against the wood while screaming into it. "Don't leave me in here like this! Everything is too tight, too big. Too painful. I'm panicking. I thought I could do this. That I could be the compliant captive and pay my penance. But I can't. I can't. Do you hear me? Come back in here!" I bang my hands on the door as hard as I can over and over.

Complete silence.

I twist my head to look back at the camera. He has to be watching. "Please! Phoenix! Phoenix! I swear to you that I'll be good. I'll be good and never give you an issue again. Just please allow me out of this room. Take the cuffs off and the plug out. Let me earn it! Let me earn it as a comfort item. Please."

Complete silence.

"Spank me! Punish me any other way. Please."

My sobbing only amplifies the silence.

My mind teeters on a dangerous cliff of sanity. I will fucking have a nervous breakdown right in this damn room if he doesn't come and help me. I can't be alone.

"Don't leave me alone!"

Collapsing to the floor, I sit on my outer thigh so the butt plug won't have any pressure on it and allow the tears to fall. I glance back at the camera and plead with my eyes.

Why do I bother?

He doesn't care. In his eyes, I deserve this.

And maybe I do. I wasn't some naive girl who didn't know what I was getting myself into when Daphne had me wait in the car while Apollo handled Mark. I knew. I knew a murder was being committed. I might as well have killed the man myself.

And now I am paying the price for it.

CHAPTER
TWENTY-TWO

Ani

I'm so lost in my misery I don't hear the door to my room open. It's Phoenix's dark clothing that catches the corner of my eye that notifies me that he has heard my repeated pleas into the camera and can't take it anymore—granting me mercy even if it's to shut me up.

Thank God. He is here. I won't be alone any longer with my dark thoughts. The mental game this man is playing is just as bad as the plug rooted in my ass.

Looking up at him with tears streaming down my face, I beg, "Please, Phoenix. I know I messed up. I know I did. But I can't be tortured like this."

"Torture?" He smirks. "You have no idea what torture really is."

"Call it what you want," I choke out. "I beg you to take out the plug. It's too big. And the handcuffs. I don't need these." I push my confined wrists toward him to emphasize my appeal.

"You don't get to be a brat and act out and not expect there to be consequences."

"I wasn't thinking." I try to control the hysteria that makes my voice sound so high-pitched that I don't even recognize it. "I was just so angry."

"You don't get the luxury of being angry while you're here. You lost that right the minute you brought my brother into your mess," he says with little sympathy or care present on his face. So cold and stoic. "The minute you put the Godwin family in danger."

"I can't do this. I can't do this." I sob. If I had any dignity left, it's gone. Vanished. Melted away in the tears falling down my face. "There is no way I can survive this. I can't. I'm not strong enough. I wanted to earn your trust and forgiveness, but not like this."

He kneels down beside me and looks me straight in the eyes. Humanity flickers in the depths. It's brief, but I see it, and it gives me hope. "You need to take a deep breath and calm down. You've gotten yourself so worked up that you're going to have a panic attack." He places his fingertip on my cheek and strokes softly. "Calm down. You're going to be just fine."

I shake my head. "I don't deserve this."

"What do you deserve then?" Phoenix asks. "Do

you think I should just ignore what you did? Trust that you won't destroy my family's lives? Trust you like my brother foolishly did with your sister?"

"No, but—"

"Would you rather I just had you killed so you are no longer a problem for us? Kill your sister? I'm sure that's what Athena and my father want."

"No," I answer as I look down toward the floor, breathing as calmly as I can.

He gently runs his fingertip along the handcuffs then dips his finger between the metal and flesh. "There's plenty of room. It's all in your head. And the plug is small."

"I know you have a good heart. I know that there is a part of you locked inside that is good," I say, continuing to cry.

"You're wrong on that."

"I saw it. We were getting to know each other. We were getting close. Intimate. I saw the kindness of your heart."

Slowly he strokes his fingers through my hair, never taking his eyes away from mine. "The minute you believe that a Godwin is kind, you put yourself at risk. Why? Because look at what you just did. You didn't fear me, and you should have. Can I be merciful? Yes. Can I treat you decently? Eventually."

"How long do I have to be cuffed? Plugged?"

He swipes at a loose hair that hangs in my eye and tucks it behind my ear with the most loving of touches. His kindness causes a whiplash of emotions in my struggling psyche. He goes from cruel to tender and affectionate in a matter of seconds.

"I just want to go home," I whine, although I do seem to be feeling better as the moments pass. His gentle touch and petting of my hair does seem to ease some of my distress.

"Your home is with me now," he says as he leans in and kisses my cheek with the most delicate of touches. "It won't always be bad. Take your punishment like a good girl, and it will soon all be over." He pulls away and looks me in the eye—so dark and piercing. "You're a strong woman, Ani, but you made poor choices. I have to make sure you never do so again."

"Trust me. I'm not ever going to again. I have to live with that mistake for the rest of my life." Though I am upset, the tears have at least ceased.

"I don't trust liars, but I understand something about you. You've had to be a fighter your entire life. I know this. And that asshole deserved to die. It's the secrets, Ani. Until you truly understand how dangerous secrets can be, how destructive lies are, you'll be here. Learning. But I won't break down the woman you are. Not at your core. I just want to break your ability to ever cross or lie to me in the future."

He kisses my cheek again and then my forehead, while continuing to stroke my sweaty hair. "You are going to be just fine."

Will I be? How can I be just fine ever again?

"I hate it!" I cry. "Why are you so cruel to another

human being? I may be your prisoner, but I am still a woman. I'm a person. I deserve some level of decency."

He nods. "I know."

"So why?"

"You're fine."

"I'm not," I argue.

"You are, so stop. Stop the hysterics. I'm trying to be nice and to be patient, but my patience will only go so far."

"Do I deserve to be treated like an animal?" It appears that my words do make a difference, but I also get the sense that there is no use trying to convince Phoenix to go against his conviction.

Phoenix places both palms on each side of my face and forces me to stare directly into his eyes. "You need to behave. If you continue to try to push me, I promise you that what you have suffered so far will be minor in comparison. Behave. Do you understand me? You have nothing to prove. Let go of that pride. Feel humiliated. Feel ashamed. That's the point. A lesson will be taught, Ani. One way or the other."

"I have already learned. Trust me," I point out. "I'm here because I don't feel I have any other choice, being degraded, and then being expected to have a baby. There is nothing more for me to be taught."

"But there is. You know this. Don't push me. Just don't."

"Is there nothing I can do? You can't truly be serious in this. I get it. I get that I need to be taught to never lie to you again. But please. I don't think you are a monster. Not truly. Please let me go. Please."

He leans in and kisses me gently on the forehead before standing up. "Being a monster is my only option. The minute I show any weakness, my enemies will strike. As Godwins, we do what we do to survive. No one gets away with betraying us. Stop begging, Ani. It's a waste of time and energy." He extends his hand to assist me up now that I am breathing and acting normally again.

Standing, I take a moment to allow the slight weakness in my legs to strengthen. Phoenix places his arm around me to hold me steady while I regain control of my body. It hasn't taken long to feel back to my old self.

"Would you like to go to the kitchen and get something to eat?" he asks. "I think you've earned that comfort item."

I nod.

He grabs my arm and leads me out of the room, down the staircase, and through a door to the left. The kitchen is dimly lit, so the shadows emitting from Phoenix's figure are all the more pronounced.

He pulls out a chair and forces me to sit down. I hiss as the pressure of sitting seems to lodge the plug even further inside my ass.

I almost ask for my handcuffs to be removed so I can eat, but the look on Phoenix's face keeps me quiet. I need to allow the man to cool down. Eating with handcuffs will be interesting, but I would rather face that than Phoenix's wrath.

Phoenix goes to the refrigerator and starts pulling out the fixings to make a sandwich. It feels as if I haven't had a meal in days. My mouth waters as he puts the plate with a turkey sandwich in front of me.

"I'm not really a cook, but I'm still going to have the chef come and prep some meals for us. The meal quality will go up."

The fact that he feels he has to justify or explain the sandwich makes me smile. At least it is an ounce of kindness. In fact, Phoenix has been quite *loving* in many ways, as insane as that is. Is that how he works? One side of him is the bad guy, one side the good guy. But maybe that's why I've been drawn to him. He knows how to offset the bad with the good. The yin and yang keep his power grounded and never out of control.

"Thank you very much. I hadn't realized just how hungry I was. This actually is perfect."

He nods and returns my smile. He heads over to a bottle of booze and pours himself a drink. "Hurry and eat. It's late, and I want to get to bed."

"I appreciate this."

He takes a long sip of his alcohol before stating, "Don't misread this. I'm not a kind person. Kindness gets you nowhere in the world we live."

Ignoring his words for now, I eat bite after bite of

pure joy. I temporarily forget that I am nothing but a woman cuffed, plugged, and captured. For now, I eat.

If I am going to survive this, I have to live one day at a time. One hour, one minute. I can't think about what will come next or risk going completely mad. One day, one hour, one minute... my new life. It is my only choice.

CHAPTER
TWENTY-THREE

Phoenix

Standing with my arms crossed against my chest, I watch the security monitor. I've just escorted Ani back to her room, and whether I want to admit it or not, I can't take my eyes off her.

I take a seat in front of the screen, propping my feet up on the table. I settle in as I always do in the evening. My television viewing before bed has become Ani.

Fucking Ani has already consumed far more of my time and my mind than planned.

I have gone too far. I saw her eyes. Real fear is lodged there.

Trying to shake off my guilt, I just stare at Ani. She doesn't deserve to feel the way she does.

Wait... What the hell? She fucking deserves it. She's a liar. A liar.

I begin pacing the room, hating that her actions still anger me. No one person should control any emotion of mine for so long.

My goal is to train her to be submissive. To teach her to never cross me or another Godwin.

There's a difference between discipline and cruelty, and I know it. I have to break her in slowly. I can't just go in full force and scare the hell out of her like that.

Did I slap her across the face? No. Did I lose my shit? No. But did I make her afraid? Yes.

I sit back down and clench my jaw as I watch Ani settle down and curl up on her single blanket.

My father treated my mother this way...

Ani is afraid of me. She is terrified. Truly terrified, and I am the sole cause of it. Shit.

Yes, my goal is to punish her, but this is different. Her pussy drips with every erotic spank or demand of a submissive act. The cuffs and plug are different. She wasn't wet. There was no arousal. She is just a scared little girl with some deep-rooted demons attacking, and I allow it.

But now... For some reason I want to protect her from all that.

Wait. No. Stop this fucking madness.

Fuck this confusion. Fuck Ani for making my emotions run crazy. This isn't me. Order and structure. Black and white. Confusion is not an emotion I battle.

Enough is enough.

I need to handle this.

I have to take control.

This woman can't have this hold over me any longer. Somehow, I have to break free.

Ani

It's late, but I can't sleep. It's not just the handcuffs and plug keeping me awake, either. So many thoughts and emotions are running through my body and mind. I should hate Phoenix, but I don't. I actually want to be upstairs in the attic with him, in his bed, in his arms. How can that be after what he's done to me? How can I feel anything but complete loathing?

Oddly, it's as if I understand him. It's as if I truly get why he is doing this. Why he has no choice. Why he feels so strongly in his actions. I can't explain it. I could never put these thoughts into words to anyone else, but something deep inside of me realizes this is the path and journey Phoenix must take. This is the road *we* must take to make our way through the darkness.

I feel there will be light on the other side, that there is an end to our story with a happily ever after.

Looking over at the floorboard that conceals the journals, I decide to take a big risk. Pushing my wool blanket over to the spot, hoping to god that Phoenix isn't still awake watching me, I carefully open the hole using the blanket as my shield to hide my actions. I also reach for the stack of books that were left as my comfort items and hide the journals within them. Feeling confident that I've concealed them enough and impressed with myself that I did all this handcuffed, I open one of them up, using the thick book to hide what I'm doing in case Phoenix is watching. To him, it will look like I'm simply reading a book.

Dear Diary,

I think my daughter killed someone today. Athena was at the top of the stairs looking down, when the butler was down below... dead. There was something in her eyes. A wicked smile on her face.

It was an accident her father was quick to say. A deadly, deadly, accident.

But dear God, I think my daughter killed a man.

I'm afraid of what this means for the future. I can tell Athena is changing, becoming colder and more distant. Her father is trying to protect her, but I fear he may be enabling her dark tendencies. Even if she didn't mean to do it, she could be capable of doing so again.

And that terrifies me.

I know she's not the same little girl she used to be. She's taken a strange liking to dark things, and I'm concerned that her fascination with the forbidden might be slowly leading to something more sinister.

I'm afraid to leave her alone, so I always keep her in my sight. But even then, I can't shake the feeling that I'm being watched. It's almost as if I'm being followed, and I can feel Athena's eyes on me even when I'm alone.

Every day I watch her with a growing dread, my heart aching at the sight of the viper in the garden she's becoming. I know now that it is only a matter of time before her wickedness is revealed. I can only pray that it doesn't spell disaster for us all.

I flip to the beginning of the journal to see if any dates were written but don't find anything to answer my questions. When was this? How old was Athena? Did she really kill the butler?

Athena has always been terrifying. She went to my school the same time I did. We were only one year apart, but everyone knew not to mess with her. And not just because she was a Godwin, but because that girl was terrifying. Even at a young age, I seriously doubted any grown man would mess with her.

Does Athena know what Phoenix is planning with me, that he's here punishing me, and then plans for me to have his baby? Maybe she's part of it. Maybe some of this is her idea. Or maybe the real truth is that if she had her way, I'd be dead. My sister and I would be dead.

Nothing about this diary entry tells me about Phoenix, however, and I so desperately want to read about things that may help me start to understand him better. Maybe I'm pressing my luck, maybe I'm tempting the fates, and Phoenix will grow suspicious and catch me in the act, but I keep reading.

Dear Diary,

Troy made me go to The Vault tonight. I had heard stories that dark, debauched sex acts occurred in the old 19th-century bank but didn't know if the tales were fact or fiction.

I'm embarrassed to even be writing this story in my journal, but then again, I never want to forget this night.

As I walked up to the entrance, I could feel an eerie presence that seemed to permeate the air. The old wooden doors creaked as Troy opened them, and a gust of cold air rushed past us. Inside, I felt a chill run down my spine as I saw the various sights and sounds of the old bank. Everywhere I looked, there were dark figures sitting in the shadows, and strange music emanating from somewhere in the depths of the building.

As I continued to walk, I heard a low, guttural laugh coming from the corner of the room. I couldn't make out who it was, but the laughter was sinister. I felt a chill in my bones as Troy grabbed my hand and led me further into the building.

We entered through the locked door and down the winding staircase. The air was musty and heavy with secrets, and I felt like I was being watched by unseen eyes. We reached the bottom of the stairs to find an ornate room filled with couches and a large red-velvet bed in the center.

The atmosphere was different here. Instead of the electricity that usually crackles in the air before a wild party, there was an eerie stillness that seemed to hang over everything.

As my eyes adjusted, I saw the people in the room— the women in the room—were all naked. Some were on their hands and knees being led around by a collar. Others were pleasing the men by sucking their cocks.

Troy led me further into the room, and I couldn't help but feel I had entered a realm of forbidden pleasures and sinister desires. My heart raced as I looked around and realized that Troy had brought me to a fetish club. This wasn't just an ordinary sex club—it was a dark, twisted place where desires of all kinds were being explored and acted upon. I could feel myself getting aroused, even in the presence of such depravity.

I knew I was in way over my head, but I also knew that I wanted to explore this new world. Anything to maybe save my marriage. Anything.

As Troy and I ventured further into the depths of the club, we encountered more and more bizarre activities, each one more perverse than the last. I had never seen anything quite like it before, and I was equal parts excited and scared.

Eventually, Troy and I found ourselves in a room with a large cage in the center. Inside, a woman was bound and gagged with rope. She was being whipped, and her screams echoed through the empty room. I could feel myself getting aroused, and I knew that I wanted to experience this world for myself. This was so unlike me. But maybe that's what I needed.

To be different.

Troy pulled me close and whispered into my ear, "Do you want to join in?" I hesitated for a moment, not sure if I could go through with it. But there was something to this place. Something I needed to taste. To see. To feel.

I nodded my head yes, and Troy smiled as he opened the door to another cage. I stepped inside, knowing my wildest fantasies were about to become a reality.

Wow. I never imagined Troy Godwin and his wife were Vault members. There isn't a single person who lives on Heathens Hollow who doesn't know about The Vault. Not everyone has been there, of course. It's exclusive and only the rich get to play in that playground. But everyone knows just how dirty and depraved it can be. People fly in from around the world to attend the dark sex parties. I had always been fascinated by them, and frankly, if it weren't for me getting with Mark so young, I would have most certainly considered being one of the girls to work the parties. I heard there was a lot of money to be made, but what tempted me the most was I truly wanted to see what was inside that bank. I didn't want to just hear the rumors. I wanted to see for myself.

I chuckle as I close and hide the journal. Freya Godwin, you dirty girl. I may not be able to ever look at Troy Godwin the same way now.

Nothing in tonight's reading has given me a peek into Phoenix's childhood, but from what I've gathered, love existed between Freya and Troy at one time in their marriage. Phoenix had to see that. He had to have seen glimpses of love.

"Phoenix," I say into the camera, not sure if he's awake and can even hear me. "What you're doing to me, it isn't you. You have to let go of the anger you have. I've apologized, and I will continue to do so every single day, if that is what it takes. But I promise you with my entire heart... I'm on your side. Your side." I take a calming breath. "This isn't you, Phoenix. I know that. I saw the real you before this all started. I've seen you. And yes, you are a Godwin, but you know your mother wouldn't condone this. What would she say if she knew what you were doing to me? If she knew just how furious you are? Would your father treat your mother this way?"

I'm taking a risk bringing up Troy because maybe the answer to the question of whether his father would treat his mother this way is yes. Maybe he would. Maybe Troy taught Phoenix everything he knows and is willing to do to me.

CHAPTER
TWENTY-FOUR

Ani

Finding a comfortable way to sleep on the floor with nothing but a blanket, with the plug and handcuffs still so tight against my flesh isn't easy, but I must learn how to accept it, or risk having continual panic attacks, which is no longer an option. I need to be strong. I have to find strength to survive. I have to. Finding my own internal peace will be the only thing to get me through this ordeal.

About an hour or so has passed since Phoenix escorted me back to the room, and I decide to take the time to really accept my surroundings and absorb them into my soul. If I can come to terms and welcome my new situation, I'll be all right. I don't know for sure what is in store for me with this man, but I must deal with the moment. My new strength will be in not worrying about tomorrow but rather focusing on today. Today, my concentration will be on breathing and comfort. Finding comfort. Rather than seeing this room as a cell, I need to change my opinion and see it as my haven. Trick my mind and trick my soul. It won't be the first time.

And it will be better than prison.

Even though I told Phoenix I would go to jail for the Godwins, I don't want that. True prison would be awful. There would be no chance to earn... comforts.

If I am a good girl.

Not a bad girl.

Maybe I can be the queen who is pampered by her king. Is that even a possibility? If I have his heir, will he feel he owes me respect and treat me better than he is now? Maybe I can work this toward my advantage. Maybe a baby is the key to my happiness. Because the truth of the matter is that anything is better than death, and I can see how maybe this entire nightmare in the manor can be better than prison.

If I can earn Phoenix's forgiveness and make him forget about my lies and secrets, there is a chance for me to have a somewhat normal life.

But having a baby?

I have always wanted to have children someday. Losing my baby with Mark nearly destroyed me mentally. I had no idea if I'd truly recover from the darkness the tragedy sent me into. As my body healed, my mind seemed to be so much further away in doing the same. I had given up hope on ever having a child again.

Being forced to conceive with Phoenix is far from how I want to, of course, but I am not against having a baby. Yes, I want love, a husband, and the normal path of creating a family, but I also gave up normal a long time ago. Girls who grow up on the Eastside of Heathens Hollow don't get to have normal.

When the door to my room opens, I'm surprised Phoenix has returned so quickly. I was hoping he would after I spoke about his mother to the camera. Asking questions about her, trying to appeal to his inner kindness, and trying to make him see what he is doing to me as wrong through her eyes would make him take pause. But I also risked angering him, pushing him too far by bringing up his past.

As I sit up to face the man in my doorway, my heart stops while I wait to see what's next.

"Do not ever bring up my mother again!" he bellows, stomping straight toward me. "I don't know how you know anything about her other than assuming it's your betraying sister. But whatever your sister must have told you is not true—because nothing she says is. I don't want my mother's name to touch either of your lips again."

"I didn't mean to make you angry," I stammer, feeling my gut clench as I scurry back toward the farthest corner of the room, terrified at the fury I see in Phoenix's eyes. "I just know a mother wouldn't want her son to act this way."

He bolts in my direction and reaches out, grabbing a handful of my hair, pulling me mere inches from his face. "Do not talk about my mother. Severe consequences for that."

"I'm sorry," I offer weakly, but I now see his Achilles heel. The sting from my hair being yanked causes tears to well in my eyes. "I won't bring her up again."

He tugs my hair harder, forcing my head so far back I stare into his furious eyes. My body nude and awkwardly posed—so exposed. "And I understand. I don't like to talk about my past either. Or parents."

Regardless of me feeling like a trapped animal in a cage, I'll do my best not to bring her up as a tool again. It was clearly enough to push Phoenix over the edge.

"And what do you feel should be the consequence for pissing me off like this?"

Clearly, sorry isn't enough.

He tugs my hair a little harder, telling me he's waiting for an answer. I have no idea what to say or how to answer correctly in his eyes.

"I don't know."

"I should spank that ass of yours."

"A spanking?" The words shoot past my lips like a bullet before I have time to think them through. Before I have time to really consider what will come from that word. But I also desperately want to repent in Phoenix's eyes. I don't like seeing him this angry with me. I want it to go away. Oddly enough, I don't want to disappoint him any longer.

Phoenix's eyes darken, and his lips set in a thin, firm line. "At least you now understand," he growls.

I want to apologize. I want to plead for compassion. I want to reach into the depths of his evil and pull out even an ounce of humanity. But I'm aware I have been poking the bear. And no, I have not expected to get away with it.

He reaches into his pocket and pulls out the key to the handcuffs. "Don't make me use these again," he says as he removes them.

It's like a vise has been released from my neck as he does so. I can suddenly breathe so much easier.

Without wasting another second, Phoenix orders, "Go stand in the corner, hands hooked behind your head, and spread your legs wide."

I can try to run out of the room, but he will catch me.

I can try to fight him off now that my hands are free, even though it is pointless. He is so much bigger. Stronger. Phoenix will get his way, regardless of how hard I struggle.

Make wise choices or anger him some more.

The choice is mine.

Placing my hands behind my head, I walk toward the corner. At least I won't have to see him as I take the punishment. I won't have to see his thundery eyes of disapproval. Maybe he'll just fuck me, and we can start the baby-making process. At least then, we will be moving forward instead of me in the limbo of hell.

"Legs spread," he reminds as I wait with my face inches from the wall.

I draw a deep breath, and do as he orders, feeling the plug move inside of me as I do so.

He approaches me then runs his fingertips along the base of the plug. "Has this stretched you? Does it hurt?"

I'm not sure how to answer. If I admit that it still does, will he only add a larger one to torture me further?

"Yes," I admit. "It's big and heavy."

Without pause, Phoenix spreads my cheeks and pulls the plug out of me, which nearly hurts as much coming out as it did going in. "I'm a fair man. I may be cruel and heartless at times, but I am fair." The heavy metal clangs as it is tossed to the floor.

I inhale deeply, as if I can finally breathe freely. I haven't expected mercy from Phoenix, but I am all the more grateful for it.

"Thank you." I am tempted to rub my ass just to feel the sensation of normal again but think better of it. I remain in position in fear that Phoenix will change his mind.

"Don't think this means you can get away with anything. Don't take advantage of my momentary softness. It's very momentary."

I nod. "Yes, sir."

"But we must replace that punishment with a new one."

I swallow hard, staring ahead at the corner, feeling Phoenix's breath against my neck.

"And when I'm done, you may wish for the plug instead."

Without warning, Phoenix places his finger at the entrance of my pussy and presses firmly inside. The invasion has me tensing and gasping, but I refuse to break position.

"I have to be honest with you, dove. I've never had another woman respond to me in the way you do. I love how wet you get for me and with little effort on my part." He pumps his finger in and out as he speaks, and all I can do is close my eyes and bite back the moan that wants to break free.

He should be wrong. I shouldn't be aroused. I shouldn't be wet. Phoenix should be wrong, but he isn't.

The building orgasm tells me just how right he is.

"I can tell just how easily I could make you come right now simply by finger-fucking you." His breath is hot against my face.

As his fingers slide out of me, I struggle not to whimper in need. He moves his two slick fingers from my pussy to my anus.

"I plan to fuck this tight little ass of yours. But like I just said, I'm a fair man. I have no desire to cause permanent damage or to make you scream in agony. The only screams I want to hear will be screams of pleasure as I fuck both holes over and over." He pushes a finger past my tight opening. "So, I'm going to stretch this hole of yours. I will train your asshole to willingly take my cock."

I shake my head though I know deep down it will do no good. He pumps his finger a few times, moving it from side to side to stretch me further.

"Some anal discipline for my dirty dove." I start to close my legs only to hear, "Stay in position or it won't just be fingers stretching you."

I open my legs even wider in the hope that he will reward me by feeling he has stretched me enough.

I am wrong.

"That's one finger inside of you." He moves his hand to add more pressure. "This is two fingers."

I gasp as I open my eyes wide in shock. The biting sting is too much. My hole won't be able to take both fingers without...

"Deep breath," he says as he lowers his lips to my neck and kisses. When I don't do as he asks, he kisses my neck again. "This will be easier if you relax. I'm not going to stop until this ass of yours is properly punished and trained to accept something much bigger than just two fingers." He kisses behind my ear, only heightening the confusing emotions and feelings ravaging my body.

He works his two fingers in and out, in and out, in and out. I whimper as he goes deeper, and I cry out when he spreads them apart, opening me for further invasion.

My knees threaten to buckle, and my hands can barely remain behind my head. With every thrust of his fingers, my body seems to be melting in place.

"Have you ever had a cock in this ass of yours?"

I shake my head. I know he wants a respectful *no, sir*, but I can barely breathe, let alone speak.

"I can tell. This little hole is virginal, but not for long."

He pulls his fingers out all the way, but only to push them back in, triggering all the sensitive nerves of my opening once again.

"Can you imagine my cock buried inside your ass?" he asks as he thrusts hard enough that I rise on my tiptoes.

"Yes, sir," I barely whisper. I can picture his penetration vividly. It not only terrifies but excites me.

I close my eyes and imagine the wicked act.

"Press your ass out more," Phoenix orders. "I want to shove my fingers deeper. Fast or I will add a third."

Moaning with a hunger I don't understand, I push my ass out as I stand awkwardly in the corner.

Phoenix pushes his fingers deeper than I think possible as he nibbles on my neck and sucks on my earlobe. Chills run down my spine as heat floods my pussy. He pulls his fingers out only to press them in with more force and deeper than the time before.

Over and over until I cry out his name. What I expect to gain from it, I have no idea, but I can no longer hold back my sounds of arousal.

"I bet you want my cock inside you right now," he says.

I nod. "Yes, sir. I do."

I am ready.

So, so ready.

He pulls out his fingers then swats me on the ass. "That's enough anal discipline for tonight. Stand in the corner for a few more minutes and think about what will come next. Then go lie down and go to sleep. Be a good girl. I continue with your training tomorrow."

I listen as he leaves and don't dare look over my shoulder or say a word in protest. A camera is on me, and I will remain in position in the corner and not move an inch until a few minutes are up. I will stand. I will think...

TWENTY-FIVE

Ani

Again and again, I wake with a lashing. I go to bed sore from the strike of Phoenix's hand on my sensitive ass. I wake to an excruciating session with the paddle and go to bed with the kiss of his belt once again. Over and over the routine continues. One comfort item at a time.

One excruciatingly earned comfort at a time.

The days are filled with other acts of submission. Long hours kneeling or standing at attention for whenever, wherever, and for however long he feels it is needed. He touches me, but never enough. And that is the worst part. Over and over he slaps, pinches, touches parts of my body and brings me right to the edge of ecstasy, only to pull away and leave me with the worst need imaginable. Every hour my hunger for him grows. Every second my lust intensifies. I dream of his touch, and I fantasize about the day he finally puts his cock inside of me.

But he never does.

That is my punishment.

That is my penance.

And oh, how I pay, suffer, and slowly earn one comfort item at a time that I no longer care if I receive. I cry. I plead. I beg for more than just a materialistic reward. I have no shame or pride left. I long for him to be near and never leave me, and when he does leave for the night, I sob for hours, waiting for sunlight to come, for it heralds the return of my monster.

If Phoenix thinks I was broken before, and that I am his dirty dove... I can't imagine what I have become now. My only strength is when he is near. My body craves him like a drug, and I am weak without him.

So fucking weak.

He is my prison guard, and yet, he has truly mastered my body. When he says I am his—that my body belongs to him—I never question the fact.

Phoenix Godwin.

And there truly is nothing I won't do when asked. Even when he hands me the phone with my sister on the other line, I tell her I'm fine and just taking some time to figure out my next step. I tell her to not bother herself by coming, and I'm actually enjoying my time alone. It's not truly a lie. I am taking time. I am considering all that is coming. My future. My future is Phoenix.

There's no baby yet. He hasn't even tried.

But where I once was terrified of the idea, I can't wait. I want that bond between us. I want that connection. I want more than what we have now. I want so much more.

"Are you a good girl or a bad girl?" Phoenix asks as he had grown accustomed to asking all the mornings he arrives in a new crisp suit with an unbuttoned white shirt at the neck.

"What do you want me to be?" I answer like I always do right before he takes his belt and runs it along my punished, upturned flesh after he has spanked me.

"Today I want you to be bad. I want you to talk dirty to me so I can punish that mouth of yours," Phoenix says.

I turn my head just enough to see him towering over me as I am bent over the bed and give a wicked smirk. "Fuck you, sir. Fuck you."

We played this game in the past. He forces me to act out just so he can punish me more severely.

Phoenix seems to like it most when I punch or kick, and especially when I call him names. My mock hatred of him seems to fuel him, though we both know it is all for show. He knows how desperate I am for more. He can see the arousal coating my pussy and dampening my inner thighs. He wipes at my tears of frustration as my stomach tightens and cramps from a growing need for release never to be granted. He makes promises that if I am a good girl, that maybe someday I will get a taste of his cock.

His torturous edging is my true punishment. Being taken to the edge only to be pulled back from the jagged ledge is the penance for my lies.

He lets me get so close, but not close enough.

I want a taste so badly.

I don't know what he is doing to me, and if this is his ultimate goal. He has turned the tables. He doesn't want me but makes damn sure I wanted him. My entire being knows this is wrong. It's a sickness rooted deep inside of me. I feel shame for my desire. I loathe that instead of trying to escape, I plot how I can tempt him to claim my body. I hate how I hunger, but I hate not having my needs met even more.

I'm not sure how many days or how many nights pass, but Phoenix has changed the woman I once was. He has broken down my walls and left me wide open for the taking. My battle scars are left without bandages, and Phoenix only opens the wounds wider.

"You have a filthy mouth, my dove," he says as he heads out of the hallway toward the bathroom.

I hold my position bent over the bed I have recently earned as a comfort item, schooled in what will happen if I act of my own free will without permission.

"I think it's time I teach you what happens to

girls with dirty, filthy mouths," he says as he disappears from my sight.

My pussy throbs at the warning in his voice. I have no idea what he has in store, and though I am sure parts of me will hate every moment of what Phoenix has planned for this morning's session, other more sinful parts of me will love every second of his evil ministrations to my body, mind, and soul.

"Kneel," he commands as he reenters the bedroom with something fisted in one hand, and a glass of water in the other.

I quickly do as he asks, licking my lips in anticipation of what's to come. A chance to earn more comfort items—items I have long lost count of. I no longer pay my penance for these items. No. I pay my penance for Phoenix. For the one day he will deem me worthy of his cock being buried inside of me.

There was a time in my life where I would have screamed and shouted at any woman who would submit to a man. Especially to a man as strict and severe as Phoenix. Mark abused me, but I never submitted. Never gave in. Never surrendered my soul, even if my body was battered because of it. My heart never belonged to Mark. My body never came alive with his dominance. But with Phoenix...

With Phoenix... I no longer care. Societal rules ceased existing the minute I walked through the doors of the manor. Life as it once was, no longer exists for me. My nightmare has become a fantasy, and my fantasies have become this nightmare.

"It's time I teach you a lesson," he says as he stands before me, places the water by my knees as well as a bar of soap, and unfastens his pants. When his hard cock pops out from its constraints, he says, "It's time I clean that mouth of yours out."

I stare at his cock in awe. It's thick, bigger than I expect, and hard—hard for me.

"I want you to wet my cock with your tongue, then rub the bar of soap all over it."

When I don't move fast enough, still processing his words in my foggy brain, he takes hold of his dick and slaps it across my face. He then presses his cock past my lips before I have a chance to do it of my own free will, though I am willing. I move my head up and down, swirling my tongue as I do so, savoring the taste of my monster.

"Get it nice and wet," he says, huskily.

He takes hold of my hair and guides my head at a speed he chooses. Up and down, I suck and softly moan against his cock. I lick every inch I can, not wanting one inch of his length missed. I all but devour him. His salty taste and the essence of his manhood flooding my senses, I coat his throbbing sex entirely.

"Now grab that bar of soap by you and coat my cock. It's time I wash your mouth out with soap, dove."

"Yes, sir," I say as my pussy aches for attention.

I pick up the white bar and start caressing Phoenix's cock with it. Small suds form as the soap mixes with my saliva. I stroke the soap up and down the length of his shaft just as I know Phoenix wants me to do.

"Now place my cock in your mouth, dove. This is what you get for having a filthy mouth. Time we cleanse it."

Not stopping to consider the awful taste or just how much this truly will be a punishment, I place Phoenix's soap-coated penis inside my mouth and begin sucking as I once had. I whimper as the dreadful taste attacks. I gag as the tip of his cock presses against the back of my throat with the soap only intensifying the sensation.

"Bad girls get their mouths washed out with soap." He tugs my hair when I try to pull back as I suck in air to help ease the turmoil occurring inside my mouth.

Using his other hand, he reaches down and cups my breast, changing my whimpers to a moan.

Mercifully removing his dick from my mouth, Phoenix spreads his pre-cum mixed with remnants of soap on my lips as he says, "Let me paint this perfect pink pout of yours. I'm about to make you my cum slut."

I look up into his eyes and nod.

He slaps the head of his cock against my cheek. "You want my cock, dove? Do you want me to punish you now with my cock?"

Fuck, yes. Fuck, yes! Although my words are lost in my own hunger begging to be satiated.

I want him so badly.

I want him to split me wide open with his cock.

My pure white sexual experiences from before about to become pitch black.

I want raw. I want depraved. I want dark emotions and desires.

Phoenix is the only one who will truly give me what I want, and what I so desperately need. And now Phoenix is here... Is it finally time?

Everything has been leading up to this. Phoenix has opened a Pandora's box of horrific fantasies and delights hidden deep within, and now that they are unleashed, Phoenix is the only one who can tame them.

"Take a drink of water, swish it around in your mouth, and then spit it out back in the glass," he orders.

I'm grateful for this, because though the soap misery has dissipated somewhat, I do wish to be rid of the residue from the inner lining of my mouth.

As I swish and spit the last bit out into the glass, Phoenix bends down and places his hands under my arms, lifting me to my feet. He then swoops me into his arms and carries me over to the bed. The tender touch and almost loving gesture have my mind spinning with the wicked, twisted lust from my naughty discipline only moments ago.

The softness is quickly replaced, however, when

he places me on my back and spreads my legs wide. Without pause, he swats my pussy, causing me to jump and cry out in surprise.

"I'm going to make these lips of your cunt swell so every time I thrust into you, you cry out in pain." He swats my bare pussy again and again. The sting only heightens my need for more.

"Please..." I beg like so many times before, but this time I feel like my pleas may be answered.

"Do you feel your penance is over? Do you feel like you've finally proven you are a good girl? A trustworthy dirty dove?"

"Yes, I swear. I am. I will never lie to you again."

Phoenix pauses, locks eyes with me. "I believe that."

My heart skips a beat when Phoenix quickly sheds his clothing. His actions are smooth and graceful, but not nearly fast enough for my need. I think about sitting up and assisting him but remain frozen. I don't want to do a single thing to have Phoenix change his mind or decide I need another punishment instead.

My heart hitches when the weight of the bed shifts as he straddles my body. This is it. I glance down at his cock, and a tiny twinge of fear sets in when I know just how much his size will be too much for me to take.

Phoenix lowers his weight upon me and positions his cock at my pussy. The meaty head stretches my hole wide as he enters, and I moan with the biting pain. He doesn't give me any time to get used to his girth but rather begins thrusting in and out at a steady pace.

There are no kisses. No caresses. No loving words of affection.

The actions are cold yet the heat between us blazes to an epic proportion of inferno. My body explodes almost instantly, finally free to release the long-overdue energy that has been pent up since my captivity started. Phoenix hasn't given me permission to come, but I don't care. I will accept whatever punishment he will deliver later for my actions. It'll be worth it.

So fucking worth it.

As I cry out his name and my pussy contracts around his cock, he pulls his face back enough so he can look into my eyes. Maybe it's the sexual energy flowing through me, or maybe it's simply wishful thinking, but I see something in his eyes.

Softness.

Emotion beyond what normally only belongs to a sadist.

Connection.

Phoenix continues to push and pull inside of me as his eyes never leave mine.

In and out, I see him.

In and out, I feel him.

In and out, Phoenix seems to merge with not just my body, but my soul.

I am his. I have been his for a long time. But at this very moment, I truly believe he is...

He is mine.

He is my monster, my captor, mine, and I am never going to let him go.

I never want this moment to end. Never.

But eventually, my body explodes again, and it is all that Phoenix needs to groan loudly and give one final thrust as he spills his completion inside of me.

Taking a few minutes to gather his senses as he breathes against the pillow beside my head, he eventually pulls his face back and stares at me again. He doesn't say anything, nor do I. But in this moment, something is different.

He is not a monster.

He is a man.

Nothing but a man.

I am not the prey.

I am a woman.

Nothing but a woman.

But we are together. We are as one. We are in this nightmare together, and we both know it.

"My seed's inside you," he states as if a medical procedure has just occurred. Any romantic bubble I thought I had, pops.

I nod, hating the thought of merely being a vessel.

TWENTY-SIX

Phoenix

I fucked up. I enter the kitchen and pour myself a scotch.

Something doesn't sit easy with me, and I can't put my finger on it. It isn't guilt. Having sex in the manor is definitely uncharted territory. Maybe it's just as simple as that.

Maybe I've gone too far. The girl has sure atoned for her crimes. That ass of hers has paid the price. I need to be done and move on.

Taking a sip, I chuckle against the crystal glass. She fucking likes it. Who would have thought? I didn't see that one coming when I planned this out.

Rare breed.

Rare breed, indeed. And the sex...

My cock twitches at the memory. Yeah. There's something about that woman.

I take a drink as I inhale air between my teeth and try to push the image of Ani out of mind.

Addictive.

Which is dangerous. I can't think with my cock instead of my head. I need to focus on the goal. I ignore the urge to march back into her room and to bury my cock inside her again.

Addictive.

She lied to me. I hate liars. I have to remember that. I have to make sure she never does it again.

But... I think I've done that.

I nod. Yeah, I have. I take another sip.

Jesus Christ, I'm an asshole. A mad man.

I'm just like my father. I've morphed to become Troy Godwin, torturing a woman. Pushing her to the brink of insanity. I'm repeating history.

It's like I'm thinking about her as a prized mare in heat and the details of mating her. It's as if this is nothing but a mundane, daily task of running a business.

My cock disagrees, however.

There is nothing mundane about that woman. Nothing.

I can't just fuck her and leave. My cock is screaming at me for more, but my core is also demanding I return to her. She's paid for her crimes. I can't keep being the monster. I have to eventually back down.

We just fucked.

I just put my goddamn seed inside her.

That means one thing. The next chapter has begun.

Once I return to her room, I say, "Your main punishment—being locked in the room—is now over. And I believe you deserve a comfort item as a reward."

Her room is complete. Every single piece of furniture or art works has been given. There isn't anything to add to it, and she and I both know that.

"Anything?" she asks.

I nod, though feeling cautious of what she may ask. If she wants freedom, I'm not prepared to give her that. I can't let her go. I can't allow her to walk out that door and leave me forever. Especially now. I glance at her belly and wonder if one time was enough.

"Let's go somewhere," she says.

I start to shake my head, but she cuts me off.

"You said I earned a comfort item. And I've done everything you've asked, so please. We don't have to be gone for long, but we both could benefit from leaving these four walls."

Thinking about how nice our walk along the beach and the trip to the lighthouse turned out, I ask, "Where?"

"You may think I'm crazy for suggesting this but—"

"Do you think I'm crazy?" I don't give her time to

answer before I add, "Maybe we are both crazy. So try me. Where would you like to go?"

"The Vault."

The surprise of her suggestion is about as powerful as a slap to the face. "The Vault? In Heathens Hollow?"

She nods. "Have you ever been?"

"I have." It's one of the few places I have felt comfortable leaving the attic or my penthouse for. Maybe it's the place's secrecy that allows me to gain a sense of comfort from it.

Her eyes widen. "Really? Is it truly like what the rumors say?"

"Depends on what rumors you are hearing."

"It's a place where sex happens. Dark sex. Kinky sex. You have to give a secret to enter," she says.

"Yes."

"Well... can we go?"

"You want this as your comfort item?"

She tosses her head up and down vigorously. "I want to go see. I want to watch."

"To *watch*?"

"To do whatever you want," she corrects. "I just want us to go and experience it. Together."

I go take a seat on the leather chair. "I'm not sure my dirty dove has truly earned an outing," I tease.

Ani picks up on her cue and quickly kneels at my feet, reaching for the zipper in my pants and pulling out my cock in one fluid motion. "Maybe I can earn some more points for this comfort item." There's a twinkle in her eye, and it's sexy as fuck.

Without asking, she places my dick in her mouth, her wide eyes looking up at me, and begins earning her trip out of the manor.

With one final push, my cock slides deeper into her throat. I groan in pleasure. "That's my good girl," I praise, almost ready to come at the sight of her glazed eyes, her stretched-out mouth around my shaft, and her lips pressing against the dark nest of hair at my groin.

None of my cock is visible; she's taken it all. I hold still for a few moments, marveling at the trust in her gaze as she is unable to suck in a breath. Drawing back, she coughs slightly and quickly gulps down air, knowing I have only just started.

Watching tears form in the corner of her eyes, I begin to thrust deep, pushing past her throat and burying my cock deeper each time. Her eyelashes flutter, and her body quivers as she continues to gag, yet she never fights me. She belongs to me, accepts my authority, and yearns for my control. I cup her face, slowly sliding out of her mouth completely, seeing the surprise in her eyes. She even reaches for my cock with her lips in a whimper of disappointment rather than relief.

I wrap my arm around her neck, forcing her back down on my cock. I feel her throat ripple as she swallows me down over and over. I'm not going to last much longer. Grabbing her hair tightly, I start to move my hips, holding her still as I fuck her face. I can't take my eyes off her mouth as it contorts around my cock. I can feel the veins in her neck becoming taut as she strains to breathe while I fuck her deeper and faster. I'm grunting loudly, letting my passion overtake me, letting myself go.

I'm not going to last much longer. My hips and thighs are tensing, my balls drawing up ready to explode inside her mouth. My entire body vibrates with need as I continue to drive into her, deeper and harder. She's panting around my cock, her throat closing around me, and I know I'm being rough, but it feels so good to fuck her throat.

No! Don't come in her mouth. I can't give her that. I need to push myself even further. Throwing my head back, I grab her hair with both hands and pull with all my might, yanking her head up.

She cries out in protest as I drag her off my cock, her eyes wide with shock and her mouth gaping. I drag her over to the floor-length mirror, pulling her down on her hands and knees in front of it. "Now I'm going to fuck you."

I quickly draw her up and over to the bed, where I toss her on her back. "No! I'm not done with you yet."

She stiffens as I seize her wrists, quickly pinning them above her head, smiling as she realizes just how much more is to come. With my other hand I cup her breast, teasing the nipple, and then slide it down her stomach to her pussy. I watch her face as I slide my fingers over her clit and slip inside her. Her mouth drops open, her eyes glassy, and her red lips slightly parted to take in shallow breaths. She looks fucking amazing lying there with her thighs spread, her hips lifting off the bed as I slide deeper into her, my thumb pressed firmly over her clit.

I hold her gaze as I thrust into her, her juices coating my fingers, her legs opening wider as she arches her back and moans. I watch as she becomes lost in the sensations.

I'm too far gone to tease her about her desperation, too horny to care about anything but fucking her.

I release her hands, grab the back of her hair, and slam my cock inside her. She cries out again in pain and pleasure, her hand slapping the mattress as she pushes back against me. I lean over her, thrusting deeper and harder into her pussy.

I flip her over, put her on all fours, bending her down slightly, causing her to arch her back, exposing her ass and her pussy as I slide my cock back inside her. I can't stop fucking her, I can't stop watching my cock thrust in and out of her. It's the most erotic sight I have ever seen, her body moving with mine, her ass and pussy exposed to me, and my cock sliding through her wetness.

My hand is still wrapped around her throat, holding her exactly where I want her. I'm so close. I need to feel her come around my cock. Thrusting harder, I reach around her body, between her legs, and press a finger against her clit, feeling the immediate tension release in her body, her pussy clamping around me. She cries out, her body shaking with her release, her fingers clawing at the blankets in front of her.

"Oh God! I'm coming!" she declares in a strangled cry, her body trembling and quivering as her orgasm rocks through her. I thrust deeply one last time, then finally let go, spurting inside her.

I continue to pump away as wave after wave of pleasure wracks through her body. I'm panting, desperate to catch my breath. Everywhere I look, there she is: the beautiful vision of her, eyes closed and head thrown back in pleasure. My heart quickens, and I marvel at the powerlessness radiating from my body.

I slowly pull out until my cock is no longer embedded inside her, and our eyes meet once more. "I'm never going to let you go," I whisper.

"I know," she replies breathlessly.

"If a man ever touches you, I'll kill him," I tell her.

"I know I'm yours," she whispers.

"Say it," I growl, pushing myself deeper into her. "Tell me that I'm the only one who will ever touch you like this."

Her eyes widen with fear.

"Tell me," I say firmly.

"I belong to you," she rushes out.

"Say it again."

"I'm yours," she murmurs, almost to herself.

"And I'm yours," I remind her, brushing my lips against her cheek. "You need this, don't you? You need me to be your Master and take control. Say it." I kiss her again, softly this time. "Say it," I whisper.

"I need this," she murmurs, her voice thick with desire and trust.

My lips brush hers once more. "I need you, too," I tell her. "I fucking need you to breathe."

After several moments of breathless silence, Ani asks, "So does this mean we can go to The Vault tonight?"

"Yes, my dove. Yes."

CHAPTER
TWENTY-SEVEN

Ani

We enter the bank—The Vault.

As I step through the door into the room, a buzzing sense of anticipation makes the hairs on the back of my neck stand on end. Hand in hand with Phoenix I descend several flights of stairs, which seem to stretch interminably, until eventually we reach the lower level.

I'm naked. Those are the rules of The Vault. And the one thing Phoenix has made sure of back at Olympus is that I follow rules.

"How many times have you been here?" I whisper. I still find it shocking that Phoenix can enter this place with ease. I don't see any elevated breathing or sweaty temples. He appears as calm now as he does in the attic.

"Enough. Depends on the theme. The Vault has different themes with each party. Not every theme is to my liking."

"What's tonight's theme?"

"Free for all."

When Phoenix opens the door to The Vault's main room, I'm overwhelmed by its sights and smells. It's a place where power and money mingle in the air. There are leather couches and armchairs, a fully stocked bar, and scantily clad women draped across the furniture. Gleaming black-and-chrome tables and chairs fill the room, providing a place for the men in dark suits to haggle and negotiate. Music pulses through the air, and the walls reverberate with laughter, the clinking of glasses, and the occasional moan of pleasure.

I have never been to a sex club before and have no idea what to expect, but this seems to be close to what I envisioned. It's dark, it's sinister, it's everything I expected it to be. The night is about to begin.

But I also sense a kind of surreal beauty to the chaotic room, something I can't put into words. It's as if I have stepped into a place of pure eroticism, a realm of sensuality and pleasure that exists beyond the laws of society. Maybe I'm just so damn happy to actually be out of the manor, that everything seems magical, but it truly does.

Phoenix sits in a leather chair, his legs spread wide and his dominance obvious. He signals for a woman nearby to come and join him. I instantly get jealous until I see he has no intention of touching her or being with her.

No, she's here for me.

Phoenix is a watcher. I should have assumed that would be his intent for the night. To watch...

He motions for me to come closer and for the woman to kneel in front of me. I stand still, unsure of what to do. He stares intently at my face, then takes his time to slowly gaze down my body. My skin heats up underneath his gaze, and my cheeks flush. I try to stay calm, but my pulse races.

He reaches out to me and takes my hand in his. He leads me closer to the woman kneeling before us, and my mind is spinning. He cups my face in his hands, and then leans in close to whisper in my ear. His words roll off his tongue like honey, and I feel my blood sizzle.

"Tonight, I want you to use her as your plaything," he says. "Show me how you want it done to you. Show me you know exactly what you want."

He traces a path down my neck with his fingertips, and I can feel myself melting. I know exactly what he wants, and I'm more than eager to comply.

The woman kneels before me, her eyes wide with anticipation and her body trembling. I run my hands over her curves and caress her skin. The heat is radiating off her—she's just as aroused as I am. I move my hands lower, teasing her as I go and making her moan softly.

I take my time exploring her body, taking in every inch of her. I move my hands up her sides, brushing my fingertips against her nipples as I go. She gasps and arches her back further in response, her body quivering with pleasure. I continue my exploration, stroking and caressing her until she is shaking from head to toe.

I trace her inner thighs with my fingers, sending shivers of delight through her body. I lean forward and whisper in her ear, my breath hot on her skin. "When you come, I want the entire room to hear it." I like this role of dominance. I like it a lot.

Her trembling intensifies, and I know she is ready for me. I draw her closer, taking her lips in a searing kiss as I slide two of my fingers into her.

My touch is gentle yet firm, finding the sensitive spots that make her moan and arch her back in pleasure. With my other hand I cup her breast as I increase the intensity of my thrusts.

Her body tenses and trembles as she reaches the brink of pleasure. With one final stroke, I bring her over the edge. Her cries of ecstasy fill the room as she comes undone against my fingers.

My lips find hers again, tasting the sweet surrender on her tongue.

She moans into my mouth, her body arching into mine as I thrust deeper. Her heat is all around me, tantalizing me with its intensity. I draw back and look into her eyes, watching as her pleasure builds.

I circle her clit with my thumb, sending her into a frenzy of pleasure. Her breathing comes in short gasps as I increase the intensity of my touch. Her tight walls quiver around my fingers as she cries out in pleasure. The sound fills the room, and I revel in every moan and sigh.

Finally, her orgasm crashes over her, and she wraps herself around me, giving herself completely to the completion. I hold her close, savoring every moment of her release.

Phoenix watches us intently, clearly enjoying the erotic display before him. He shifts in his chair, his arousal growing with each passing moment. His gaze is burning into me, but I don't look away. I continue to pleasure the woman, exploring her body and pushing both of us closer and closer to the edge.

Finally, when I feel she has milked my fingers for the last time, I press my lips to hers and praise, "That's my good girl."

Phoenix grins, clearly satisfied. He stands and moves toward us, his hands running through our hair. He leans in and kisses us both, sending shivers up my spine.

I should be jealous that he's kissing another, but instead I press my fingers that were just inside her to his mouth and allow him to lick her juices off my hand.

He moves around us, lingering and caressing our

bodies. His hands roam and explore, making us both moan with pleasure. He takes one of my nipples in his mouth, gently sucking and licking, then moves to the other, treating it with the same care.

His hands wander further down, tracing circles on my stomach before sliding between my legs. He uses one hand to part me, while the other slides up and down, teasing and tantalizing me until I'm breathless and shaking with need.

With one more kiss, he stands and moves away. I'm left panting with desire, my body aching for his touch. He grins again, the hunger in his eyes sending a thrill through me. Tonight is only the beginning.

"I just watched you give someone else pleasure, but now I want to watch someone else make you scream while your eyes are locked on mine."

He motions again to a man who has been sitting and watching, stroking his dick while I finger fucked the woman.

The man eagerly approaches, his heavy and thick dick in hand.

"Please my little dove," he tells the man. "Please her while I watch."

I examine Phoenix's face, his eyes, unsure if he means what he says. "I thought you said no man can ever touch me."

"Without my permission," he says. "I'm giving it. I'm controlling it. You are mine to give."

The man approaches me, his eyes filled with hunger and lust. He caresses my hip, and I lie down on a bed of pillows at Phoenix's feet, my body quivering with anticipation.

The man starts to stroke his shaft while his eyes roam my body. He puts on a condom, and with every inch it lowers down his length, I wait for what comes next.

His fingers then find their way inside me, exploring me and sending waves of desire through my body. I gasp and moan as he gradually increases the pressure and intensity of his touch.

The man takes position between my legs and I lock gazes with Phoenix. The energy in the air is palpable as this man's gaze rakes my body.

He then pushes his cock inside me, slowly at first but then increasing his speed. He fills me completely, my body shaking with pleasure. I cry out, my eyes locked on my lover's as he watches in pleasure. With each thrust, my orgasm grows until I am screaming out in pleasure and tears.

I'm barely aware of the man pushing himself inside me, thrusting deep as Phoenix watches. His gaze is so consuming that it almost feels like he's joined us, like his body is touching mine.

"Fuck her harder," Phoenix orders the man inside of me. "She likes it rough."

The man obliges, pushing himself deep inside me and grinding against my most sensitive areas. I feel like I'm going to explode as wave after wave of pleasure crashes through me. I scream out with each thrust, my orgasm growing more and more powerful.

The man grunts with each thrust, his body shaking with need. Phoenix watches us hungrily, his eyes never leaving our entwined bodies. I call out to him as I near my peak, begging him to join us, but he refuses.

He only wants to watch.

"Stick a finger in her ass as you fuck her," Phoenix demands, handing the man a small bottle of lubrication. "Stretch her ass."

The man does as he's told, taking hold of the bottle of lube, applying it generously, pushing his finger inside me and stretching me with each thrust. I gasp as I'm filled up, my climax intensifying. I gasp in pleasure as the fullness overwhelms me. His finger presses deep inside, and I can feel my body opening to be fucked in the ass, if that's what Phoenix wants.

I only want to give Phoenix what he wants.

His finger presses even deeper, and my body opens even more. I let out a long, raspy moan as my body calls to have Phoenix take over. But instead he watches me, his eyes dark with desire. Primal need blazes in his eyes as he watches, and it only makes my primal urge for more to grow.

The man slides another finger inside me, pushing deeper and rotating them slightly. The sensation is electrifying, and I push back against him, wanting more. I shiver as sensations course through me, and I begin to get closer and closer to orgasm. The world around me spins with each thrust.

I cry out in pleasure and in pain as another finger pushes inside.

Three fingers. Three fucking fingers are inside my asshole while this stranger still fucks my pussy.

Phoenix looks on with approval as the man's fingers work in and out of me, spreading me wider than I thought possible. His hands move faster and faster, pushing deeper and deeper into my tight hole. I'm on the brink, and Phoenix notices.

"Does it hurt, my dove? Is he stretching you?" Phoenix asks.

"Yes, yes."

The man moves his finger around in circles, stimulating my inner walls as he thrusts his cock in my pussy and his fingers in my ass. The sensation is overwhelming, and I'm rewarded with waves of electricity.

It hurts so fucking good.

I moan and beg for more, but at the same time shaking my head and begging for no more.

"Add another finger," Phoenix directs, and I cry out at the thought of how much it will push past my limits.

"No," I whisper, but I don't put up a fight.

I tighten around the man as he adds a fourth finger, pressing deeper and deeper inside me. His fingers work together in perfect harmony, hitting all the right spots and pushing me even closer to the edge.

It hurts, but I don't want him to stop. I want to be pushed to the edge.

Finally, Phoenix joins us and slides his hard cock into my ready ass. He pumps it in and out, pushing deeper with each thrust. All three of us moan in rapture as our bodies move together in perfect synchronization.

The hedonism builds and builds, until I'm vibrating with madness. Phoenix and the other man know exactly how to stroke my body, each movement more delicious than the last. Soon, I'm moaning uncontrollably, begging for them both to take me over the edge.

I have the man's dick in my pussy, and Phoenix's cock in my ass. Push, pull, in and out.

They both thrust their hips forward and back, faster and harder as I scream with animalistic need. Their cocks rub against each other through my thin inner wall, and it sends a wave of ecstasy through my body.

The sensations mix in a storm of carnal delight, until I can't take it anymore. My back arches and my body quakes with ecstasy as they fuck me in perfect harmony.

The sensual feeling is so intense I can hardly draw a breath.

I'm on the brink of another orgasm when Phoenix suddenly stops, causing me to scream out in frustration.

He smiles wickedly at me before pulling out

completely. "I want you to come all over this man's cock."

The man goes faster and harder, thrusting deep inside me as he brings me closer and closer to the edge. My entire body trembles as I reach my climax, and I cry out as I follow Phoenix's command and come on the stranger buried in my pussy.

Phoenix smiles triumphantly and leans down to kiss me softly. "That's my good dove. Such a dirty, dirty dove."

We lie still in the deep silence, connected in a way that can't be described. It's a comfort so profound I can feel it down to my bones, and I'm almost lulled to sleep. Then his voice comes again, cutting through the air.

"It's time to get up," he says. "I'm ready to take you to the attic."

I groan at the thought of movement, but then he presses his hand against my back, and a shiver of anticipation runs through me. What does he have planned next?

"I want you all to myself," he says, as if reading my thoughts.

A lump forms in my throat as I anticipate all the ways he will make me tremble. His hand sears my skin as it trails down my spine, wrapping around my waist and pulling me close. My body is a quivering mass, my desire stoked by his whispered promises.

"The attic?" I ask, wondering if it means my

punishment is over. If I've fully earned his trust and am allowed back in his domain.

My breath catches as Phoenix rises from the ground, standing before me in all his glorious perfection. His sculpted body and strong features send a wave of renewed desire through me, and my skin heats up with pleasure. His gaze is a magnet, drawing me closer until I'm standing right in front of him, his hard cock pressing against me.

He takes my hands in his, and I swear I can feel sparks shooting between us. His full lips brush against my knuckles, and my eyes flutter closed as his hot breath ghosts over my skin. I want to throw myself into his arms and surrender to all the sweet pleasures that await me, but I remain still, content to savor the moment.

He pulls me closer and brings his lips to mine. His kiss is fire, igniting a passion that threatens to consume me. I want to cry, to sob, to thank him for trusting me again. For forgiving me.

But then I'm not sure he truly has.

I grip his arms as if my life depends on it and enjoy the taste of his delectable mouth and do my best to focus on the now. Stop worrying about the future when this minute is absolutely perfect.

CHAPTER
TWENTY-EIGHT

Ani

The days continue, as do the regular, routine punishments. Phoenix has only fucked me one more time, and it is not the same as before. He simply pushes me against a wall and quickly takes me from behind in an animalistic way. None has been as intense as the first. I long for even a glimpse of that connection we had when we were first together. I hunger for it as I once hungered for his cock to be inside of me.

I want all of Phoenix.

I want to know what is behind his tough exterior and why he gives me little of who he is inside. There is more. So much more.

But he is cold. So, so cold.

I see small glimpses. He is still as strict as ever,

but I also receive tender touches here and there. He carries me to bed after a session and holds me as I fall asleep several evenings. He had bathed me, brushed my hair, and has started taking every meal with me in the dining room or upstairs in the attic.

Yes, he is still a severe disciplinarian, but when I am his perfect dove and submissive like he wants me to, he usually rewards me with kindness, even if it is just in small doses. Because I hunger to see and to feel more of that connection, I constantly search for it in his eyes and in his actions, and I know without a doubt that I can see it. I most certainly can feel it. Not all the time... but the times do exist.

Yes, I am still earning my comfort items.

I am still a prisoner.

But there is something different in the way he watches me. In the way he touches me. And even in the way he punishes me.

There are still constant reminders of my reality, however. He often demands to have a close-up recording of many spankings where I must hold my butt cheeks spread wide so he can see my anus as it, too, is spanked and prodded for his viewing. It is also expected for the tears to flow. Even if I don't particularly feel like crying, I know it pleases him. I think I understand deep down what he wants to see —my pain, my suffering, my miserable penance.

He wants me broken... possibly so he can be there to pick up the pieces.

And whenever I perform as he wants, he will

reward me with a caress, or a touch that makes my heart soar. But he also wants to see me as a captive hating every minute of her stay in the manor, and I play the part perfectly.

If Phoenix only knew.

If he only knew just how much my body craves the penance.

He isn't the monster. *I* am the fucking monster. I want and actually like every single lick of pain. I ache for the next fix. I absolutely writhe in agony when I am without one of his touches. I am an addict, and Phoenix is the only one who can deliver the drug I crave.

After a deep breath while I eat my breakfast in the attic, I allow a wave of optimism to enter my psyche. I'm still naked, but I've never felt warmer. I'm not sure if it's because Phoenix is giving me more and more of a leash, or that today is a new day, but I do have a new sense of hope. The despair and shadows that threatened to conquer me and swallow me have long vanished. I feel a renewed sense of strength as each day passes, at least enough to get through another day. One day at a time.

I feel him approaching me before a single sound is made. Phoenix has entered the attic with two fresh cups of coffee. Something about Phoenix's presence causes erotic tingles throughout my entire body. I have a strong feeling that sex with Phoenix is something I will never experience with someone else. Not to this level or intensity. When I was at The

Vault, I was with another man, but he was nothing without Phoenix. Nothing.

Even though my body aches from last night, I want my hands bound above my head as I scream no while Phoenix thrusts his cock into me. I want him to take me. God, how I fucking want to be taken. I want nothing more than to feel Phoenix in the most intimate of ways over and over. I want to be the woman tied to his bed, sucking his cock and giving over my full submission. I want to feel him spread me as he presses his body to mine. I want Phoenix more than I want anything in my life. I lust, I obsess, but more than anything... I crave his hard hand of discipline again.

How can you love the monster? It's a sickness, a contagion, no doubt, but I can't deny the feeling.

Phoenix approaches me with a domineering presence, causing my heart to stutter. He slowly stalks over, stands before me, and places the mugs of coffee on the table where I sit. He places a palm on each side of my face. Very closely, he examines my eyes.

"I hope you plan on obeying today."

I escape his glare and stare at the floor. "Yes, sir."

He lifts my chin so I am forced to look into his eyes again. "I hope you have been learning your lesson, no?"

I simply nod.

"Maybe we should take another trip to The Vault for my good girl."

I nod. "Yes."

"Do you want another man to fuck you as I watch. As I direct each move?"

I nod.

"But you belong to me. Only belong to me," Phoenix says, as he strokes the back of my head. "Should I still give you your daily lesson?" He has a wicked gleam to his eye.

"I will not forget the lessons ever," I admit, hoping that will be enough to prevent another punishment.

"Regardless, I may want you to feel the sting of my lash into the next day," Phoenix says. "I want every time you sit to remind you that I could whip you daily forever."

"I will remember," I whisper.

"I know you will," he says as he hands me a mug and then sips from his own. "Which is why we are leaving Olympus Manor and going to Seattle."

"Seattle?" I'm not sure I'm excited to hear the news or sad. I like his attic, and I've only got to be in it for the night.

"Consider it a comfort item," he says. "I can't expect you to be locked away, and like you said yesterday, it will be good for us to get out. I have the helicopter coming this morning to pick us up and bring us there."

"I'd like that. Very much."

"But first"—he places his mug back on the table —"stand up and bend over the table."

I pause for a moment, not wanting to do what he asks, but at the same time, I do. The confusion in my body and mind almost paralyzes me.

"Now," is his only command.

As if his deep voice is a spell, enchanting me to do his bidding, I do just as he asks, staring into his deep, dark eyes as I willingly bend over the table in his attic. Everything I do, everything I think, is traitorous to the depths of my core. I shouldn't want this. I shouldn't crave it. I should be screaming, clawing, hating this man with every living inch of my body. But I don't.

When I place my palm against the table's wood, Phoenix puts his hand atop mine, lacing his fingers and taking hold. I feel his breath on my neck as he presses his body against my spine. The rough fabric of his pants rubs against the bare flesh of my bottom and thighs.

"Did that man fuck you good at The Vault?" he purrs into my ear as he runs his free hand along the edge of my hip.

"Yes."

A sharp spank to my ass reveals he does not like my answer.

"Yes, *sir*. That man fucked me good," I correct. The saliva in my mouth dissipates as the nerves take over. Will he be angry today, even though it was his idea? Will he be jealous now that he has time to process what he watched? Does he regret taking me to The Vault?

"And did you like it?"

I nod, which again earns me two hard swats to my ass. My pussy throbs with each slap. I hunger for more.

"Yes, sir. I did." One thing is for sure. I will never lie to Phoenix again.

He runs his fingertips along the surface of my upturned butt and dips between the crease, running them from my anus, to my taint, to my pussy, to my clit. "Look how wet you are." He pushes a finger past my folds, into my pussy, and begins pumping it. "What gets you so wet, my dove?"

"You," I barely say between my gasps.

"Elaborate." He adds a second finger to the one already finger-fucking me.

"Your dominance. Your control. You."

He removes his palm from mine and uses his hand to start spanking me while he fingers me at the same time. The combination of pleasure and pain has me moaning and writhing against the table's coldness. The spanking is not gentle, and his fingers thrust firmly inside me.

Rising up on my tiptoes with every thrust, I finally cry out. "Please!"

"Please what?" he asks as he pumps and spanks, never easing up in the slightest.

"Please, I can't take any more." I don't truly want him to stop, but I need more. I need so much more.

"Do you want to fuck me?" he asks.

"Yes."

"Why do you want to fuck me, if I just fucked you last night?"

I don't answer.

"Do you need a belting instead of a fucking? Answer me, or I will whip this ass of yours, and it will be far worse than the one I gave you last time."

"Because I'm a cum slut. I'm *your* cum slut," I admit between deep moans, hardly believing such crass words are escaping my mouth.

"My cum slut," he repeats as he pauses in the spanking but keeps his two digits still firmly planted inside my cunt.

"Yes, sir. Always."

Phoenix pulls out his fingers and stands me up, turning him to face me. "Well then, let me give you some more cum."

With strong fingers he digs deep into my scalp, gripping my hair tightly as he wraps the other arm around my waist, crushing me against his body. His mouth descends on mine with violent intent and an undeniable hunger, devouring me with each sweep of his tongue. I'm captured in his embrace as his lips press harder and his tongue dives deeper into my willing mouth. I can't breathe through the intensity of the kiss, my moan only stoking the flames of his passion further as he growls in response. Breaking away just long enough to grab my ass and yank me back into him, he plunges his tongue into me once more, claiming me as if I'm his own. I'm lost in dizzying pleasure and desperate for more.

The sensation of his tongue claiming mine is all-consuming, my hands splaying over the taut muscles of his back as he presses me against the wall. He digs his fingers into my flesh, his hard length pushing insistently against me. I quiver in anticipation as he lifts me onto the table, silverware clattering as he sweeps it away.

He cups my breasts, and I bite back a moan. With skilled precision he pinches my nipples and tugs gently, setting off sparks of pleasure that have me pressing into his touch. When I'm so close to shattering, he withdraws and looms over me with an unspoken question in his eyes.

"Who do you belong to?"

A wave of shame courses through me, and my cheeks flame with humiliation. His knowing smirk sets my righteous anger ablaze, but before I can lash out at him, I remember where we are. Defeat evident in my posture, I meet his gaze and answer softly "You, sir."

He grins wickedly as he lifts me from the table and carries me to the nearby chair. He slides his hand around my neck, his breath hot on my skin. His fingertips blaze a trail of fire up my inner thigh. A feral hunger is in his eyes as he kneels between my legs and drives his tongue into me.

The sudden sensation causes me to gasp, my breath hitching in shock. I grip the chair's arms as I lift my hips to meet him, desperate for more. He teases and pinches my nipples while his tongue works its magic between my legs, sending wave after wave of pleasure coursing through me. His fingers press into my hips, holding me firmly in place as he takes me to the edge of bliss and then pulls away, taunting me with his touch. Frantic and panting, I beg him for more, pleading with him to take me over the edge as only he can do.

Desperation and arousal war within me. I'm quaking with need, desperate for my release.

"Who do you belong to?" Phoenix growls, his deep voice a silken caress against my skin.

"You," I plead, my voice fluttering. "I belong to you."

"Beg me, and I'll give you freedom," he murmurs, tracing my body with his hands until I'm shaking beneath his touch. "You'll no longer have to remain in the guest room."

"Please!" I whimper, my body trembling beneath his hand. "Please, I need you! I don't want to have to leave you."

His grip tightens, and he pushes himself against me as he commands, "Tell me."

"I'm yours!" I cry out, shuddering with the force of my orgasm, unable to hold back my rapture. "All yours, Phoenix!"

He leans down and claims my mouth in a passionate kiss as he thrusts into me, filling me completely as he unleashes his own ecstasy. He grips my hips, and I arch into him as wave after wave of pleasure washes over me.

With a low growl, he pulls out of me, taking a moment to gaze down at me with a wolfish smile. Something is changing in Phoenix. I truly believe he's released his anger toward me, but there's more. Though he hasn't offered a toothy grin, or allowed himself to laugh. I'm starting to notice peeks of a smile here and there. I see some light shining through his constant brewing storm.

"You're mine, Ani. No one will ever have you but me."

CHAPTER
TWENTY-NINE

Phoenix

We enter the penthouse overlooking Seattle, a sprawling cityscape of steel and glass, shimmering and shining in the light. The view of city is a tapestry of lights and skyscrapers. The clouds are purple, pink, and orange, as if a god had exploded a box of crayons in the sky. It's raining, the droplets streaking against the glass of the floor-to-ceiling windows that master the far wall.

This penthouse is a rich man's home with a view. It reeks of money but also loneliness.

The living room is lined with beautiful furniture, each piece delicately upholstered and crafted with care from a nameless interior designer Athena hired. I don't care what the apartment's interior looks like, but my sister does. All I care about is the wall of windows which offers a stunning vista of the city below, the sparkling waters of Puget Sound, and beyond.

I like to see the world. I just don't want to walk within it.

The room is silent, save for the chirp of a bird perched on the balcony outside. I step closer to the window, feeling the warmth of the sun on my skin, and a gentle sense of peace settling in my heart.

Home. Though it's not the same as Olympus Manor, it most certainly still feels like home.

Safety. Ani and I are most certainly safe.

Comfort. We can be very comfortable here... forever.

"Oh my god. You have a view of the Space Needle. Of the entire city." Ani spins around to face me with wide eyes. She's wearing a yellow dress, and although I have loved every second of her being naked at my whim, I have to admit the bright, cheery color on her only elevates the light she exudes.

"Views are important to me considering—"

"Considering you never leave your house," Ani finishes for me.

Ani means well, and she's just trying to understand, but I can't help but feel judged. I draw a deep breath and try to explain myself.

"It's not like I'm afraid to leave my house. It's not fear. But it's not like I have a choice in the matter. It's something I've been dealing with for a long time, and it's hard to explain."

Ani looks at me sympathetically, her dark eyes full of understanding. She reaches out and grabs my hand, squeezing it gently. "It's okay. I understand."

But do I? Do I even understand myself?

Leaving Heathens Hollow and flying in the helicopter took every ounce of strength I had. No doubt Ani saw the demons taking hold of my throat and strangling me the entire way of the trip. I didn't say a single word to her the entire trip, but she also didn't expect me to or push me to. I appreciate that more than she can know.

I fucking hate being this way.

The walls of this penthouse are a reminder of what I could have been and what I am. I had the opportunity to see the world and experience so many things, and yet here I am, living in a bubble of security, hiding from reality.

I've chosen the safety net of a life of seclusion and comfort, but I wonder if I'm missing something more. Maybe there's more out there for me than the secure life I've created for myself. But the thought of taking that risk terrifies me, so I stay put. I remain in my own little world, safe, secure, and fucking lonely.

I don't want to be this way. I don't want to be scared of taking a chance because I'm afraid of the unknown, but it's hard to quiet those fears when they are so deeply ingrained within me.

Ani puts her hand on my shoulder and squeezes it gently. She looks into my eyes, and a part of me feels she understands what I'm going through. She understands just how penetrating darkness can be.

For a moment, we stand there in silence, taking in the view from my penthouse. The Seattle skyline stretches out before us, twinkling softly in the evening light. The Space Needle stands tall and proud, a beacon of hope and possibility.

As I watch the city below, the darkness inside begins to ebb. Ani's presence beside me is a balm for my soul. Maybe I can overcome this internal prison after all. Maybe I can be brave enough to step outside my comfort zone and experience the world beyond my walls. Maybe her light can defeat my darkness.

"I like the way you furnished it," Ani says, leaving the window for the first time and assessing her surroundings.

"You can thank my sister for that. Athena is the Godwin designer. We don't even bother to try to argue or go against her vision."

"You must be glad she's on your side. From what I know of your sister, she'd win a fight against the Devil himself."

"Sometimes her bark is worse than her bite, but yes. I'm glad she's on my side."

Ani grins and surveys the rest of the room. She admires the furniture and the art pieces, noting the details and craftsmanship.

"It's like a little palace," she says.

I smile at her remark, but I feel a twinge of sadness. It is a place where I can hide from the world and shield myself from all the ugly realities that come with living life on the outside.

Ani crosses over to one of my favorite paintings, an abstract landscape Athena picked up in Paris a few years ago. Its vibrant colors and unique style never fail to captivate me. My sister understands art, and she understands me. She knew it would be the perfect fit. I find it fascinating that it's the first piece Ani goes to observe.

"It's beautiful." Her voice is filled with admiration.

"It is." My eyes never leaving the painting. "My sister chose it, and it's always been one of my favorites."

Ani turns away from the artwork and looks at me, a gentle smile playing on her lips. I think she's sensing how much this place means to me.

"It's like your safe haven," she says softly.

I nod, my throat suddenly tight.

"It is," I whisper. "It's where I come when I need to escape the chaos and find peace from Olympus. It's a break from... memories."

Ani returns to my side, takes my hand in hers, and squeezes it gently. Her touch is warm and comforting, and the approaching darkness takes a huge step back.

My phone vibrates in my pocket, and I know who it is without even having to see. "The bedroom is down that hallway." I point as I pull out the phone.

ALTA HENSLEY

"Why don't you go and settle in. Make yourself at home. I need to take this call."

I wait until Ani is halfway down the hall and getting out of earshot to answer. When I hear the bedroom door close, I say into the phone, "Hello, Athena. Couldn't give me ten minutes before checking in?"

"Who's the woman?" she asks.

Leave it to my sister and her intensive intel. I don't say anything to mostly tease her. It's just a matter of time until she'd find out the answer on her own.

"I know you flew in the helicopter. I know you are at the penthouse. And I know you arrived with some mysterious woman. Who the fuck is she?"

I still don't answer.

"Phoenix! This is serious. Have you run a background check on her? Had her sign an NDA? Who the fuck is this chick?"

"Ani Parker," I answer.

"Daphne's sister?" I hear her deep inhale. "Are you fucking her?"

I don't answer, but I think my silence is answer enough.

"Holy shit. I figured you to be a eunuch or something. Damn." She pauses. "So is it just fucking or something more?"

I'm not ready for this talk. I'm not ready to share Ani yet. I've liked keeping her all to myself.

Not waiting for an answer, Athena asks, "Does

she know what that means? The Godwin family is like a thorny vine that is not going to ever let her go."

"Ani and I will be staying here for a bit," I say.

"Can you trust her?" Athena asks.

"As much as you can trust anyone." I struggle not to say what I really want to. Yes. Yes, I can trust her.

"Okay… Phoenix?"

"Yes?"

"Are you happy? Right this second, are you happy?"

"I don't know what happy feels like to say yes. But I'm feeling something," I confess. "Something different than I've ever felt before."

CHAPTER
THIRTY

Ani

I shouldn't have brought them—the journals—but I couldn't leave them behind when Phoenix told me to pack my bags for Seattle. I have been reading them almost every night. I have developed a sort of kinship with Freya. I understand her, and through her words, I now truly understand Phoenix. He comes from the same level, if not more, of darkness I do. So much childhood pain. So much pressure from his father to be perfect. So much yelling, shouting, threats of everyone's lives. Poor Freya was miserable. And from all the passages I read in the journals, it sounds like every member of the family is just the same.

Medusa Enterprises and Poseidon Industries are empires built on shattered souls. Skulls of their enemies are the bricks to the buildings.

The Godwins ranging from Troy's branch of the tree to his two other brothers are toxic. The family tree is full of poison. And the island they own—Heathens Hollow—is the belly of hell. I have always thought the Eastside is the worst part of the island, but in fact the Eastside is simply poor. Hades truly rained down fire on the wealthy who reside here. So many secrets. So many torrid tales. And Freya knew them all.

When I met every Godwin at Daphne's wedding, I felt so much less. I felt like a stain in their pool of pure white. But after everything I've read, I realize Phoenix is like me. He's so much like me.

I can hear him on the phone in the living room and decide to take this time to read a little as I wait. My nerves are shot since Phoenix told me to get dressed and we walked out the door of Olympus. I should be ecstatic that I'm being treated like a human again, but I am uneasy. My safe little bubble has been popped, and I'm back in the outside world. But at least I have the journals and Freya. Something from that bubble.

Dear Diary,

I thought about jumping off the cliff today. About jumping to the sea below and swimming with the mermaids. I want to see Poseidon for myself and pray he's a more forgiving God than the Gods I've been living with up until now.

But as I walked to the edge's cliff, Phoenix stood by my side, took my hand in his and said, "If you jump, we jump."

I was taught to never take life lightly, and here was my son offering his own. We stood there, just looking at each other with his offer hanging in the air. It felt like a choice between two worlds, between two lives. I wanted to take his hand and jump into the unknown together, to save him from his own darkness. Maybe we could find light together. But something else held me back.

I'd like to say it was because I was a good mother. But it wasn't. It was fear.

Fear of the unknown and fear of what we might find on the other side. So, I stepped away from the cliff, and with tears in my eyes, told him no. I wanted to keep him safe, even if that meant condemning us both to the same fate.

As I walked away, I saw something out of the corner of my eye. It was a dark figure shrouded in shadows staring out our bedroom window, laughing. Troy. He seemed to be mocking me for my decision, like he knew I was afraid.

I quickly looked away, not wanting to make eye contact. But his silent laughter swirled around me as Phoenix and I made our way back home.

As we walked, I couldn't shake off the feeling of impending doom. It felt like Troy's presence was always looming, always watching, always waiting for the right moment to strike. I knew he was a part of Phoenix's past, a part of his darkness, and I wonder if he was the reason why Phoenix had offered to jump with me. Was he trying to escape his own demons?

Once we were back home, I sat Phoenix down and had a serious conversation with him. I told him that I couldn't let him throw his life away, that I loved him, and I would always be there for him, no matter what. But I also told him that he needed to face his own demons head-on, to confront them and overcome them.

I was a hypocrite.

He looked at me with tears in his eyes and whispered, "I don't know if I can do it, Mom. I'm scared."

I hugged him tightly and whispered back, "I know, my son. I know. But we'll face it together."

As we sat there, holding each other, I felt nothing but dread. Because I knew that Troy wasn't going to just disappear. He was a part of Phoenix's life, and he would always be there, lurking in the shadows, waiting for his chance to strike.

I didn't jump from the cliff that day...

Hearing Phoenix approaching the room, I quickly hide the journals among my belongings and try to steady my breathing. It is a bad idea to read the journal knowing it could be something dark and even sinister. But this... fuck. Poor Phoenix. Poor

Freya. Jesus Christ. How could anyone survive that life?

"Did you settle in okay?" he asks as he enters the room. He crosses over to me, moves a strand of my hair, and examines my face. "What's wrong? You look pale?"

I see worry in his eyes as he towers over me. "I'm fine. Really. I think I just got a little airsick on the ride over." It's not a lie, I actually did get queasy. "But I feel fine now."

Phoenix's eyes blaze as he scans my body from head to toe. "Could you be pregnant?"

Hearing the question makes my heart stop. Could I be? Maybe. But I doubt it. Other than feeling a bit ill on the helicopter ride, I don't have any other symptoms. "I don't think so. It was just the trip." I smile. "Don't worry."

"I'll always worry." He reaches out to touch my belly. "I can't wait to see you when you're carrying my baby." His voice is low; a tremor of anticipation trickles along my spine.

My face heats, and I look away, earning a caress of my ass, from his beefy hand, lifting the fabric of my dress. His mouth closes on my neck, teeth grazing my skin as he sucks.

"Take off your dress," Phoenix orders.

I fumble with the buttons at the front of my dress, and he reaches out to take over. He moves his hands slowly and deliberately, like he's savoring the

273

moment. When his fingers brush my skin as he unfastens each button, goosebumps rise on my arms.

I breathe a sigh of relief as the dress slips from my shoulders and puddles in folds of fabric at my feet.

When Phoenix leans forward to kiss me, it seems like a natural thing to do. I haven't kissed many men, but even if I had, I think I'd be hard pressed to find a man better at it than Phoenix.

I fling my arms around his neck, and he kisses me hungrily, like he can't get enough of me. He strokes my body, exploring every inch of my skin. I pull one of his hands to my breast, and his thumb skims the sensitive peak. I gasp at the pleasure, and he takes it as a sign to deepen our kiss. His tongue slips between my lips, and the pleasure radiates from my very core.

We lose track of time, our kiss slowly intensifying until we are both breathless. He pulls back and looks into my eyes, a satisfied smirk playing on his lips.

"I think I could spend eternity with you," he whispers, gazing into my eyes.

My heart swells, and I can't help but smile back. I reach up and pull his face to mine once more, and as our lips meet again, I know that I would, too.

"Could you live in the cave with the monster?" he asks.

"I like the monster," I say with a smirk. "I know he'll fight to the death for me."

Phoenix lifts the corner of his mouth and wraps

his arms around me. I nestle into his embrace, feeling the warmth of his body coursing through me.

"The monster likes you," he whispers, pressing a gentle kiss to my forehead. "So much so, he could devour you."

Phoenix takes my hands in his and our fingers interlace, sending shivers up and down my spine. "This is where we stay for now. Where no one can hurt us or take away what we have."

His words comfort me, and I relax into his embrace. In this moment, I know this is where I belong—with him, in this place of safety where nothing else matters.

With a deep breath, Phoenix presses his lips against mine and wraps his arms around me tightly. "I'm not going to leave this room without a fresh load of my cum in that sweet little pussy of yours." Phoenix's gravelly tone and the vulgar words cause a catch in my belly. Phoenix strokes hard fingers between my thighs as I watch him effortlessly rid himself of his own clothing. "I want you to smell who you belong to."

Once naked, with his erect cock on full display before me, he approaches, pulls me over toward the edge of the bed, and sits me on his lap.

Phoenix strokes my pussy's tender flesh. "So wet for me, so wet for what I have planned," he purrs with approval. "Are you sure you want to be fucked so soon? Are you sore from the last time?"

I nod, knowing he wants to know just how sore I am. "Yes. And yes, I'm sore."

He repositions me so I'm straddling his lap. He presses a hand onto the flat of my stomach as my hips grind against him in silent need, like my sex is an offering to a god.

I need him like I need air to live. My nipples bead as he takes hold of my breasts, and I ache to be claimed.

The large head of Phoenix's cock enters me without preamble, thrusting into my core, where my flesh is far more sore and swollen from Phoenix's prior fucking than I expected. I gasp in surprised discomfort, focusing on accepting his girth. He holds my hips still with his big palms until my enflamed muscles accept his thick presence. Then he thrusts again as his eyes lock with mine.

"This pussy belongs to me. I will never allow you to leave me. Never."

Even the thought of leaving this man gives me a pang of sadness, but I quickly shake away the emotion as Phoenix thrusts deeper inside, his balls slapping up against me.

He then leans toward me and presses his lips to mine as he presses even deeper with each movement, grinding his hips against me, until I feel stretched. Full.

"Do you like how my cock spreads you?" Phoenix asks when he breaks away from the kiss. His voice in my ear is a gritty caress, a velvet growl, as he moves his hands over my breasts, then nipples, pinching tightly. I desperately want so much more. I have a hunger that makes me wonder if it can possibly ever be satiated.

"Yes." I do. My whole body comes alive under the power of his words and body. Phoenix grinds in deeper as he palms my breasts.

"Do you want me to spread both holes? Tell me." Phoenix's voice holds a devil's smile, but there is a question there, like he wants to be sure I like his aggression, and that I truly am giving myself to him and it isn't all take.

I do. I have never had a need so strong before. His dominance beckons, as if I can hear his masculine blood pulse beneath his flesh. A drumbeat demanding I march along. I can't think, just arch my back and press my hips downward, seeking more of Phoenix, wanting to pull him deeper into my core.

He pinches a nipple, making me jerk under his hand. "Do you want me in your ass while I fuck you there until you scream?" His voice is insistent; his breath runs along the sensitive hairs on my neck as he speaks.

Him never letting up in his assault has my mind spinning and my body humming along to the rhythm of his fucking.

"Yes," I moan.

"Tell me." Phoenix's teeth close around the sensitive skin of my earlobe. "Tell me you want my cock. You'll like it when I fuck you in the ass with it.

Tell me you want my cum inside your ass and then feeling it drip down to your pussy."

I'm panting now, my pussy leaking wetness around Phoenix's dick.

"Tell me. Tell me you want it bad."

"Yes, I... I want it." My stomach convulses again at his low hum of satisfaction. "I like your big cock." I gasp, reveling in the spikes of pleasure that shoot straight to the sensitive nub between my thighs as the filthy words leave my mouth. "Please fuck me in the ass so I can feel your cum seep out of me."

He lets out a long-satisfied groan at my words and thrusts even deeper, spreading me wide.

He brings something out of me I've never known before. A part of me I never had the chance to experience. He has shown me the salacious, raw woman inside who asks for what I want, and like it.

"Say it again." Phoenix's voice is a growl.

I answer with a ferocious growl of my own. "I want you to fuck me hard." I've never felt so powerful as when Phoenix swells within me. I look into his dark, lust-filled eyes and add, "Take me in the ass. Claim me there." I thrust downward, clenching my internal muscles around his cock, waiting for him to give me what I so desperately need.

He roars as I clamp down on him like a vise, and then he pulls out of me roughly. He lies on his back and positions me so I straddle his body, placing the tip of his cock at my tight back entrance.

"This will hurt," Phoenix warns.

"Yes!" I pant. God, I want it to hurt. I want to feel the pain.

He grunts, surging forward, holding me immobile so I can adjust to the size of his dick stretching my ass. I want to scream, to moan, to beg for him to stop, but at the same time, I want to beg for him to begin. Wave after wave of conflicting emotion and feelings wash over me. Pain versus pleasure. Submission versus resistance.

Phoenix eases past my puckered entrance, thrusting slowly, setting a tempo for our bodies to follow. In and out, back and forth, he fluidly controls my body. The pressure, the fullness, the bite—so much that I have no choice but to succumb fully to his control. I release everything to him and truly become a slave to his mastery.

"Harder," I say, pressing down, while Phoenix pulls slowly out of me, only to have him thrust in once again. "Fuck me harder."

"Say it again," Phoenix demands.

"Harder."

"You're mine," Phoenix announces, followed by a deep and guttural moan.

He pulls my face down and places his lips firmly on mine. His tongue twirls as my heart soars.

He then moves rough and fast, pumping furiously until I feel the hot jets of his climax deep within, and a screaming release tears through me, leaving me shaking and gasping for air. My quivering walls milk him dry while we both regain our composure. A warm heat flows through my veins. He holds me, preventing me from collapsing fully while he keeps his cock still firmly implanted inside of me.

I can't speak, not that I would know what to say if I could. The smell of sex mixes with the room's thick silence. Even though we are physically joined as one, we are distant and deep within our own selves. Pleasured, replete, satiated, and yet... there seems to be a sense of longing cast over our intertwined bodies. His seed flows through me, but at the same time, I feel more confused than ever before.

Have we made a baby yet?

Is a part of the monster inside me?

I must have fallen asleep because when I wake, I'm spooned up against him in the bed as normal couples would after lovemaking. Legs are entwined, arms are heavy as they possessively hold me close. My back is to Phoenix's warm chest, and my breasts are held in his hand. I have never felt more comforted and safe in my life.

His heavy breathing as he sleeps seems to blend with mine. Our heartbeats seem to beat as one. Little space separates us as flesh morphs into a single body.

I can picture this as my future.

Always in his arms. Always his to be held.

"You're beautiful," Phoenix murmurs against my ear.

I don't tense or wonder what will come next. I don't fear this man but feel a level of satisfaction and contentment that I will never be able to put into words. My body hums, and I have never felt more alive or free in my entire life as I lie trapped in his arms.

There is so much I want to say, but I don't want to break this bubble of euphoria. I want this single moment to last forever.

"Go to sleep, dove," Phoenix says as he clears the little bit of space that separates us to kiss me on the neck. So gentle. So loving. So... everything I could ever want. "Sleep."

CHAPTER
THIRTY-ONE

Ani

The next time I wake, a single ray of sunshine penetrates the fog surrounding the apartment and illuminates the room. I don't know how it has happened, but somehow, the tiny splinter of light has made me feel warm. When I realize why, I feel a sudden surge of emotion. Phoenix's broad frame is draped behind me, holding me close as he sleeps.

The larger-than-life figure makes me feel small, and so secure in his embrace that I can hardly move. I feel his every breath, inhale his aroma, and feel like I could drift in and out of sleep for a lifetime. But then his body presses against mine, and I realize it's impossible to doze off any longer. His skin is soft against my own, and I hold my breath to keep from giving away that I'm awake. I lie there for what feels like an eternity, until finally his breathing slows, and he releases a heavy sigh. I'd stay here forever, in his arms and surrounded by his scent, but eventually I muster up the courage to slide away.

I look up at him, watching him sleep peacefully, and somehow I know that nothing ever felt as right as being in his arms.

"Come back to bed," he mumbles, not opening his eyes, fooling me in making me believe he was asleep.

"I was going to start breakfast."

"It can wait. Bed now."

Knowing that I'll spend a lifetime following the commands of this man, I crawl into bed and back into his arms.

The feel of Phoenix's morning erection pushing against my butt is far more delightful than eggs and bacon. His hips start rocking and grinding against me, arousing desire in my soul. I hook my leg over his, giving us a temporary bond.

He slides his callused hand up to cup my breast. His gentle touch leaves me wanting more, so when he pinches my nipple, I murmur encouragement. His grip gets stronger as he moves to my other tit.

Not knowing how much time we have before he retraces his steps, I reach back and slide my hand between my butt and his hardness, rubbing him through his boxer briefs until his hips start thrusting in an unmistakable rhythm. His breath quickens just as I grope for his unencumbered cock, pulling down his boxers to free him from any restraint. Phoenix's fingers travel down my chest and slip to my bare pussy. I want him to come closer to me, but his actions suggest something different. Instead, he slides his hand around and grabs a cheek of my ass in each hand while pushing his hips forward. His cock is hard against me, and it pulses with anticipation.

He moves his mouth to my ear and whispers, "More?"

I answer yes without a moment's hesitation, my body tingling with anticipation as he rubs himself against me. His kiss starts gentle and slow, but soon picks up in intensity as our bodies move together in perfect unison.

Slowly, he slides inside me inch by inch until we are both groaning with pleasure thanks to being so deeply connected. He continues gripping my ass as our hips thrust in harmony. The heat between us is almost unbearable as we reach the height of passion together.

He removes one hand from my ass to stroke my hair softly while I moan in pleasure from the intense connection that only comes from being so close to another person during sex. Our breathing becomes labored before finally slowing down as we descend from our high together and collapse into an exhausted embrace.

We lie there for a while afterward, not wanting the moment to end just yet before reality sets back in. Finally, Phoenix pulls away after giving me one last lingering kiss on the forehead, getting up without saying a word as though he doesn't want to break the spell between us.

I lie there a few moments longer, basking in the afterglow of our passionate encounter.

Eventually, I force myself to get out of bed, my body still filled with pleasure and intensity.

"Can I ask you a question?" I begin as I watch him pull on a pair of gray sweats, his chest bare, muscled and delicious.

He turns to face me, an eyebrow raised.

"Why do you call me dove?"

"Because of a story my mother used to tell me," he begins. "The Phoenix wasn't just a bird but a creature of fire and fury, who had lived for hundreds of years, but had never known the joy of true love. Then one day, the Phoenix's eyes fell upon the delicate form of a turtle dove. She was small and pure, with feathers as white as snow, and the Phoenix knew that it had found its soulmate.

The two birds flew together to a hidden corner of the forest and built a nest as their home. Here they were able to bask in their love, despite the mocking of other birds who did not understand their devotion. The Phoenix's burning wings were a stark contrast to the turtle dove's soft feathers, and they were a beautiful sight to behold, like two flames united in perfect harmony. No matter what those around them said, their love was strong, and nothing could ever come between them.

But as the Phoenix's life drew to a close, it knew that its death would come soon. All it could think of was the love it had for its beloved turtle dove, and the thought of living without its love was unbearable. In an act of selfless devotion, the turtle dove chose to die and join the Phoenix in the afterlife. When the Phoenix rose from its ashes, so too did the turtle dove, and they were reunited in a new life."

I gaze into Phoenix's eyes and can feel the intensity radiating from his soul.

"That's a powerful story," I murmur.

"It is," he replies softly. "It's a testament to the power of unyielding devotion and eternal love. It tells us that even when the Phoenix passes away, it still remains with its beloved turtle dove in each new life, and that kind of love will never die."

"It's tragic, though," I whisper, tears glistening in my eyes. "The Phoenix dies."

He nods gravely. "Yes, it is a tragedy, but it's also a symbol of the cycle of life and death, and of the power of true love that transcends time and space."

"But you haven't truly answered my question," I say. "Why call *me* dove?"

"I call you dove because you are the one who completes me. The one I am willing to die for, the one I am reborn for." He takes my hand, his gaze burning into mine with passionate intensity.

My heart swells with emotion at his words.

I don't know how long this softness will last, as

Phoenix burns cold just as quickly, but I'll take it and relish it while I can.

I get out of bed, wrap my arms around his neck, and press myself closer to him so I can kiss him deeply. His lips are warm and inviting as our tongues meet in a passionate dance. We linger in our embrace, exploring each other's souls with our lips.

The intensity of the moment is too powerful to ignore, and my heart opens to him like never before.

He holds me tightly against his chest, and I melt into him, feeling like I have returned home after a long journey. Maybe it's too good to be true to believe that we can conquer any challenge that comes our way and live out our days in blissful harmony, but I want to tell myself that. I want to believe it's possible.

"I love you," I whisper softly against his cheek.

The words hang in the air between us—frozen.

Did he hear me?

Maybe he did and doesn't feel the same.

I wait. And I wait. But I don't hear the words in return.

I have to change this. I have to fix this. I can't let those words break what we're building. Trying to pretend I never said them to begin with, I blurt out, "I need you. I need to feel you inside me again, and again, and again."

Return to the sex. Return to the part of our relationship I understand. The part of us that works effortlessly.

Phoenix takes me in his arms, pressing my body to his as he kisses me deeply. I feel the warmth of his lips as they move against mine, taking me on a journey of pleasure and passion. His hands are gentle yet insistent as they explore my curves, eliciting delicious moans from deep within me.

His kisses are hot against my neck, and he lowers me back to the bed as he moves down my body, exploring every inch of me. I melt into the sheets as pleasure washes over me. His touch is pure ecstasy as he brings me closer to the edge of pure bliss.

My heart rate quickens as I become lost in the sensation, wanting nothing more than to be with him forever in this moment. Our tongues dance together in perfect harmony; each movement takes us further down the path of desire and passion.

"May I please suck your cock?"

"Yes," he says with a grin. I lift my body from his so that I'm kneeling between his legs. But when I realize he isn't going to open them up to allow me access, I pivot to look over at him. "Straddle my chest. I want to look at your ass and wet pussy while you suck my dick."

I feel myself blush with each lascivious command he gives me. So, I do as he asks, placing my leg over his body as I turn around and sit down. Now, he's able to feel the wetness that's started between my legs. Leaning forward, I then kiss the tip of his penis.

"No, start with my balls," he commands, making me lean further forward until his cock is pressed against his abdomen and I'm holding his testicles in my other hand.

The moment my tongue flicks out to lick him, I feel his hands on my butt cheeks. I stop suddenly to see what his next command will be.

I flick my tongue out again and begins to stroke along the smooth and velvety skin of his scrotum, rolling his testicles around in my grip. They're heavy and full, so as I take one into my mouth and start gently sucking on it, rolling it around in my mouth, he lets out a groan of contentment. Using my other hand I continue to stroke up and down the length of his shaft while squeezing lightly at times as I release the one testicle and switch over to suckle its twin into my mouth.

"Rim me."

A sharp slap to my butt startles me, but I resist the urge to stand; instead, I lift my ass higher and my ponytail slides over my shoulder to caress his groin. I stick out my tongue and trace the incredibly sensitive skin between his scrotum and his anus. His cock twitches in my hand as I again lick the area before carefully exploring the rim of his anus. I open and close my mouth, unable to form words as Phoenix pushes a finger into my butt. His grip tightens around my waist, keeping me from sitting up.

"You're such a naughty girl, aren't you?" His voice fills the room.

I smile and turn away, lowering my head again.

"Yes, yes, I am," I confess before taking another swift lick.

My tongue is tireless as I glide over his skin, savoring and delighting in his body. He starts to probe my rectum with his finger, and my delicate nether area contracts in response to the forbidden act. I don't stop, despite society's expectations of what a 'good girl' should do. I circle my tongue around his puckered hole one last time before being ordered to move back up to his penis. I pause for a moment, allowing his finger to further penetrate me, as I position myself for another nibble on his testicles. He teases me for not jumping into place quickly enough, so I press my lips against his opening and give it a final kiss before sliding his shaft into my mouth.

"Go ahead. I want you to thrust yourself onto my fingers as you suck my member." For a split second, I think I have misheard him, but the fingers re-enter to be certain of the command. I shiver a bit and submit, moaning softly as his digits penetrate deeply. Dropping my head, I open my mouth and let him glide in his head. With my tongue, I spread his pre-cum over the top, then suckle it while moving one hand up and down with the other cupping his slick testicles, giving them a gentle roll.

Phoenix grabs my hair, pulls me away from him, and flips me over as I land on the bed. Knowing what's coming, I hang my head off the edge of the mattress and lift my ass in the air.

"Ask for it," he says, his eyes piercing mine.

"Please," I whisper. He stands behind me, and I sense the cap coming off a bottle. The familiar sensation of lube being poured onto my skin follows, and I prop myself up on my elbows so I can look back at Phoenix, who is sitting in a chair and stroking his manhood.

"Are you sure?" he asks again, looking intently at me.

"Yes." My voice trembles slightly.

THIRTY-TWO

Ani

My anticipation is almost unbearable as I feel Phoenix's fingers slide between my legs, slick with my arousal. He pushes them deep, scissoring inside me as I moan uncontrollably, widening my tight opening in anticipation of what is to come. His cockhead presses against my back entrance, and I tense as I wait for him to take me, knowing he won't exceed my limits.

"Yes," I beg, desperate for his possession. "Take me. Take my ass."

"Good girl," he growls. "Push back and open yourself. Let me in."

I obey, feeling the intensity of the moment crushing around me like the heat of a furnace. His fingers create a steady rhythm of pleasure that loosens my muscles enough for him to enter me. I cry out as he pushes deep, claiming me as his own with a possessive thrust. My breath catches as he presses his hardness against my entrance. I cry out as he plunges deep, pushing through my tightness. His fingers dig painfully into the soft skin of my neck, forcing me to stay still, no matter how much I want to resist.

"Oh God! Oh God!" I chant as Phoenix hammers into me, pleasure and pain blending into an overwhelming sensation that nearly makes me faint.

His thrusts become increasingly rough, each one driving deeper than the last. He doesn't let up until his entire length is sheathed inside me, and finally he stills, pressing himself to the hilt until his balls slap against my pussy. I am filled with a terror that is strangely exhilarating—an intense awareness of how powerless I am in this moment and how truly owned I am by Phoenix's relentless desire. His every move claims me in a way that is indescribable.

He ravages me, his fingers digging into my ass, his palm striking against my skin, each moment of connection further driving me to the ultimate height of pleasure I have ever experienced. I am no longer just a woman. I am an entity of pure pleasure, writhing beneath him, my nipples hardening, my hips rising to meet his relentless pounding. He entwines his fingers in my hair, yanking my head back, and leans down to devour my mouth with his own. His teeth catch onto my lower lip, tugging it before moving up to nip the flesh of my neck and shoulder. Each sharp sensation amplifying my insatiable craving for more.

"Harder! Oh God, yes, harder!" The need is uncontrollable, threatening to consume me from within. He brings his free hand between my legs and his fingers clamp around my clit while he thrusts three fingers deep inside me.

"I'm coming!" I scream without a second thought as the waves of pleasure reverberate through me.

My body shudders, and a liquid heat drenches me as he continues to pound into me. His roar fills my ears as he slams inside me, pumping his seed deep into my core with every rock of his hips. For the first time in my life, I see explosions of light behind my eyes as I quiver beneath him, feeling his cock still twitching within me, and oh God... the bliss refuses to abate as he continues to tease my clit with every thrust. I still keep coming.

"Phoenix!" I choke out, the intensity of my emotions tearing me apart. My vision blurs, and my body shake as he wraps his arms around me. I'm gasping, my back arching in ecstasy as he holds me close and whispers in my ear.

I'm coming so much. So much wetness. So wet. So fucking wet, and with each wave, blackness takes over until I see nothing but darkness.

I open my eyes to find myself cradled on his lap, Phoenix gazing down at me with a satisfied smirk.

"What did you do to me?" I ask breathlessly, my heart pounding in my ears.

"I gave you la petite mort... the little death, my dove. You are now reborn." He leans down to capture my lips in a passionate kiss.

My body trembles as I recall my last memory before waking, the indescribable pleasure that had left me mute in its wake.

"That was so fucking hot, Ani," Phoenix growls. "Your ass around my cock. It was the hottest, softest velvet, yet powerful as a vise when you squirted."

"The bed is soaked," I mumble, embarrassed.

He pulls me back and looks me in the eyes. "It won't be the last time." He tilts up my chin. "You let yourself go. I fucking loved it." He presses his lips against my forehead. "And then you fainted in pure ecstasy."

"I'm sorry," I whisper.

He shakes his head and tightens his grip on me. "Don't be sorry. It was the most amazing thing I have ever experienced, and I can't wait to make it happen again."

I melt into him, accepting the truth in his words. Yes, I have given him not only my body, but my trust, which has set me free to bask in pleasure without inhibition.

I died in his arms and have been reborn like the phoenix rather than the dove.

The raw desire inside me has me repeating the words I said a short time ago. "I love you."

And just like before... silence.

But this time it doesn't hurt. It doesn't sting. I speak my truth just as my body has.

He tenses but doesn't let go of me, and for now I'll accept.

I'm not a fool to believe the darkness has left him, but right now, all I feel is light.

THIRTY-THREE

Ani

I think I fucked up. Actually, I *know* I fucked up.

Ever since I declared my love for Phoenix, he seems so distant. He's reminding me of the brick wall of a man he was at the manor. I had felt that each brick was slowly being removed, but with three deadly words, I have rebuilt the impenetrable structure.

"The sea," Phoenix says after my evening belting that he's still doing even though we have been staying in the penthouse for two days now. "It's a reminder of the power of the gods. Of Poseidon, the ruler of the seas."

He turns to me, and I can see the intensity in his eyes. "Do you know the story of Poseidon?"

I shake my head, not sure where he's going with

this. He's been so sullen lately I'm cautious and feel as if I'm walking on eggshells.

"Poseidon was a god among men," Phoenix continues. "A ruler of the seas, and a master of the earth. He was feared and respected by all. But he was also a jealous god, and he would do anything to protect his power and his kingdom."

My sense of unease grows as he speaks. It's like he's not just talking about a mythological god, but about himself.

"Poseidon would stop at nothing to protect what was his." Phoenix's voice is low and menacing. "And that's what I'll do, Ani. I'll protect what's mine, at any cost."

My heart races as he speaks. He's not just talking about the sea, or about Poseidon. He's talking about me.

"You should be carrying my baby by now," he blurts. "It's been a month since we started, and something tells me that you're with my child."

It's as if ice cold water has been thrown on my quivering body. My heart freezes as my knees buckle, and I fall to the floor. I look up into Phoenix's stunned face with wide eyes and shake my head in denial.

Baby.

I don't want to think about having a baby.

His baby.

Every time I do, it makes me panic. It's too real. Too...

A baby will bring us back into reality.

With furrowed brow, he kneels down and takes my hand in his. "What's wrong? Are you sick?" The concern on his face is foreign, and I take a moment to absorb a new element of the man I long to know more about.

"I'm not sick." I can't breathe normally, and my body grows clammy.

Phoenix wipes a loose strand of hair from my face and places his palm on my forehead. "What's going on, Ani? Do you need a doctor?" He pulls my shivering body against his and cradles me.

"What happens then?" I ask in a whisper. "When I do have your baby?"

"Once you're pregnant, I'll start making plans to move you out of state to one of my properties to have you carry the baby with the best medical staff at your disposal."

His words confuse me. Why would he want to leave Seattle? And if not staying in Seattle, why not Heathens Hollow? "Why would you have us leave the state? Where?"

"Just you for now," he says.

"Wait. What?"

"You'll raise the baby and be very well cared for. You won't be trapped away in this penthouse or manor anymore. I'm sure you can't wait to be able to truly be free and be out in the sunlight where you belong."

His words aren't making any sense. He's been

using words of possession when it comes to me. He says I'm his. He says *forever*. He hasn't hidden his control over me in the slightest. Why would he even think of sending me away? "Why won't I stay with you?"

Phoenix surprises me when he kisses the top of my head and still holds me securely in his arms. "You paid your penance and then some." He kisses my head again. "If you stay here, my family will swallow you up and spit you out. I won't have that for you or for my baby. And if the secret ever gets out about what you, Apollo, and your sister did... I want you far away where you can't be found."

"I don't understand."

"This has been the plan all along. You paid for your crimes. You are giving me the baby. You've done more than enough."

"So you want me to go into hiding? Where?" A deep wave of grief attacks every part of my being. I have no idea why. I should want to be free from the penthouse, the manor, and free from my constant punishments. Once I have the baby, I would have paid for my lies, my sister's lies, and what we did, and this all can stop.

"I'll make sure your housing and financial needs are always met. No baby of mine will ever be without or ever be in danger. Luxury and comfort will be yours. I will take part in raising our child, of course." Even though he says the last part, there is something in the way he says the words that seem...

302

uncomfortable. As if he doesn't know what being part of raising a child really entails.

"But what if I don't want that?" I say as I tilt my head so I can look up at him.

"Don't want what?" His eyes darken. "Would you rather go to jail? You don't exactly have a lot of options here, Ani. I hope you aren't stupid enough to think you can fuck with—"

"What if I don't want to leave here?" I swallow hard. "To leave you."

Phoenix recoils as if I have just slapped his face. "What are you talking about? Of course you want to leave here."

I shake my head. "No. I don't."

Phoenix shoots to his feet, and his concern is quickly replaced with fury. "Have you lost your mind? You are about to be free. No more captivity. No more punishments."

"But also"—I sniff as the tears finally fall from my eyes—"no more you. At least not in the same way. Not the way I had grown accustomed to having you. And I don't want that."

"You don't know what you're talking about," he snaps. He shakes his head. "Of course you want to leave here. What person in their right mind would want to stay?"

"Me. I want to stay. To stay here with you. I don't want it to change. Baby or not."

"Ani."

"Is that so wrong?" I move myself into the

kneeling position I know Phoenix likes me to assume. "I don't want to leave you. You said I was a bad girl. You saw that in my soul the minute you laid your eyes on me, and you were right. I am bad. I have bad thoughts and bad needs. But with you, I feel like all the bad thoughts are realized and experienced. I feel safe with you and comforted in your hands, no matter how firm they are. You called me a pain slut, and maybe you're correct in that as well. I do like it. I love it."

"Your new submissive tendencies don't need to be constantly explored. You don't have to be here to know that sexual side of yourself." He says the words between clenched teeth. "I can't understand why you would want to stay here under these harsh elements that I created."

"Is it so odd that I would want to stay with you all the time?" I ask.

"I'll still be in your life," he says. "You'll have my baby, after all. I won't go too long without checking in."

"But not daily. Not often, right?"

"I can't have you here. Living with me. Not forever."

His words hurt. I don't like reality. I don't want reality.

"Why not? Why can't you open yourself up to the idea of changing your life for... me and the baby?"

"That wasn't the plan," he says quickly.

"I know, but can't we at least sit down and talk? About our future?"

Hope replaces the sadness in my heart. My idea seems like a good one and one that maybe Phoenix will consider.

"You have no idea what type of world I live in." Phoenix goes over to the window and looks out, leaving me staring at his broad shoulders and strong posture that only makes me crave to be in his arms once again. "I'm here by choice. It's what I do. Who I am. But this isn't you. You belong beyond these walls."

"But you aren't asking me what I want?" I am being far more daring and bolder than I would have ever done before, but I have to fight. I have to do something. Phoenix will slip between my fingers if I don't do everything I can to stay with him once the baby comes.

"I know what being a Godwin means," he answers. "It isn't safe for you or the baby to be caught in the web of this family. Yes, the baby will be born a Godwin, but he or she will be protected by me until they are strong enough to battle without my shield."

"But don't you think we'd be safer with you at all times?"

"That's not part of the plan. Part of my life is that I always stick to the plan," he says, still staring out the window.

"But can't we alter it just a bit?" I counter. "There

is so much I don't know about you, but I do know that there is some sort of connection between us. There is something deep inside of us that deserves exploring. Yes, you awoke sexual desires I never knew before, but I know there is more than that. Tell me that I am wrong. Am I nothing more than just a woman who is paying her penance for lying to you? Have I misread you completely?"

"I don't know you," he says as he turns to face me. "Not beyond these walls."

"You know more about me than anyone ever has before. The real me. You have stripped me naked from the inside out. You said I was yours. I am. I truly am."

"This conversation is over. The sooner you wrap your head around what will be expected, the better."

"No!" I scream. "I won't. For your plan to work, you need me to agree. Once I'm not a prisoner, you won't have full control, and you know it. So no, I won't be cast off to raise the baby alone with occasional paternal visits. I won't do it."

I stand up and charge toward him. I am completely out of control, but the thought of being forced to leave him is far worse than the thought of staying and whatever discipline he will issue for my outburst.

"And I know something happened to you as a child," I add. "I know something happened to your entire family to make you be this way. I found journals by your mother. I read them. I read about you and everything your family experienced. And I don't judge you, Phoenix! I understand you. I feel you. Your black is my black. That abyss you swim in is the same murky waters I have. Don't you see that? Don't you see that there is more between us? I told you I loved you, and I fucking meant it!"

Phoenix meets my charge and takes hold of my shoulders to stop me. He then grabs my neck and squeezes. "Do you have a death wish? Have I taught you nothing? I told you to never mention my mother. And where are these fucking journals?"

"At the manor," I squeak. This is my first lie to Phoenix since my penance began. I don't know why I don't tell them they are in the next room, but I'm not ready to let them go. Not yet. Maybe they will help me figure out a way to soothe this beast before me.

"Don't ever try to understand my family. Never again."

"Why are you not listening to me?" I demand with wild eyes and fury building inside.

He squeezes my neck some more. He applies just enough pressure with his fingertips to make breathing difficult and to show me he is the one in control. "Because this is who I am. I'm a monster, not a husband. Don't try to picture me as a man that I'm not."

"I don't have to picture it. I feel it," I say with strangled breath. "You said yourself. You may be a natural monster, but I am a natural prey." His hold on my neck loosens. "I was just a poor girl from the

Eastside of Heathens Hollow. No connection other than with my sister, and even that in the last few years was distant. I was in an awful relationship and lived a miserable existence. Until you, Phoenix. Until you set me aflame with the things you did to my body. I felt alive while here. I don't want death. And that was exactly what my life was before you. Death. So please, Phoenix. Keep my soul alive. Don't allow my soul die. I want you to push past your boundaries and your thick walls."

His hand on my neck moves, and he once again grabs a fistful of my hair. I hiss as the sting intensifies, but as I am about to beg for more, Phoenix brings his lips down upon mine. Passion erupts as he presses his tongue inside my mouth and dances it within. A kiss from my captor. His breath merges with mine as our bodies come together and our kiss intensifies.

"You don't want this," he says between his claiming of my mouth.

"I do." I hold onto his shoulders, hoping to never let go. I hope desperately Phoenix will not force me to let go of the only thing—the only person—I want. I want this man and his attic.

Breaking the kiss but still holding me close, he says, "I'll think about it. That's all I can give you now."

Fresh tears cloud my vision as I stare into his stern expression. Defeated, I shake my head as I look at my bare feet and whisper, "It's not up to just you,

Phoenix. I've done everything you have asked, but our future needs my input as well. I ask you to consider that. Consider me. Not the prisoner. But me. Me."

Phoenix tilts my chin to make me look up at him and kisses me again softly but then nips at my lip. "I'll think on it. That's all I will say for now."

CHAPTER
THIRTY-FOUR

Phoenix

"Ani's losing her mind," I begin as Athena and I have just finished a meeting with our staff about moving from the Seattle penthouse. Ani is going to Spain, and me back to Olympus. They have their new orders, and I am confident all will run smoothly. I like the penthouse, but I'm uneasy, edgy, and my home is back at Olympus.

Ani is still asleep, exhausted from our fight last night, and I'm grateful to have a break from her pleading eyes. I have had a long talk with Athena, filling her in on everything. Even the murder. I know I can't keep her in the dark about everything. My sister will figure it out eventually, and I need her on my side to help fight off my father and the toxic world of Godwin hell. I don't want anyone knowing about Ani and the baby.

"We'll move her soon," Athena says. "I'm sure the walls are closing in on her."

"It's more than that."

Athena pauses, looks deep into the screen at me to study my face.

"Don't ask me how, but I think she's falling in love with me," I add.

Athena smirks and rolls her eyes. "I think *you* are losing *your* mind. Maybe the walls are closing in on you."

"Athena..." I run my fingers through my hair and sigh. "You're welcome to watch the video of our talk, but it wasn't pretty."

"Just tell me, and save me the time."

"She doesn't want to leave me. She said so. She wants a life with me and the baby."

Athena's eyes widen. "Baby? Is she pregnant?" She shakes her head.

"No guarantees but a high chance."

"Jesus Christ. I wouldn't have guessed this in a million years."

Baby. A baby... I can't believe I'm even having a discussion about a baby. About *my* baby.

Jesus, is this all really happening? The plan all seemed good at the beginning, but now that reality is kicking in, a surge of panic hits me hard.

"But this isn't about the baby. I really think she's in love with me."

Pushing back the thoughts of fatherhood to focus, I rise and pace the room, which often helps me process all my emotions.

"It's probably just hormones," Athena offers.

"No. It's more. You didn't talk to her. I did. She wants to stay with me. She doesn't want to leave Seattle without me."

"After what you just told me you did to her... That's insane. She should hate your guts."

I nod in agreement. "She should. She should want to fucking kill me." I look Athena square on. "But she doesn't. Far from it."

Athena is right, however. The thought *is* insane. Ani in love? How could this be? I essentially kidnapped her. Made her fear for her freedom and her sister's. Forced her into submission. Yes, it was clear she enjoyed much of the punishment, and her body came alive under my touch, but that was physical. How in the fuck could she be falling in love with me? How?

"It's that Stockholm syndrome shit or something." Athena nods as if she has just explained it all away. "I'm sure as soon as she's out of your grip, she'll want you dead and hate your very presence."

I nod slowly, taking in her answer. "Possibly."

"And it doesn't matter really," Athena adds as I sit down and study Ani in the monitor. The camera in our room is positioned on her and zoomed in perfectly.

God, she's beautiful as she sleeps. So angelic. So perfect. So...

Athena's words snap me out of my thoughts. "We continue as planned. If she's pregnant, we move her to a location away from Medusa, Poseidon, and all our other enemies. I've been looking into a villa in Madrid that looks like we could compound the hell out of it. It would be a good setting for her to stay during her pregnancy and should make her happy. I think keeping her there for nine months will be an okay amount of time, but we'll want to move her and the baby soon after. I don't like the idea of her staying in one place for a year. Considering you want to keep this quiet from Dad... Well, it won't be easy unless we keep her moving. Father is distracted with Medusa business, and you've never really been on his radar so—" She grimaces. "Sorry."

"Don't apologize. It's true." I shrug. I gave up hope a long time ago of ever having a close relationship with the powerful Troy Godwin.

"What about you? Are *you* ready to leave and return to Olympus?" Athena asks.

"Yeah, I am. I miss some of the comforts of the attic. Plus, I need to get back to the daily oversight of Medusa's security. I think there are some cracks forming we need to get sealed up."

"What about Ani? Are you ready to leave her?"

My stomach twists, and an inexplicable lump forms in the back of my throat. "The time together has been fun. I'm not going to deny that. The kinky sadist in me has been able to run free. There's a physical connection, for sure, but it's not like she'll ever be out of my life. She'll be carrying my baby. She's in my life, one way or the other."

"How often do you plan on seeing her in Spain?" Athena asks, but it's a question she already knows the answer to.

Not often enough.

"I need to get back to my life. Full time. You know this," I say.

Who am I trying to convince? Athena or myself?

Athena nods slowly. "But from what you are saying, it sounds like she wants to be part of that full-time life."

"Which is crazy. In a goddamn attic?"

"You don't need to choose the attic, Phoenix, and you know this."

"And you know what being a Godwin does to people. What it did to Mother," I say, to counter the idea of a happily ever after. "The last thing I want to see is Ani jumping to her death because she sealed her fate by marrying me. No one deserves that. No one."

"Our mother was different." Athena's jaw tightens as she spits out the words. "She was weak. She didn't have the strength to fight for our family."

"How do you know Ani isn't weak?"

Athena shrugs. "I don't, but I think you know just how strong Ani is. Otherwise we wouldn't even be having this conversation."

"True," I agree. "She's not weak."

"But even if you wanted this woman as your wife, there is no way to have that normal family where you come home at the end of the day to a homemade meal and family laughter like some suburban fantasy. It's just not who you are. Who any of us are."

"I don't know. It sure as hell looks like Apollo and Daphne are about to live that perfect white picket fence dream," I say.

Athena rolls her eyes. "Doubtful. But whatever. I couldn't care less if they do."

"Yeah, well... you are right. It's not who I am. It's not who I will ever be." I release a deep breath and return my attention to Ani asleep on the monitor. "Ani may think she knows what she wants. But she has no idea."

"Then stick to the plan."

"Ani said there are journals of Mother's at the house," I say. "I'm having the staff search for them."

"Why bother?" Athena shrugs.

"You aren't curious what's inside?"

"She's dead. Dead. Let's move on."

Picking up on her tone, I do just that. "I'll work on security in Madrid." I like that I now have something to focus on other than Ani and her idea of an impossibility.

"Fine, but let me ask you something first. Be honest," Athena says in a low voice. "Do you have feelings for Ani? Do you love her?"

I look back at the monitor, lean back in my chair,

and fight the urge to study every single curve of Ani's body, which I often do. "Yes." I run my hands through my hair. "Fuck."

Athena studies me and then says, "Fuck. Fuck. Fuck."

"It makes things messy. Complicated. And if she's carrying my baby, I think my feelings are only going to grow more for her."

"Spain," Athena says. "Distance. You need it. She needs it."

"It's the only way. I need to focus. Stay on course."

I sit back and continue to watch Ani sleep peacefully as my mind tells my heart lies.

Stay on course.

Stay on course.

CHAPTER
THIRTY-FIVE

Ani

I sit and watch Phoenix eat. Waiting for him to look up at me. Hoping that maybe just once he will acknowledge my presence in any way except to punish me. Is it possible for Phoenix to feel anything toward me? Can he ever be anything but an authoritative disciplinarian? Do I not have any hold of his heart at all?

I haven't had my period, and though I don't know for sure, there is a part of me that knows I can very well be pregnant. My time in the penthouse is limited. Once he knows I'm pregnant, this wicked game of keeping the princess locked away in the tower will be over. Reality will set in.

Though Phoenix and I share a connection, it's going to be hard to convince him of that. He has punished me several times, sometimes severely and other times with a lighter hand. He tolerates little and has zero patience. Some of the times are deserved for acting out due to boredom or raising hell because I feel like the walls of the penthouse are often closing in on me. But there are times that he will pull the belt from his pants and take it to me simply because he can.

Does he know how much I like it? I do. His dominance. His power. The bite of the leather against my flesh. The act of being punished nude before him. I love it all. Crave it even. Maybe it is my soul desiring the punishment for never being happier when I should be miserable. Or maybe it is simply the fuel I require to light the fire within. Regardless of why, I wait in anticipation for the next strike of his hand. But unlike with Mark, it's never on my face. Never any place that causes any *real* harm. Just my bare ass causing me to become instantly wet.

And then there are times he softens. He never punishes without soothing afterward. He takes his duty of aftercare seriously. He kisses, he holds me close, and cuddles me into his muscled chest while stroking my hair repeatedly. He bathes me and cares for me in ways I didn't know possible. The more Phoenix punishes, the more he loves. The yin and yang of his sadist self is more than I could ask for. These months at the manor, and now at the penthouse, are the most fulfilling relationships I have ever experienced.

I try my best not to think about the day I will have to leave him. If I bring it up in conversation, he bends me over and sears my behind. It is not to be spoken of in his presence. It is clear he had a mission. A plan.

Fighting back tears, I decide that I need to speak with Phoenix, even though it will result in punishment. "Phoenix," I say tentatively. "I was hoping I could discuss something with you." I have to act now. I need to bring it up in my own way before he shuts it down completely without any input from me.

He looks up from his meal with annoyance in his eyes. "No."

His sharp answer takes me by surprise, but I swallow back the lump in my throat and carry on. "Once I'm pregnant—"

He looks up at me with wide eyes. "Are you?"

"I don't know," I answer honestly. "But once I am—"

"My sister and I have it all planned out," he says. "You have nothing to worry about, but your time paying for your actions will be over. So, you should be happy about that."

"So, when I leave the penthouse—"

Phoenix swallows the last bite of his meal before speaking in a deep and menacing voice. "We will discuss this once we know you are definitely pregnant. No reason to discuss this now."

"I want to stay with you. Not be shipped off to some hidden location."

"No."

"I don't want to leave you. I don't want to leave Seattle."

"I don't care."

"I don't believe you," I say without pause. "I think you do care, and no matter what you say, I think you feel the same way about me that I feel about you."

"This conversation is over."

"Phoenix..."

"I said no," he snaps.

"How can you stare at me like that and feel nothing?" My voice cracks and wavers. "Am I truly nothing more than a body? Just a surrogate for your baby?"

"That's what you are."

His words shatter my heart. Why does he have the power over me to do so? Why am I drawn toward a man who has never led me to believe there was anything more? He has only caused me pain—both physically and mentally. So why? Why do his words stab at me? He hasn't made any promises. He has never whispered sweet nothings about the perfect future together. I should know how he will act. I should know how he will feel. But my heart has taken over.

"I have sat across from you at this table for days. We have had sex. You have demanded my submission in the most intimate of ways, and I have given it to you. Please. I know you have to feel something more. I can feel it in your touch."

"I touch you in order to keep you in line. To make you pay for your betrayal and to guarantee it will never happen again. Nothing more."

"Not true."

He looks at me with the most severe warning I have yet seen.

I clear my throat and try to keep my voice calm and steady. "I can see. I notice what you do. When you spank me, you also dip your finger between my folds to see that I am wet. My arousal is important to you. When a punishment is over, and I'm crying, you wait with me until my tears cease. You want to care for me. You want to give me comfort because you feel more even though you aren't capable of admitting that to yourself. You want this because you do feel something for me. I know this. I feel this. You are lying if you say otherwise."

"Ani..." His warning sends a shiver up my spine, but I don't stop. I can't. I'm not wrong. I can't be. He's just too stubborn to see.

"I'm not asking for love right away. I'm not asking for you to be someone you aren't or can't be. I'm just asking for you to be honest. This hasn't been easy for me. I'm not usually this open and free with my feelings, but you made me this way. It's because of you that I can say how I feel. I hunger for you. You wake up a passion inside of me that salivates to be quenched. You spark a flame inside. When we made love—"

"We fucked." His voice vibrates off the bare walls.

"Maybe," I say calmly, "but more than just a body part entered me. I felt it just as I know you did. I had your *seed* as you like to call it, blending within me. Something happened at that moment. A bond. I can't imagine losing it forever while I bounce around like an expensive piece of artwork never to be appreciated or touched. I want more out of life." I pause for a moment, preparing for the rejection I am sure will follow my next question. "Was I the only one who felt it? Did you not feel the connection with me? When we were together?"

"I felt it," he admits. "I fucking felt it."

Phoenix begins pacing, his aggravation visible in his posture. I sit and wait for the storm to erupt. I am asking for a severe spanking by continuing, but I have to, if even the slightest hope exists. He turns to me and points to the hallway. "Ani. Leave. Now. Go back to the room. I need... time."

I rise quickly and run to the room. Not out of fear, although I am scared of Phoenix's wrath, but because I don't want him to see how truly devastated I am.

Have I got this all wrong?

How?

How can I be so off?

How can this be so one-sided?

I'm in my room crying when a knock sounds at

the door rather than it just being opened like every other time. With the mood Phoenix is in, he would never knock. Never.

I quickly dry my tears. "Come in."

Phoenix opens the door and gracefully enters the room. "Ani, I can see... no, I can feel that I have upset you."

I look into his deep eyes and say nothing. I meet his gaze and allow him to truly see my pain. I want him to see how the thought of not being with him once we confirm I am pregnant causes anguish like no other. I understand I am simply a surrogate now, but that doesn't mean I like it.

Phoenix pulls me into his arms harshly. He presses my head to his chest with more force than I am prepared for. "It kills me to see you hurt. I want to never be the cause of your heartache." Without releasing his grip, he continues, "But what you want is not possible. It's not the way your life should be. Even if I could safely keep you with me at all times, a life in the attic is no way to live. It's just a matter of time until you lose your mind. Our child deserves a sane parent."

I pull from his strong embrace. "I don't care what we do as long as I'm with you. And our child deserves to have both his or her parents. Not just me." I sniffle and wipe away the tears, trying to regain my composure. "Anything is better than me being cast off alone."

"You won't be alone. You will have around-the-clock security watching over you. We will give you staff as well to help with cooking and cleaning. You won't be alone."

"But that is alone! It might as well be. What kind of life will I have with no real connections?"

"A better one than you would have with me. Look at me. I'm not the man you are picturing. I'm not that white picket fence dream." He pauses as if he may change his mind but then quickly snaps out of it. "And you won't be alone. You will have the baby. And who knows, we may want a second child down the line."

I shake my head. "You are a coward. You are too scared to let me in. To let any form of love in." I pause to drum up the strength to tell Phoenix my true feelings. "I love you. I love you so much. Even though you may never return the words, I'm at least not a coward and can tell you how I truly feel." I look back up into Phoenix's deep blue eyes. "But I know my baby, and I deserve more. So, if you can't say the words—"

"I love you, too," he cuts in. Sighing, Phoenix shakes his head. "I can't give you what you need."

"Then take me someplace else. Find a place besides the manor or the penthouse, besides the properties everyone is aware of, and build something fresh. Anywhere else."

"I can't do that, and you know it. I have responsibilities that keep me here. I can't just run off and play house. The slightest show of weakness, and others will move in."

I reach out for Phoenix's hands and pull him close to me in desperation. "Figure it out. Fix this problem as you fix everything else with your business," I suggest, feeling hopelessness take over all sense. "You are a man who doesn't take no for an answer."

Phoenix wraps me in his arms and kisses me on top of my head. "Ani, this is final. I have nothing to offer you. This is not the way to live. I can keep you safe, and that's the plan. Regardless of what you may think of me, I don't wish you unhappiness. I know what I have planned for you might not be what you planned, but if you have my baby inside of you, there's no other choice. I have to keep you both safe."

I close my eyes for a moment, searching my entire being for the power to not burst in tears and beg to be loved. I have to maintain some pride. I have to do something. Anything but feel this pain and rejection.

Cold.

Survival.

Put that wall back up.

Just be a pain slut and nothing more.

Try, Ani. Try.

"Fine. Forget I even tried. Let's just go back to the way it was. Fucking." I tentatively press my palm to Phoenix's chest. "Let me taste you." I lower my hand to the bulge in Phoenix's pants. "I want to feel your cock between my lips." I quickly undo his pants, releasing him from his confines. "I want again."

Phoenix stands still, never making a move to stop me in my mission. I consider this a sign to continue. I kneel, softly place his hardened cock on the base of my tongue, and close my lips tightly around him. Looking up into his eyes, I move my mouth up and down along his shaft. Phoenix never looks away.

I tighten my lips and work my tongue in small circles along the entire length. His taste, his smell, and his entire aura consumes me, but I focus only on the task. Nothing more.

Phoenix reaches for my hair to stop me. "Ani," he moans. He's losing control. Good. Let the man lose some fucking control.

I look up into his eyes with his cock still in my mouth. I lower my mouth down to the base of his cock and slowly back to the tip. Removing his penis just enough to speak again, I rasp, "Watch me, Phoenix. Watch me suck you off."

I know he likes the dirty talk.

I know exactly what he likes.

I have been trained.

Trained. Just not loved.

Phoenix closes his eyes and throws his head back in euphoric surrender. I have won this battle. I smile wickedly at my success and continue my quest to please Phoenix like he has never been.

"No. Stop," Phoenix orders. "This isn't right."

"Nothing about this is right," I snap as I fall to

the floor, not caring to stand. "I guess I am nothing but a fucking breeder."

"I'm sorry, Ani," Phoenix says as he lifts me and places me on the edge of the bed. "I know what's best."

I lie down on the bed and turn my back to him. "Fine. I understand. It's just a matter of time until I'm fat with swollen ankles anyway." I take a deep breath so my voice won't crack and reveal my pain. "I'm tired. Can you leave so I can get some rest? I've been tired lately."

"Let's have you take a pregnancy test," he says.

"Don't bother," I mumble. "I know I'm pregnant. I know."

At least the baby will love me.

THIRTY-SIX

Ani

As I finish washing out my mouth from my new morning ritual of throwing up my breakfast, the butler from Olympus Manor knocks on the open bathroom door. His presence doesn't surprise me, even though I've only seen him a few times before, and always while he's serving us food. And I had always been naked.

This time, however, I'm fully dressed in a light, summery floral dress with pink high heels. He doesn't say a word and hands me a letter. The words on the note are like a punch to the gut, but they should make me happy:

. . .

A dove has wings for a reason and doesn't deserve to be inside a cage.

~Phoenix

I haven't seen Phoenix for a full day, which can only mean one thing. "Has he left already?" I ask, staring at my reflection in the mirror and leaning against the sink for support.

"He returned to Olympus Manor," the butler replies.

"He's not coming back to Seattle." I already know the answer. I knew it the minute he had left the room, that what we had was over.

"No. But all the arrangements have been made for you to leave as well. Is there anything you want to pack or bring with you?" the butler asks.

"Well, that all depends. Do I have to earn my comfort items in this new place you are taking me to, or will I have access to a bed at least?" I ask with a smile. I refuse to cry. Absolutely refuse. Damn those tears that burn my eyes.

"Everything will be provided for you there. Mr. Godwin wanted me to tell you that you'll have a generous allowance as well, so I'm sure you can purchase anything that wasn't thought of. Also, there will be a full staff waiting for you there to assist with you and..." the butler looks at my stomach. "There will be people there to help with you and the baby."

Fury builds inside of me, but it's no match for the overwhelming despair and sadness that overpowers all other emotions. "I'm fine. I can go anytime you're ready."

"Mr. Godwin has asked me to make sure you call your sister and inform her you got a job overseas. To explain your absence to her."

I nod. "Yes, of course."

"Would you like me to write a script out for you?"

"I've got it." Daphne's been so distracted lately that she won't pick up on my blatant lies. Plus, she'll be so happy to hear that I got a job and won't be returning to the Eastside of Heathens Hollow.

"After the phone call, we can leave."

I won't ask where we're going. I don't care. I won't ask when I'll see Phoenix again. I don't care. I won't ask any questions about my future. I don't care. It's just me and the baby I carry. No one else. Just us.

As I step into my new home, an older man in a pressed gray linen suit with a baby blue tie says, "Welcome to your new home, Mrs. Godwin."

I correct him by saying, "My name is Ani Parker," and then look over his shoulder to find a place to sit. My journey has exhausted me, and I'm suffering morning sickness, night sickness, and every-hour-of-the-day sickness. All I want is to find a bed and sleep for days.

The man offers his arm to assist me, and I take it out of need as I worry my knees will collapse underneath me. He tells me that my room is ready if I want to rest, and that dinner is still a few hours away but can be pushed back if I'm still napping. I agree, and he leads me up the stairs to my room. The butler, whose name I now know to be Dio, is trailing behind me, tells the man that he will be staying for a few days to help me get settled in and train the staff on what Phoenix Godwin expects for Mrs. Godwin.

Although I am too tired to tell them to stop calling me by a name that isn't mine, I take in the Spanish villa, which is fully furnished with rustic furniture and antiques. Romantic paintings of the countryside and small Spanish villages hang on the aged walls of yesteryear. The smell of savory food being cooked in the kitchen adds to the idyllic environment, but it is just another version of a prison, and this time, I will be alone.

The man who introduces himself as Ricardo shows me to my bedroom, and I half-expect to see the room empty, as my room was when I first began my penance. However, it is far from that. The beautiful bed dominates the room, with a carved wooden headboard and engraved flowers that match the nightstands, the large armoire, dresser, and small desk and chair beneath the window. Everything in the room is custom made, including the patchwork quilt on the bed.

Ricardo leaves me alone to rest, but not before telling me that there is a private bathroom behind the door on the right of the armoire, fully stocked with all the hygiene items I could need, as well as towels and washcloths. He assures me that if I need anything, I should not hesitate to ask. As I collapse on the bed, I make a mental note to ask Ricardo about ordering some pregnancy books, as I know nothing about pregnancy and have no one to guide me.

I try to let the exhaustion wash over me and quiet my mind, but I wonder where Phoenix is, and if he will want to be involved with the pregnancy at all. As I try to fall asleep, I know that this is not some romantic love story where I have a doting spouse to be with me every step of the way.

This is madness. Complete madness. I place my hand on my belly. How long will it be before I start showing? I've been a loner in my previous life and don't have any girlfriends who went through this. I don't have a living mother to guide me or some trusted aunt. Though I know Daphne would love to be here by my side, this isn't a possibility, either. It's just me.

I roll over to my side and try to allow the pure exhaustion to wash over me and quiet my mind. A clock ticks a few doors close downstairs, and heavy footsteps go up and down the stairs.

I need to sleep. Sleep. Sleep.

Would anyone other than Phoenix care about this baby in his family?

Go to sleep, Ani. Go to sleep and stop thinking about them. You aren't a Godwin and never will be. Stop!

I can't remember the last time I've been this tired, and yet I can't fall asleep. My mind won't cease for even a moment.

Why has Phoenix done this to me? How can he just leave without saying goodbye? I'm carrying his child. Shouldn't he have at least escorted me across the world himself?

How could I have gotten this so wrong? Yes, it started off as me fucking up by lying and him making sure I paid the price. But there was more between us. I truly believe that. Our bodies respond to each other... correction. My body responds. Clearly, I'm nothing more than just a fuck for him.

So why am I mad? He hasn't broken any promises. He told me from the beginning what to expect. He's only following through with what he's always planned to do. Do I really have a right to be mad?

I'm not mad.

I'm heartbroken.

CHAPTER
THIRTY-SEVEN

Phoenix

"Dio said they arrived safely," I tell Athena. "He said that Ani was sick for most of the trip."

Athena looks up from the papers that scatter a large table that she uses as a desk when she visits me in the attic. "Sick? Is she all right? Do we need to get a doctor out to the villa?"

I'm not used to seeing worry cross Athena's face. She rarely shows any emotion, and worry is something she rarely does. If she does worry about anything, she does a damn good job concealing it. Our father taught us early on in life to not reveal emotions. They make us weak. The Godwin family will not survive if there is weakness present. A face that is impossible to read makes a strong, feared man.

That belief has served us well up to this point.

"He assured me it was just pregnancy sickness, but I'm going to have a doctor check her and the baby out tomorrow. I'll have someone come to the house," I say. "I haven't given the house staff any set rules or restrictions on whether I will allow Ani out of the house or not."

Athena takes a long moment staring at me before she looks back down at the papers and gets back to work. We sit in silence, which is what we often do when we are stewing on something. One thing about my relationship with my sister is we aren't impulsive in our speaking or actions. Plus, all the talk about Ani is crossing a line we've never really crossed before. It's personal talk. Athena doesn't like personal, and I'm the same. If we don't have to discuss business, then we pretty much keep to ourselves. It's clear we both don't want to talk about Ani, or the baby, more than we have to. That much is obvious.

"I'm concerned we may not have enough security there," Athena says casually without looking up from her reading. "Our dear uncle is planning a big move for Poseidon. I can feel it. I can smell it. I don't want there to be any collateral damage. I wouldn't put it past him to somehow utilize Ani and the baby to attack us."

"Then we'll get more." I will have Dio arrange that before heading back to the States. Athena isn't an alarmist, but she has exceptional foresight and can almost see what is in store for us. I've never doubted her hunch.

"It doesn't seem fair to keep her locked away inside, however. Not everyone is a hermit like you, dear brother. You already did that, and well... you had promised her that once her punishment was over, it was over."

"True, but she's carrying my baby. A Godwin. So, I have to take her safety into consideration from this point on. She'll never just be a normal woman walking the streets of the Eastside of Heathens Hollow again. Life has changed. Once people get wind that another Godwin heir is being added to the family tree, she'll be a marked woman from that point on."

"She may be more of a prisoner now than she was in the manor," Athena says.

"It's our reality. Her new reality."

"I know Spain was my idea, but she's a long way away if she..." I can see the wheels spinning in Athena's head.

"Needs us?" I answer for her. "Yeah, I've been thinking about that."

"And who is this Ricardo guy looking after her? Do we even know anything about him?" Athena asks, obviously not focusing on work any longer. "How do we know our uncle or even our father can't get control over him?"

"He's vetted, but I already asked Dio to grill him and watch his every move while he's there. We may want to have Dio stay in Spain a little longer than planned. Just to be sure," I say.

"I've been thinking about our grandfather a lot lately," Athena says.

"How so?"

"He was a feared leader of the family. No one gave him shit. It was known to never mess with Cronus Godwin."

"Yeah. So? We're feared as well. Our father most certainly followed in his footsteps, too."

"Right. Some would even say we're feared and respected even more."

"Your point?" I'm not sure what she is getting at.

"Our grandfather was able to rule with an iron fist, but he was never that way with Grandmother. He loved her. Cherished her. There wasn't a thing he wouldn't do for her. He was the same with us when we were young. He softened at home, but no one ever saw that side of him beyond our four walls."

"He was a good man," I agree.

"So, why are you completely ruling out doing the same? Is it so unheard of that you can't have a family?"

I point to the attic. "Look around, dear sister. I think the answer is clear."

"It doesn't have to be, brother. You have a son or daughter coming."

"You've never been one to not just get straight to the point. Where are you going with this?"

Athena leans back in her chair. "When you came

340

up with this crazy idea of having Ani pay for lying to you via her body, and then having your baby, it was crazy. But you do you, brother. No matter how much of a psychopathic idea it may be. And I saw your point about having a baby to keep the Godwin family name alive and not just be the child of Daphne who both of us will never trust. But the reality is, you started a family. Whether you want to face that fact or not, you did."

"So, are you saying you want my psychopathic ass to raise this baby? Try to be a good father?"

"I'm just wondering why you've ruled that out?"

I lean forward on the desk and lock my eyes with my sister. "We've talked about this and all the reasons why."

"I know. I guess I'm second-guessing your decision. It feels weak. Like the decision was made from a place of fear. I don't like the way that feels," Athena admits. "We are motherfucking Godwins. We don't cower in the shadows."

I know what she is talking about. Ever since leaving Ani on the bed with her heart ripped out, I couldn't shake my own level of sadness. I did feel weak, but then again, I've never claimed to be a strong man. I've left that role for my siblings.

"She deserves better than me," I say.

Athena smirks. "She sure as fuck does. I won't argue there."

"So, what are we saying here?" My heart speeds up, and my brain swirls with possibilities. The heavy, thick depression that has been plaguing me since my arrival back in the attic seems to be dissipating as our discussion progresses.

"You told me Ani said she wanted to be with you. She said she loved you."

I nod.

"You have a woman who sees you for who you are. She knows what you do in the shadows and isn't asking for you to quit being who you are. She's open to your darkness. She's willing to have your baby and not demanding anything for it."

"Not to mention her sexual tastes mesh with my kinky ass," I say with a small chuckle.

Athena makes a gagging sound and scowls. "Too much information."

"But she did lie to me. She got Apollo into what could be a mess later. She's still Daphne's sister."

Athena's smile fades. "True, and there is a part of me that wonders if I can truly ever trust her to be part of the Godwin family. I don't trust. I don't forgive. I don't allow someone in. I know this. And you're the same way."

"We don't trust, or we risk everything for letting our guard down. It's how we survive. Or at least, it has been our creed up until now."

I pause for a long moment. "I think I'm over all that. My gut tells me she isn't the person I believed her to be. I see good," I admit, or maybe even defend. Athena hasn't seen what I have, but Ani is... more than what I ever gave her credit for.

Athena surprisingly nods in agreement. "I think you're right. You've always had a good gut instinct."

"Let me ask you a serious question," I say. "If I marry her. Claim her and the baby as mine forever. Do you really see her becoming part of the Godwin family? Or do you see her resisting like Daphne did?"

"Only you can answer that," Athena fires back. "Do you love her?"

"Well, I sure as fuck wasn't planning on falling in love with the woman when this all began," I answer.

I stand up and pace the room. I don't do relationships. True relationships. And the women I've had in the past—no matter how insignificant they were—I have never loved. Quite the opposite. I am overprotective, over-possessive, and what is mine is mine, but I never love.

Mine.

Ani is not just mine... I love her.

Am I going to be all right with that fact? It has given her power. My love will forever be a chink in my armor.

"And what about raising our father?" I begin. "He's toxic. You know this."

Athena smirks. "We're all toxic. Nothing is going to change that. But something about Ani tells me she's accepted that fact."

I sit back down and stare at my sister. "I know for a fact that I want Ani. I want this baby. I have no idea how everything else will work, but I know the basics.

There is a primal need inside me that wants her in my arms. Never to let go."

"I think you have your answer," Athena says.

"I do, too. My gut is screaming for me to listen to my heart and to tell my cautious mind to shut the fuck up." I run my hands through my hair and take in a deep breath. "Jesus Christ. Am I really considering this? What am I saying here?"

"I think you need to take the Godwin jet to Madrid," Athena answers.

THIRTY-EIGHT

Ani

"You can go fuck yourself," I say as I try to slam my bedroom door in his face.

How dare Phoenix just show up here and try to enter my room as if nothing had happened. When Phoenix's shoe blocks the door from closing, I add, "You said my penance was over once I'm pregnant. Well, I am. So, now you have to leave me alone."

"I'd like to come inside," Phoenix says. "Hear me out, and then I'll leave if you still want me to."

It is odd to hear him ask permission and not just demand his way in. There is no aggression, no threats, no intimidation. That alone has me backing away as he opens the door fully and enters.

"I expected you to remain in Olympus Manor... in the attic," I say softly.

"I was," Phoenix says.

I have my hand on my belly protectively until I notice him staring down at where my palm sits.

"How do you feel? Dio said you were ill during the travel here," Phoenix says.

"Just morning sickness," I answer shortly. I don't know why he's in my room appearing to care, and it unnerves me. "The doctor arrived this morning and examined me. Everything is fine, and the baby is fine. He said the heartbeat sounded healthy."

Phoenix lights up before me in a way I have never seen before. His usual dark eyes sparkle as he continues to stare at my stomach. His eyes are fixated as if he can see the baby inside.

"I'm about six weeks along," I add.

I have no idea why I am not seething any longer or at the very least afraid that he'll treat me like he did in the manor. I should be calling him every name in the book but instead am excited to talk about baby news with... the father of my baby.

"When will we know the sex?" Phoenix asks.

We? That word seems so foreign to me.

"In about twelve more weeks. It's also too soon for the doctor to tell if I'm having twins or not. He said with you having twins in your family, it's likely I could."

After a moment of awkward silence, Phoenix speaks up. "Why don't we go for a walk? One of the reasons I liked this place when buying it was that it sat on a few acres of beautiful countryside. I think we should go check it out. Some fresh air could do us good."

It's unlike Phoenix to want to go outside so easily, but this is a different place. Not his home. Not his safety zone. Does he feel like the walls are closing in on him just as much as I do? Now that we aren't in the manor, the energy between us is different, off in many ways. Uncertain, for sure.

I am angry. But not really.

I am hurt. But also happy he is in front of me.

I am confused... very much so.

"The shoes you bought for me in the closet are a little too big," I say as I go to find a pair to put on. "But I was reading in a pregnancy book the doctor gave me that I could expect my feet to expand and swell. So, I guess that's a good thing."

"I'll get you more shoes," Phoenix says.

I have no doubt. I am sure that when it comes to materialistic items, Phoenix will buy me whatever my heart desires. The thing is... I am not a materialistic person. I want so much more. Things that don't cost money, and things that this man clearly isn't willing to give.

As we head outside, Dio is standing by the front door with two other men in suits.

"All is secure," Dio says. "Cameras, sensors, security gates around the full property. I personally toured the premises myself."

"Thank you, Dio," Phoenix says. "There's an envelope inside on the kitchen counter waiting for you. But I'd like you to stay for a few more days. I will need to brief you on some security business for Medusa in the States I will want you to handle while we are here." Phoenix places his hand on my lower back as we take the stairs down.

"How long do you plan on staying?" Dio asks.

"A while. I don't plan on traveling unless need be while Ani is pregnant," Phoenix announces. "And then I don't want to leave the baby right away either."

My heart stops as I glance at his face to see if he truly means what he says.

Staying?

He's staying?

For months. For almost a year maybe.

With me?

"We'll talk more and go over everything after our walk," Phoenix says, stepping closely beside me.

I am nestled next to his body as we begin to stroll a dirt path leading into a mass of trees. The sun feels good on my face, and though the boots I wear are a little big, it feels good to stretch my legs and feel normal in the fresh air. We walk in silence. Side by side.

Not as a captive and captor. Not as a beauty and her beast.

Phoenix is the first to break the silence as we are several yards from the house. "It's nice to be in the country. The land is pretty spectacular."

I haven't said a word since we walked out the

door. I have no idea what to say. I have no idea what the hell is going on. Phoenix seems... different.

"I have made a decision," Phoenix says. "I would like to stay. With you, with the baby, and I want to..." Phoenix seems to be struggling to find the right words.

I simply walk on. I am scared that if I chime in at all, he will suddenly go back to his closed-off, no-emotion self. I am terrified that what I heard him say to Dio is just a momentary lapse of judgment, and he will suddenly change his mind and hop back on the first flight to Seattle and then to Heathens Hollow.

"I shouldn't have left you," Phoenix says. "I know that now. I shouldn't have done a lot of things." He sounds remorseful, which is odd. He always is so focused on his decisions and his actions.

"When you confessed your feelings to me." Phoenix reaches for my hand and takes it in his. "You weren't wrong. There was a bond between us. There was something so strong that it scared the holy hell out of me. After the lie, my plan was to never love you. To never care. But I do. I care, and I love you. As hard as it is to say those words, and to admit the feelings, I do."

Holding his hand, walking beside him, strolling the countryside in Spain... we are talking about an epic love story right out of a romance novel. But this is too good to be true. This is so polar opposite of what I had before. This is not the future I accepted as mine. It just can't be.

When did my beast turn into prince?

I pull away from him and freeze.

He walks in front of me so he can stare directly at me.

"I don't deserve you," Phoenix says, "and I don't have the best of situations to offer. In fact, a life with me won't be easy. Being a Godwin is fucking messy. I hide in the attic to avoid what being a Godwin truly means. I never want to face my reality. I prefer the safety of four walls, a self-imposed prison, over staring down the Godwin curse. I lost my mother because of that family, and I don't want the same for you."

"I told you I understood the Godwins," I say. "I understand your mother."

"Just because you read some journals, doesn't mean you will truly understand. My father is... well, there are no words in the dictionary that can describe that man. My sister—as much as I love her —is a fucking sociopath, and my brother is just as bad."

"But it's your family. Yours. And"—I place my hand on my belly—"this baby's."

"I'm going to continue to battle this agoraphobic bullshit day in and day out for you, but I can't promise it won't win. I can't tell you that I won't expect us to be locked inside all the time. And if you say no, truly say no and not want me in your day-to-day life anymore, I will accept that answer. Choosing me is not part of your punishment for the lie. I'm done dictating; I'm done demanding. I'm done truly punishing," Phoenix says with his eyes locked with mine. "Well..." Phoenix smirks. "I'm done punishing for the lie. I still have my... needs."

I chuckle.

"I'm not a changed man. In fact, the reality is, I am who I am. Still a fucking monster in the attic."

"I told you from the beginning that I knew who you were. And I had accepted that," I say. "But you shattered my heart. You rejected me and made me feel as if I was the only one who felt there was more between us."

"And for that, I'm sorry," Phoenix says. "I'm sorry for a lot of things when it comes to you. I can't fix it. I can't take it all away. All I can do is move forward from this point on. If you allow me to."

I take a step backwards. "And what does this future look like? How do you see this playing out?"

"With you," Phoenix answers. "The two of us together raising the baby as a family."

I look at Phoenix and study his face.

"It won't be easy," Phoenix says, "and if you marry me, I have to warn you that Godwins marry for life. There is no divorce as I'm sure Daphne has told you. But you and the baby would be protected legally, and my assets would be yours in the eyes of the law."

I don't care about all the legal details. Or about money. I want to know what this really means.

"I have demands of my own," I have the courage

to say. Not wanting to lose my will to speak my mind, I quickly continue. "I don't want to be locked away in some tower like Rapunzel. I don't want to be away from you. I understand you will have Medusa business, and I'm not asking to be involved with it, unless you ask for help, that is. But I am asking to not be shut out. I don't want to be treated like some naive little girl and kept in the dark by you."

"Fair enough," Phoenix says.

"I also..." I swallow hard as my stomach twists in nerves to reveal my truth. "I also don't want you to be soft on me. I like the firm hand. I fucking crave it."

"Oh, I won't be soft. Trust me on that," Phoenix says with a small laugh that is lined with a delicious promise that causes my pussy to throb.

"Do you truly love me?" I'm not sure how I've summoned the inner strength to simply ask what I really want to know from him.

"I don't think I know what that means. I'm not sure I can one hundred percent say yes. At least not the normal kind of love," Phoenix says. "But I know I don't want to live without you. I know that I want you by my side as we move forward with our lives. I can't imagine myself being with any other woman. And I know that I want to make sure you are protected, cared for, and treated as you deserve every single day we are alive. My version of love is no doubt fucked up. It's not going to be the tender kisses and red roses kind of love. I'm not an easy man, but with that said, I would never disrespect you or harm you in any way. Once you agree to be mine you will see a side of me that will nearly suffocate you with my kind of love."

I can taste the tears on my lips as they fall down my face. This man is saying everything I have hoped to hear one day. He is promising his truths, and his heart—no matter how dark and twisted they are. He isn't promising me he will change. He can't even promise he can leave the attic. And that's fine by me.

I want to enter his world. I want him to let me in.

And he is. He finally is.

"I love you, Phoenix Godwin. I love every fucked-up part about you."

I take his hand and let him lead me back to the villa. As we reach the door, I hesitate. There's still a small part of me not sure if I'm ready for this, if I'm ready to be pulled into Phoenix's world of power and wealth. Of secrets and isolation. But as he gazes at me with those intense eyes, I know that there's no turning back.

I take a deep breath and follow him into the villa, ready to face whatever comes my way.

"Can you live in my life? My rules? My darkness?" he asks, closing the door behind us.

"Yes," I say, because I want nothing more.

"Are you sure?" he growls, the desire in his voice causing my body to tremble.

"Yes," I gasp, barely able to breathe. "I'm yours."

His eyes blaze like fire, and he pulls me against him, possessing me with a fierce kiss. His hot lips move hungrily over mine, claiming me as his own. He pulls away, his voice a low rumble. "Do you understand?"

I nod and swallow hard, my entire body trembling.

"Say it," he orders.

"I'm yours," I whisper, my voice thick with emotion. "Only yours."

CHAPTER
THIRTY-NINE

Phoenix

I can't get her back to the villa fast enough.

I'm being pulled to her. An invisible tether connecting us effortlessly tugging me forward. She lifts her shirt just above her belly, letting me see what I have created, tucked away in her warmth.

The realization that a part of me is inside her nearly buckles my knees. I am overwhelmed by the love I have for her—for this unborn child that is a fraction of us both. It's like being within a dream, the kind from which I never want to wake.

I cautiously reach out bring my hands to rest on her stomach, feeling the gentle rise and fall of her breathing. My own heart beats wildly, as if it is searching for its other half.

I need her. I need her in my arms. I need her

beneath me. I need to be inside her. She is the only thing that can make me whole. I need her like I need the air to breathe.

My heart is racing as I move closer to her. I can feel the heat from her body, and I want to be near her. I want to touch her. I bring my hands to her hips, gently caressing her skin. She responds to my touch and moves closer. She looks up at me with a smoldering stare that sets my whole body aflame.

Our lips meet for the first time in what feels like decades, as if every emotion between us has been given its own voice. Passion, desire, and love all find their way into our kiss. Our bodies press against one another in perfect alignment, as though each piece of us is meant to fit together perfectly.

We explore each other's bodies with our hands, exploring every curve and dip with newfound reverence. Our intensity robs us of breath; a wave of emotion washes over us both as we discover just how much we need one another.

Time stands still in this moment, suspended by a force beyond space or understanding. As our souls intertwine in the most intimate of ways, I know without hesitation that she is my home. I will never truly be whole until she is at my side once again.

I lean in closer and whisper in her ear, "I want you, Ani. I want you so desperately it hurts."

She draws a sharp breath, and her body quivers beneath my touch. Before she can say anything, I press my lips against her neck, sending waves of pleasure coursing through my body.

I move my hands down her body, tracing the curves of her waist. I start to lower my head and nuzzle my face in her cleavage when she grabs my shoulders and pulls me up to her. Our eyes lock, and we both know that this is our moment. I capture her lips with mine, and we both moan in unison.

I wander my hands down her body, and soon I'm slipping my fingers beneath her panties. She trembles in anticipation as I stroke her warm wetness. She throws her head back, her breaths coming in short gasps as I teasingly circle her clit with my thumb.

I inhale deeply, pressing my body against hers. Her heat radiates through me, and I let out a soft moan as I drown in her scent. She looks up at me with pure desire, and I can no longer suppress the ache that has been growing inside me for so long. I slide my hands around her waist and pull her close, pressing my lips to hers in a deep, passionate kiss.

With urgency, I press my body against hers. She gasps as I slip a hand between her thighs, tracing my fingertips along her most sensitive parts. Her warmth beckons me closer, and when I gaze into her eyes, I see the same desire that I feel.

I reach for her waist and hoist her up, pressing her against the wall. She wraps her legs around me, and I capture her lips with mine, tasting every inch of her. I explore her curves with my hands, running them over her skin, eliciting soft moans from her.

I've never enjoyed touching a woman as much as I am with her.

She's carrying my child inside this body, and I feel as if I must touch and touch and touch again.

I want to be gentle. I want to make love, but the primal need inside of me needs to take her hard, deep, with all the aggression that is sizzling through me to claim her as mine. Truly mine.

We come together in a flurry of heat and movement. I thrust deeper, faster, and harder into her as she screams out my name. The intensity of our connection only grows as I feel her body quivering with pleasure beneath me.

I press my hips against hers, my hands roaming her body. Her heat surrounds me, her desire driving me on. I reach down and grab her hips, thrusting harder and faster. She gasps, her eyes wide with ecstasy as I drive into her.

My body trembles as her amazing tightness envelopes me. She gasps my name, her fingers digging into my back as our pleasure builds. I kiss her deeply, tenderly, savoring the sweetness of our connection.

I move faster, pushing harder and deeper into her with each thrust. We come together in a frenzy of passion, our bodies writhing in what seems to go on forever.

I toss her onto the mattress and slowly crawl

onto the bed and over her body. Bracing my weight on my hands, planted on either side of her head, I gaze down into her eyes. When I smile, she smiles. And when I kiss her, she kisses me back. Her lips part, and I dip my head to kiss her. When she opens her mouth wider and lifts her head to meet me halfway, I take her bottom lip, sucking it into my mouth until she moans and then giving it a nip until she gasps. Only then do I kiss her, softly, gently, until she reaches up, wraps a hand around my neck, and pulls me closer.

She wraps her legs around my waist, holding me against her as we kiss. Her hands move from my neck to my ass, and then they dig into the muscles on either side of my spine until they reach the curve at the top of my ass, where they grip me tight as if trying to pull me inside of her. That's when she starts to whimper as if in pain and when that doesn't work, she begins to whine as if she is frustrated beyond belief. When that still doesn't work, she arches her back beneath me and releases a cry that makes it clear what she wants.

I turn onto my side and pin both of her hands above her head with one of mine.

"You're killing me!" she whines, arching her back.

A wicked smirk spreads across my lips as I hear her snarl. I respond by leaning forward and delicately tracing the outline of her right nipple with my tongue. Her nipples are my favorite type of temptation, changing from a light pink when soft, to a captivating dusky coral as they stand firm. I shamelessly indulge in their flavor, only stopping when she begs for more.

I snake my hands beneath her supple ass and lift her into the air as I plunge deep into her. A thunderous scream erupts from her lungs as I fill her with my passion and pleasure, leaving her panting and wanting more. My body is still as I wait for her to adjust to me, until finally my movements begin to draw out the desire that was hidden away in her soul.

I devour her lips with mine, my tongue demanding possession while I claim her body with a possessive ferocity. I take her fast and hard, driving relentlessly deeper as she gasps my name and claws at my back. She begins to peak, and I keep going, pushing her further until she screams in pleasure, each contraction pulling me closer and closer to my own release. I grit my teeth, determined to keep going until I take her to the crest again.

My cock is digging deeper and deeper into her tight little hole, pushing her to the brink of pleasure. My balls tighten as I drive hard and deep into her, pushing her further and further until she's screaming for me to stop.

"You're so fucking tight," I growl, pushing against her with all of my strength, feeling my orgasm come close.

"You're so fucking big," she pants, her body tightening around me as I fill her completely.

"Does my cock hurt you, dove?" I demand, thrusting like a wild animal.

"Yes," she gasps, "but hurt me more. Hurt me deep and hard."

Her back arches, and her muscles tighten around me, pulling me deeper inside her. My intensity is building within me, and I cry out, my voice echoing off the walls as I drive into her one final time.

We both collapse afterward, exhausted and trembling from the fervor of our lovemaking. Our breathing is heavy and ragged as we lie there for a few moments, savoring the afterglow of our union.

Finally, we pull apart and look into each other's eyes with adoration and love. We share a soft kiss before snuggling up close to one another in comfortable silence, feeling closer than ever before.

I'm not a man to cuddle, but something inside of me demands to pull her into my arms. To protect. To hold onto like she's mine and will forever be.

I move my hand along her naked body, feeling the silky softness of her skin against my fingertips. I peck her shoulder then hug her waist, our closeness in the aftermath of our pleasure still strong.

My erection remains, yet I want nothing more than to stay with her like this. To be with her. To be one.

She kisses my cheek and rests against my chest. Our breathing slows, receding into a tranquil tempo.

For the first time ever, I feel like I could drift off right here in this bed with her tucked securely in my embrace. I have never felt such a thing for anyone else before, nor have I ever considered it. I trail my fingers gently across her face and tilt up her chin so I can make eye contact. This is the first time I have ever wanted something like this to last. This isn't just a one-time thing. I have plans for us.

I kiss her lips softly, and when I pull away, she has a sleepy smile. Her eyes sparkle, and she looks up at me with a content expression.

This is how lovers fuck, and I can't say that I mind.

As our breathing slows, I press my forehead against hers and whisper "You are truly mine now." She smiles up at me, her eyes still filled with desire as she wraps her arms around me and whispers "I've always been yours."

Her eyes meet mine, and she smiles softly before pressing her lips to mine. Our kiss is soft and gentle, filled with promise and devotion.

My arms wrap around her waist as I deepen the kiss, our tongues entwining in a passionate dance. She moans softly into my mouth, her body trembling in my embrace. I can feel her warmth against me, her need for me a shimmering heatwave.

We break away from the kiss reluctantly, both of us breathless and trembling with desire. I look into her eyes and see something I can't put words to: love, passion, commitment... It's all there in her gaze.

I brush my fingertips over her cheek before carefully tucking a stray strand of hair behind her ear. I smile at her before leaning back in for another kiss, this one slower and more tender than the first.

She wraps her arms around my neck and pulls me closer to deepen the kiss even further. We move together as one, exploring each other with an intensity I've never felt before.

We break away eventually but remain pressed against one another until we're both breathing normally again. We pull apart just far enough so that we can look into each other's eyes once more; hers still filled with emotion and mine burning with passion for the woman I can now call mine forever.

She is my dove in the flames of my fire, and that will never change.

FORTY

Phoenix

We're back in the manor, but this time it's different. This time I have Ani. She's here by choice, and I'm no longer trapped between four walls. I still use the attic as my office, and I still hate most people. Ani has assured me that some things don't need to change. I am who I am, and that's fine. She says that she loves my grumpiness and to never change.

I take a break from my work and walk down to our bedroom. It's next to a smaller room we've decided to turn into the nursery. Olympus Manor isn't exactly our house as it belongs to the Godwins, but neither Ani nor I feel any place is truly home other than where we fell in love. No one in the family seems to mind that we've taken up residence here. My father barely said two words when I told him the plans that Ani and I have to live full time on Heathens Hollow and call Olympus home. I am grateful for that, and when it comes to that man, I'm not grateful for much.

I'm not ready to ask her to marry me. I'm not sure why. I think it feels too normal, and I'm far from that. Also, by marrying her, I truly expose her to the Godwin rules. I feel this need to protect her from that. To keep her safe from the strangling vines. But I am committed to giving this woman everything I have until the day I die.

Ani is lying in the bed, her stomach growing bigger and bigger with my twin boys every day. She's reading a book, but she's frowning. Tears are rolling down her cheeks. Ani's hormones have been out of control, but something tells me this is different.

Rushing to her side, I say, "What's wrong, dove?"

Her big eyes look up at me, and she asks, "Promise you won't get mad?"

I'm unable to control my emotions. This is not a skill I feel I'll ever master, so instead of lying to her, I swipe a tear from beneath her eye and say, "Tell me."

"You've been working all day, and I was getting bored. So I decided to read some more from your mother's journals. I want to know everything about her and your family to tell our boys someday when they ask about their grandmother. I know you asked me to put them away and keep them out of your sight..."

I did. And a familiar rage begins to bubble up inside of me at the mere mention of my mother.

"But I feel there's something you need to read."

I open my mouth to refuse, but Ani pushes the open journal my way.

"Just one entry. That's all I ask. But I really feel you need to read this," she presses.

"Ani..."

"You said your mother committed suicide, right?" she asks.

"Yes."

She pushes the journal to me again. "Then you really need to read this."

Dear Diary,

I told Troy that he was going to have to kill me. And I meant it this time. There is a madness inside of me. An insanity that Troy only makes worse. I need to get out. I need to be free. I need to do something. Anything. And if trying to escape means Troy kills me... then so be it.

I prepared myself for his fury. I readied myself for his storm. But instead the man I once loved looked into my eyes with sadness.

"I don't want you to go," he said. There was no demand. No threat.

"I have to."

"What about the children?"

"They're being pulled into our darkness, and the best thing I can do for them is to set them free from it."

Leaving my children will be the hardest thing I could ever do, but I'm already gone. I'm simply a hollow ghost walking the halls of this manor. I haven't been a mother for a very long time.

"They won't understand how a mother could just leave them," Troy said, but there was no judgement in his voice. No anger. He was simply stating a fact.

I nodded, knowing he was right. "I have to," I repeated.

Troy remained quiet for several long moments before he finally said, "I'll let you leave on a couple of terms."

I looked up into eyes with surprise. That wasn't the answer I was expecting.

"If you leave, you can never come back. You can never reenter their lives again. Never. I'll set you up in a house where you will stay and remain hidden from this family. You'll have a generous allowance and never need another thing. But the children are never to know you exist. I'll tell them you died. It will be easier that way for them."

"You'll let me go?" His words didn't sound real to me. For years his threats have kept me prisoner, but now he was willing to allow me to leave.

"You'll die."

"I'm already dead."

And just like that, Troy gave me what I had been asking for years. Freedom. I needed to walk out the door of Olympus and never look back. I needed to rid myself from this cancer and set my children free from inheriting my disease.

RIP Freya Godwin.
It was the only way.

I toss the journal on the bed and stare at Ani in disbelief. She's waiting for me to say something, but I have no words. Instead, I take out my phone and call the only person who will know how to handle this or know what to say.

"Athena," I say when she answers the phone.

"Is something wrong?" My sister can always pick up on my emotions.

"It's Mother." I draw a deep breath as I stare down at the journal cast to the bed. "I don't think she killed herself."

Athena releases a heavy sigh. "We've discussed this. Does it really matter if she was the one to jump off the cliff or if someone actually pushed her? She's dead. And this happened a long time ago. It's long due we let this go."

There's ringing in my ears. "Athena... I think our mother is still alive."

Are you ready for Athena Godwin's story?
Vipers Are Forbidden **is next!**

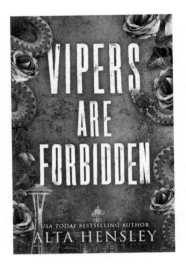

Vipers Are Forbidden

It's impossible to enter a pit full of vipers and not get bit.

Until you meet me, that is.

My venom is far more toxic than the four men who have declared me their enemy.

They seek vengeance and launch a twisted game of give and take.

I'll play in their dark world, because it's where I thrive.

I'll dance with their debauchery, for I surely know the steps.

But then I discover just how wrong I am. Their four, not only matches, but beats, my one.

. . .

With each wicked move they make, they become my obsession.

I crave them until they consume all thought.

The temptation to give them everything they desire becomes too much.

I'm entering their world, and there is no light to guide my way. My blindness full of lust will be my defeat.

Yes... they are the vipers and are forbidden.

And they are the end of my beginning.

About the Author

Alta Hensley is a USA TODAY bestselling author of hot, dark and dirty romance. She is also an Amazon Top 10 bestselling author. Being a multi-published author in the romance genre, Alta is known for her dark, gritty alpha heroes, sometimes sweet love stories, hot eroticism, and engaging tales of the constant struggle between dominance and submission.

She lives in a log cabin in the woods with her husband, two daughters, and an Australian Shepherd. When she isn't battling the bats, and watching the deer, she is writing about villains who always get their love story and happily ever after.

Facebook: https://www.facebook.com/AltaHensleyAuthor/
Amazon: https://www.amazon.com/Alta-Hensley/e/B004G5A6LI
Website: www.altahensley.com
Instagram: https://instagram.com/altahensley
Bookbub: https://www.bookbub.com/authors/alta-hensley

TikTok: https://www.tiktok.com/@altahensley
Join her mailing list: https://landing.mailerlite.com/
webforms/landing/c9b6n3

Also by Alta Hensley

Gods Among Men Series:

Villains Are Made

Monsters Are Hidden

Vipers Are Forbidden

―――――

Secret Bride Trilogy:

Captive Bride

Kept Bride

Taken Bride

―――――

Wonderland Trilogy:

King of Spades

Queen of Hearts

Ace of Diamonds

―――――

Dark Pen Series:

Devil's Contract

Dirty Ledger

Dangerous Notes

Spiked Roses Billionaires' Club:

Bastards & Whiskey

Villains & Vodka

Scoundrels & Scotch

Devils & Rye

Beasts & Bourbon

Sinners & Gin

Evil Lies Series:

The Truth About Cinder

The Truth About Alice

Breaking Belles Series:

Elegant Sins

Beautiful Lies

Opulent Obsession

Inherited Malice

Delicate Revenge

Lavish Corruption

Gold In Locks

Sick Crush

Secret Bride

Captive Vow

Ruin Me

Delicate Scars

Ingram Content Group UK Ltd.
Milton Keynes UK
UKHW040720170423
420292UK00004B/329